A VENUE OF VULTURES

BOOK 1
THE RANCHO EXOTICA MYSTERIES

PATSY STAGNER

FIRST EDITION

A

VENUE

OF

VULTURES

PATSY

STAGNER

JPS
PUBLISHING
COMPANY

Ordering Information:

For details, contact JPS Publishing at systag48@yahoo.com.

Print ISBN: 979-8-35094-799-1
eBook ISBN: 979-8-35094-800-4

Printed in the United States of America on SFI Certified paper.

Only an unjust bard would condemn the vulture
for feasting on the flesh of the fallen.
—Anonymous

1

Thunderous sounds like a rousing game of bowling reverberated from the metal roof and shot Avery out of her comfortable chair. Spilling coffee onto the area rug, she stepped over the stains to stare out floor-to-ceiling windows. Her sister rushed from across the room.

"What's that godawful noise?" Claire asked.

They stared with dismay into the backyard.

"Am I seeing what I think I'm seeing?" Since her health scare eight months ago, Avery needed to check with her sister to make sure the elaborate tableau before her was real and not an illusion supplied by her brain's faulty electrical wiring.

"What do you think you're seeing?" Claire said.

"Birds... really big birds?"

A billowing black blanket of turkey vultures spread across the backyard. Although a common sight in the forest surrounding their home, the number of vultures in the yard was exceptional. Towering over the birds, a buckeye tree held its own among the loblolly pines in their rivalry for a place in the sun. It was the only tree in the thick grove whose leaves had begun to turn and fall in the early Texas October.

As senior citizens, the sisters had retired to their gated community in the Piney Woods of rural East Texas and expected to live out their lives in peace and tranquility. Based on the vultures—legendary as harbingers of death—settling in the grass outside, that dream wasn't panning out too well.

"Hush, Bodhi. Lie down!" Avery feared the high-pitched bark of the cocker-shepherd mix the sisters had adopted from the local shelter might incite the vultures. Being a good boy, he flopped to the floor but continued to whine and squirm with excitement.

Avery ventured one step out the back door, and a tentative Claire followed. Neither dared move farther for fear the amassing birds would rouse and suddenly attack. Nonsense. Avery knew turkey vultures did not stalk and kill their own prey. They feasted on whoever might have died of natural causes—which in Texas meant being squashed by a speeding vehicle on a state highway.

"Something's dead," she whispered. "Something nearby." The sisters took two more tentative steps onto the patio.

"Something big, judging by the number of buzzards," Claire said. More steps revealed scores of vultures on the metal roof. One skid-landed like a skydiver making a shoddy touchdown. Others drummed their wings and clacked their claws performing a bird war dance.

"Vultures," Avery said. "Turkey vultures. Not buzzards."

"Whatever. Guess we need to check it out. The Wildlife Committee wants us to report the death of any animals." Claire hesitated. "I'm not eager to find a rotting deer carcass."

"Cheer up. Maybe it will be something small, like a squirrel or a possum. Then it won't stink as bad."

Back inside, Avery beckoned the dog. "Come on, Bodhi. Let's go chase some birds."

Bodhi leaped up and bounced around the sisters. Avery wished she had half the dog's energy. Still in pajamas, they donned hoodies to guard against the cool morning mist. Avery pulled her long hair into a loose top-knot, proud that she only had a little graying around the temples. In a royal blue hoodie she'd color-coordinated with her pajamas, Claire preceded her sister outside with an excited Bodhi dashing after them. When the trio advanced into the yard, the startled vultures rose into the sky with a susurration of wings that whispered an unknown language.

"They're so big up close." Claire, the normally calm sister, sounded nervous.

As if he could fly, an exhilarated Bodhi charged after them. Avery followed, flapping her arms and chasing the departing birds like a lunatic. Claire lagged behind, laughing. Avery knew she looked ridiculous but didn't care. Having control of her own body, no longer being at the mercy of the medical system, elated her.

After they had expunged the birds, Avery and Bodhi joined Claire. They followed the vultures' flight toward the 15-acre forest on the opposite side of the sandy-bottomed creek. An arched wooden bridge straddled the stream and connected the five-acre lot on which they'd built their house to the adjoining woodlands.

After Avery's illness, she had attempted to persuade Claire to retire from their stressful jobs as legal assistants. An unconvinced Claire argued that their 401(k) account balances were a bit shy of retirement ready. But her sister's charming description of the reasonably priced 20 acres of heavily wooded East Texas property, the lure of the quiet safety of a gated community, and the worsening of downtown Dallas rush hour traffic convinced Claire it was time to go.

Halfway across the bridge, Avery stopped.

"The smell's stronger," she said. The unique yet familiar odor of death permeated the close atmosphere of the dense trees. Sniffing the air, Bodhi wrinkled his nose.

"We're getting close," Claire said.

Beyond the bridge, the creek continued to flow and reflected the tall surrounding hardwoods. It snaked through their property, serving as a jagged border between their acreage and the adjoining lot upstream. After following the stream, the sisters stopped when the stench grew overwhelming.

"There it is!" Avery froze, trying to comprehend what she saw. On the embankment, a dark, undulating shroud of feeding fowl covered a carcass, each vulture politely sharing their bounty with the others. In the surrounding trees, newly arrived birds awaited their turn as if cueing up for a popular concert.

For a moment, Avery thought the buzzing in her brain had returned. The fuzzy state she and Claire jokingly labeled "brain fog." She closed her eyes and massaged her temples.

"What's that called?" Claire whispered, as though not wanting to disturb the birds. She gripped her sister's arm.

Avery shook her head—recovering from what had been nothing more than a fleeting disorientation. "A wake of vultures," she told Claire. "Nature's undertakers servicing the animal world."

Her sister shuddered. Bodhi threw himself into a barking frenzy, the black and white fur around his neck standing up like a starched collar. The shroud lifted to reveal a figure clothed in camouflage. Face down, his features disappeared into the soft sand. An army-green hat fell back from his forehead, and his booted feet sunk into the murky water.

"Bodhi, sit." Avery snapped her fingers and pointed at the dog. He hesitated for a second, then sat. "Do you think he's dead?" she asked Claire.

"Based on the presence of the buzz… uh, vultures… I'd say yes." Claire shot her sister a look that suggested she too feared the return of Avery's brain fog. When Avery met her stare with a straightforward gaze, Claire turned back to the body. "Definitely dead."

A shiver ran up Avery's spine in response to the autumn chill. Or finding a deceased person in their forest, more likely. Probably a hunter, but what was he—if indeed it was a he—doing on their property?

"I'm calling 9-1-1." Claire pulled her cellphone from a pocket and punched in the numbers.

"Wait a minute!" Avery snatched the phone from her sister's hand. She canceled the call, then moved closer to the corpse, staying downwind to avoid the smell. Claire plodded behind her. "He's dead in our forest, and we discovered the body. That makes us immediate suspects. Are you sure we want to report it to the police?"

"Suspects? We don't know what killed him." Claire frowned. "Right now, it's just an unexplained death. We must report it. What choice do we have?"

"We could move him across the creek. The Johnsons own the lot next to our forest. We can drag him over there. Make sure he's on their property. That way, it would be somebody else's responsibility."

"Don't you think the police will realize he's been moved?"

"We can cover the drag marks like they do in the movies. Sweep a leafy tree branch across them."

Claire rolled her eyes. "What about the fact that his feet are wet from being in the creek? Or there isn't any blood where we dragged him, but they find his blood on our creek bank? You watch enough of the Investigation Discovery channel to know better than that!"

"Well, crap!" Avery's breath came in labored bursts. "Something like this isn't supposed to happen in a small-town gated community. That's why we retired here. To get away from Dallas crime and traffic and stressful jobs. And now this!" She tried to suck air into her lungs, but it felt as if her chest had collapsed.

"Are you okay? You're not having a panic attack or... something else—"

Avery caught a deep breath. "No, no, just some minor anxiety. I'm fine." Of course, Claire was right. They had to report the body. Her fear had clouded her thinking.

Claire's phone pealed. Both sisters jumped at the loud jangling tune she had set for her smartphone. A startled Avery dropped it into the creek embankment's soft sand.

"It's 9-1-1 calling back." Avery brushed off the phone and tossed it; Claire caught it against her chest. "Okay, report it. Looks like we don't have any other choice." They were doing the right thing, if not necessarily the convenient one.

Claire gave Avery a relieved nod. At least her responsible sister looked happy.

"I'm going to the house to call security." Avery felt a little flurry in her stomach even though she hadn't mentioned his name—Jay Vidocq, the handsome Head of Security at Rancho Exotica. This might be an opportunity to get better acquainted with him... and vice versa. "He needs to know too. I'll take Bodhi."

Avery cast a backward glance at the body. A twinge of melancholy accompanied by a touch of guilt reminded her it wasn't just a body, but a real person whose family was missing them. Not an opportunity to promote her love life or, more realistically, create one where none existed. She and Bodhi crossed the bridge, Avery thankful to leave Claire to deal with the emergency dispatcher, and the dog prancing along as if he'd had the greatest adventure of his life.

2

Avery despaired at the number of golf carts lined up in front of the house. The police had not arrived, and yet the Rancho Exotica rumor mill had already churned out more than a dozen spectators.

Formerly a hunting ranch, Rancho Exotica consisted of 2,000 acres of platted lots surrounded by a high game fence. None of the lots were smaller than an acre, and most of them were larger. The former owner, who ran into trouble during the 1980s savings and loan scandals, had been forced to sell the acreage when he and his partner were convicted of fraud and banished to a Texas prison.

A developer snapped up the land but kept the exotic animals who had been born and raised there. Exotics such as zebra, Père David's, fallow, and axis deer roamed the acreage, free from being hunted and managed by the development's homeowners' association. Property owners, with dogs and grandkids in tow, drove golf carts around the maintained roads searching for wildlife. Rural Texas's low cost of living and the development's animal-friendly environment convinced the sisters it was their Garden of Eden.

Alas, there was one serpent in the Garden. The HOA's Wildlife Management Plan recommended the white-tailed deer be thinned every year by hunting. The flourishing community frowned upon shotgun fire, so they hunted using bows and arrows. Each property owner could choose to allow harvesting or not. The sisters emphatically chose "not" and made the best of it.

Living at Rancho Exotica had given them a dozen other reasons to be happy, but the carnival of golf carts parading outside their residence was not one of them.

The carts dared not venture onto the 100-foot driveway sloping up to the garage, nor near the bridge leading to the forest and, ultimately, the crime scene, as Avery now thought of it. But still, they came. Some walking their dogs as an excuse to check out the action, some blatantly stopping their automobiles before the grove of pines that served as a half-pulled curtain between the house and snooping eyes. Onlookers parked beyond the grove and walked back to join the others in their carts.

Avery jumped when the doorbell rang. When she looked out the window, Jay Vidocq greeted her with a reassuring wave. He had shown up driving his red golf cart and looking like a Calvin Klein brief commercial—albeit wearing pants.

When Avery had returned to the house, she fed Bodhi his breakfast, which he scarfed up in 15 seconds. While she waited for Jay, she took the opportunity to swipe on a little makeup and throw on jeans and a cute top. Ten years younger than most of the men in Rancho Exotica, Jay kept himself fit by regular visits to the gym. Other neighborhood men practiced the more popular mode of exercise—standing over a backyard grill or sitting for hours on a boat or the pier wielding a fishing rod.

Jay smelled of fresh country air flavored with pine needles. He pushed the long sleeves of his V-necked white cotton knit shirt above muscular forearms. It contrasted nicely with his dark hair. Bodhi greeted him with a short bark and wagging tail, and Avery pretended not to be giddy with his heady presence.

"Wanted to check in with you before I went down to the forest." Jay scratched the dog behind the ears. "Are you okay?"

"Why wouldn't I be?" Avery wondered if he had heard about her health problems. It put her on the defensive.

Jay raised his gracefully arched brows. "Finding a deceased human being on one's property is a shock for most people. I've seen rookie cops throw up when they get a whiff of their first corpse."

"I'm not that squeamish." Avery tried to get the peevish tone out of her voice. "Claire does get car sick, and sometimes acid reflux if she has too many sweet drinks on top of a full stomach." Attempting to curb her over-sharing tendencies, Avery clamped her mouth shut. Jay's closeness made her lightheaded.

"I'm thrilled you're doing so well considering the circumstances." He didn't sound thrilled.

"It seems surreal. Our beautiful forest contaminated by a gruesome death."

"I'm sure the deceased's family will feel the same."

Avery flushed. "I'm sorry. That was an awful thing to say. There's a human being down there. Somebody's loved one. I left my sister to keep the vultures off the body, uh… off him."

Jay winced but his severe expression softened. "Do you want me to tell those people in the street to go away?"

Avery looked out the window at the milling crowd. She could almost hear what they said: Everything's different since the sisters moved to Rancho Exotica. They're not like us.

"Let them stay," she said. "Don't want them to think we're trying to hide something."

Avery led the way across the bridge. A venue of turkey vultures roosted in the dark treetops, silent except when the occasional flapping wings of a recent arrival banged their way to a perch. As though taking her turn sitting vigil with a terminal hospital patient, Claire balanced on a thick, rotting log and stared at her cellphone.

* * *

After Avery and Jay had relieved her of her body-watching duties, Claire left them to wait for the police and returned to the house. Now, dressed for company in sharp-creased jeans topped with a burgundy twinset, she pushed a cart carrying a pitcher of fresh lemonade and clear plastic glasses filled with ice down the long driveway leading from the house.

Even though the clear autumn day had turned warm when the sun climbed above the treetops, the number of bystanders lingering on the street surprised her. They lounged in their golf carts or mingled beneath the pines, amassing like the birds who hovered in the trees surrounding the dead body. Waiting for the misfortune of others to feed them. Seemed like death attracted species of every type in one way or another.

Claire pushed her cart through the crowd, overhearing bits of conversation.

"Thanks for the lemonade, Claire."

"Needs more sugar."

"We've never had a suspicious death before."

"Shouldn't the cops be here by now?"

"Is someone dead? What happened?"

"Do you know who it is?" Finally, someone Claire recognized.

Bart Downs, famous for being one of the few bachelors in all of Rancho Exotica, boasted a nice head of hair for an old coot. Now, he needed a good haircut and a wardrobe consisting of something other than baggy Bermuda shorts and a stretched-out T-shirt.

"Looks like a hunter," Claire said. "He's lying face-down, clothed head to toe in camouflage." Maybe she shouldn't share the details. The police might want to keep some things confidential. She was good at keeping secrets, unlike her sister Avery who treated everyone like her personal therapist. Claire admired her sister's unearned trust in people, but her tendency to be so open often proved uncomfortable.

"Don't think it could be a hunter," Bart said. "The whole world knows you don't allow hunting on your acreage."

Of course, he would correct her. Unlike Avery, who avoided him because of his inevitable contrarian positions, Clare felt slightly more tolerant toward Bart. She enjoyed testing her debating skills on occasion, but today she was not in the mood for a quarrel.

"I see Jay's golf cart in your driveway." Bart pointed toward Jay's bright red vehicle. "Is he down at the crime scene with your sister? Alone?" Claire didn't like the insinuating way Bart said that. And it wasn't a crime scene. Not yet anyway.

"Don't worry," she said. "He's safe from Avery."

"Is she okay now?"

"She's always been okay." Although not bothering to keep the annoyance out of her voice, Clair's impatience didn't seem to affect Bart.

"He's married, you know."

"I heard he was separated."

"For the moment. His wife kicked him out of their house a couple of months ago. He lives in their Winnebago in the neighborhood RV park. Claimed he volunteers too much. Stays busy all the time and doesn't pay enough attention to her." Bart barked a raw laugh. "Typical woman. Always wanting a man to be something he's not. My girlfriend keeps trying to get me to marry her. But I don't see the point."

"Neither do I." It astounded Claire to hear that Bart had a girlfriend. Guess there was someone for everybody.

* * *

Avery and Jay took over the log Claire had vacated earlier. She maintained a distance between them that was neither too far to appear unfriendly nor too close to look pushy. Jay had spent the last few minutes looking at his cellphone. Avery wished she had hers, so she'd have something to do besides fidget. They hadn't gotten off to a very promising start, and she was afraid to open her mouth for fear something ridiculous would spill out.

"You're sure Claire called emergency services?" he asked.

"Yes, she was on the phone when I took Bodhi back to the house and called you." We're not senile—not yet anyway.

"The police probably think it's a natural death, which would explain their tardiness."

Avery snorted at the term "tardiness," like school kids who failed to return to the classroom after the bell rang.

"What's the rush?" she asked. "He's dead. Why else would the vultures be after him?"

Jay cut her a look, and she blushed when she remembered the serious-ness of the situation. And that her snippiness wasn't the way to make a friend. She blamed it on her nerves.

"Don't you think it's a natural death?" she asked. "No reason to think otherwise, is there? Surely, no one here would murder someone. Could have been accidental."

"Could be."

He seemed disinclined to talk about the body, so she decided to broach another subject. "Aren't you kind of young to be retired?"

Looking up from his cellphone, he appraised her. "I could ask you the same question. And I'm usually the one doing the interrogating."

"I'm older than I look. But why did you leave the police department? If that's not too personal."

"I'm a cop cliché. The things we see… the things we do… it got to me." He stared into the distance as if envisioning all the troubling things he'd been through. He looked older now that she saw him close-up, as if his years of stressful experiences had etched fine lines into his face.

"I watch a lot of true crime TV shows," Avery said. "The cops in them say things like 'you can't unsee what you've seen.'" A prolonged pause hung between them. She had the feeling he did not particularly enjoy talking about his life as a police officer.

He cocked his head in her direction, sighed. "That's true. But you try." His wistful smile revealed how attractive his crinkled eyes looked. Avery resented that the same feature merely made her look old. Life was so unfair.

"Claire said you volunteered at the Sweetgum PD."

"Big difference between a small town and Big D. Murders in Sweetgum per year—zero." He glanced sideways at the corpse. "Well, one… maybe. In Dallas, 250. Big difference. I was a detective for the homicide division. In Sweetgum, I mostly hang out around the coffee pot, answer the phones, and do grunt work. No real responsibility, and that's the way I like it." He scooted off the log and moved toward the body. "Think I'll check him out, see if I recognize him." He turned back. "Whatever your age, it looks good on you."

"Really? I… uh… I mean, uh… thank you!" Avery stuttered, thrown off balance by the compliment. She quickly glanced beyond him at the corpse. "Be careful. Don't want to contaminate the crime scene."

Jay laughed as if she'd made a joke, then scuttled down the creek bank as the sandy shore shifted beneath his shoes. Feeling for a pulse, he bent and placed two fingers on the corpse's neck. Seemed pointless to Avery. You can't put anything over on those vultures. The dead man lay face down, so Jay tilted the head slightly to one side and slipped his cap back an inch. Avery winced, thinking he shouldn't have moved anything about the body, but he was the expert. From where she sat, Avery couldn't see the man's face, but Jay's lit up.

"Do you recognize him?" she asked.

When Jay stood, his gaze went past Avery. She followed his look. Halfway across the bridge, Claire escorted two strangers toward them. Jay jumped away from the body sending the lurking vultures into anxious flight. When the group reached the log, Claire introduced them.

"This is Detective Butler Castellan and Coroner Wendy Martinez." Wearing a meticulously tailored gray suit, the detective reminded Avery of the actor Idris Elba. The coroner looked equally serious and formal in her black pantsuit and severe bun.

"We've met," Jay said. "I work with Butler and Wendy at the Sweetgum Police Department." Handshakes all around. "I'm surprised to see you two here so soon. We don't know if it was accidental or intentional."

"Not like they had anything else to do," Avery whispered to Claire.

"Guess they decided to skip the middleman," Claire responded, and they both giggled, clamming up quickly when the others shot them disapproving glances.

"Anyway," Jay continued, "I checked the victim for life, but nothing. He's a resident here at Rancho Exotica. Looks like Thorne Mondae. Spelled M-o-n-d-a-e. He and his wife have lived here about five years. Big house over on Ridgeview Court."

"Uh oh," Claire muttered under her breath. Avery's stomach dropped.

The detective wrote down the information in a flip-top notebook he pulled from his pocket. The coroner merely nodded.

"This way." Jay led them down the slope toward the body.

The sisters exchanged a panicked look.

"What if it wasn't accidental?" Claire asked.

"Then it looks like," Avery said, "you're about to become the prime suspect in a murder."

3

Two weeks ago

Claire tripped down the road behind Bodhi, who pulled her along like a water skier behind an out-of-control boat. The dog turned to bark at a squirrel, stopped to pee on a bush, twisted back to where they'd just been to smell, then lunged forward. Claire was exhausted. Happily, they were on the downward stretch. The house appeared at the bottom of the hill.

Beside the paved roadway, a souped-up UTV sat unoccupied, an orange traffic cone perched behind it. That meant a hunter must be in the forest nearby. He had parked the vehicle on the side where her acreage began. Could he possibly be hunting in her forest?

She surveyed the inside of the UTV—a two-seater with a convertible flatbed—but saw nothing. A loud thrashing in the woods, and an eight-point whitetail leaped the creek and clamored up the embankment. He stopped for a moment, staring at her, then stampeded across the pavement into the trees. He must have been frightened by the hunter.

"Mr. Hunter!" Claire shouted into the forest. "Are you in there? Hey, you're on my property." She stopped, listening for a reply. When none came, she raised her voice. "Hey, you, hunter. Get out of my forest right now! I'm calling the Wildlife Chairperson. And Security."

Bodhi barked and strained against the leash. Claire tried to hold him with one hand and dial her cellphone with the other, but the dog pulled loose and rushed into the woods.

The phone went to voicemail. "Bitty? It's Claire on Waterfront Road. There's a hunter in my forest. Can you come right now?"

Then she dialed Jay Vidocq who agreed to come immediately.

Claire started toward the woods to look for Bodhi, yelling for the dog as loud as she could. "Bodhi! Come here right now. That hunter is going to kill you. Come here, doggie."

"Hey lady!" The voice came from the other side of the street. Claire whirled, and a man in full camouflage regalia stood with a crossbow resting against his chest. His face puckered into a sour frown, and he moved the bow to a defensive position. "I'm right here. What's with all the commotion? Why are you yelling?"

"Don't point that bow at me!"

Bodhi charged toward her, panting, and she grabbed his leash. Jay skidded his golf cart to a stop and jumped out.

"What's going on?" he asked.

"This crazy woman is interfering with my hunting," the guy in camouflage said. He pushed back his hat, swiped sweat from his forehead. "I was up in the stand. Heard all this shouting and came down to investigate."

"Why's your car parked by my forest?" Claire asked. "I thought you were on my property."

"It was muddy over here, so I found a dry place. Didn't want to get stuck. You and your sister haven't exactly kept how you feel about hunting a secret. I wouldn't come anywhere near your property."

"You're near it now," Claire said.

"Looks like this was just a misunderstanding," Jay said. "It's over now. Thorne, it's getting late. Why don't you call it a day and start fresh in the morning? Claire, do you want me to drop you off at your house?"

Sulking, the hunter threw his gear into the UTV. "It's against the law to interfere with a legal hunt," he said to Jay. "I'm calling the game warden about that woman." His glare reminded Claire of an angry pug.

"It wasn't intentional," Claire said. "But do what you need to."

He leaped into his vehicle and peeled out.

Jay watched after him. "Boys will be boys."

Claire shook her head, directed Bodhi onto Jay's cart. "Isn't that always the excuse?"

"Nice vehicle," Jay said. "A BMS Beast 1000. Equipped with the best standard package in the off-road industry."

"Sorry if my eyes just glazed over," Claire said.

"Not information you'd be interested in. But it's typical of Thorne Mondae. Nothing but the best for him."

For a minute, they rode in companionable silence.

"Sorry I got you involved in this." Claire put her arm around Bodhi to keep him from jumping off the cart, sniffing his fur fresh from their walk in the clean country air.

"It's my job to settle differences between neighbors," Jay said. "I like your dog."

"You used to be a cop. Guess that's good practice." She tickled behind Bodhi's ear. "He's a good boy. Adopted from the Sweetgum shelter when we first moved here. Our other dog and cat died recently. They were old."

"Sorry for your loss. I'm a volunteer at the Sweetgum PD. Just for fun." He gave Bodhi a pat on the head. "Thorne Mondae is a powerful guy. But even if he calls the game warden, you'll be okay. If they accuse you of interfering with a hunter, they must prove intent. Which is not present in this case, so they'll drop it."

At the house, Claire thanked him, told him she would call Bitty, the Wildlife Chairperson. Tell her the issue had been resolved.

When Jay stopped by a few days later, Claire led him to the office.

"Thorne Mondae did call the game warden," Jay began. "The warden requested that I warn you to be more careful. And that was the end of it. Just Thorne being an ass."

Later, when Claire told Avery she was off the hook, her sister said, "I'm relieved. We need to avoid any ongoing disputes with our neighbors. I've seen too many episodes of 'Fear Thy Neighbor' on the ID channel. A squabble starts over nothing and ends with one guy shooting the other and getting life in prison. And all because his fence may or may not have crossed over a property line!"

4

While Jay showed the detective and coroner around the scene, Avery tracked him like a drug-sniffing dog. It seemed impossible, but it appeared as if he might be interested in her. She hadn't had a love connection in years and wasn't sure she wanted one. But didn't being retired create a whole new life and an opportunity to reinvent oneself?

When she and Claire first moved to Rancho Exotica—it sounded like a couples' sex retreat—they refused to be defined by their ages or the term senior. They reverted to their somewhat marginally misspent early twenties, enjoying the lack of fear and carelessness of youth. When Claire had met her future husband, she settled down, but Avery clung to the reckless and crazy life promulgated by the 70s. She partied by herself or with friends or friendly strangers without heed for her own safety or best interests. The 80s brought an end to the partying, but Avery never regretted allowing herself to be irresponsible and carefree even if her body ended up paying for it in the long run.

Okay, so things weren't exactly the way they were back then. A few things had changed in the past 40 years. Today, Avery didn't use drugs, except for her blood pressure medication. And getting drunk proved impossible since a touch of arthritis prevented her from bending over a low-slung toilet to throw up. As for sex—within her demographic, the dating pool had dwindled to a thimbleful and, based on the over-60 incontinence statistics, there was a 50% probability it had pee in it.

But, comparatively speaking, the sisters were still attractive and young at heart. And, after discovering a number of Internet dating websites that provided a smorgasbord of lonely old geezers searching for a couple of feisty 60-something-year-olds, Avery announced, "We're hot again!"

Jay sat on the rotting log. Silently, Avery slipped onto the opposite end. Claire stood nearby, wearing an expression that said she would prefer to be anywhere but here. Detective Castellan surveyed the forest as if counting every tree. He motioned Claire to come closer.

"This property belongs to both of you ladies?" he asked.

"Yes," Avery said. "The house sits on five acres; this forest is a total of 15. It's more or less bordered by the creek where the victim… where Mr. Mondae is uh, lying."

"The vultures started divebombing our house," Claire said. "We discovered him when we followed them to his body." She rubbed her arms where goosebumps appeared. Damp from the morning mist, her dark hair curled around her temples. She made sure to color the pesky gray on a regular basis.

"Did you see anyone else? Before or after you found the victim?"

"No. We'd just gotten out of bed. We were having coffee."

"He's a hunter," Jay said. "But the sisters don't allow hunting on their property. No reason why Mr. Mondae would be here since hunters are assigned certain areas. No one would have been assigned to this acreage."

"Do either of you know the deceased?"

No one said anything for several seconds.

"We know who he is." Avery took a deep breath. "But we don't socialize." Before anyone could interject, she said, "Do you think he had a heart attack or a stroke?"

Detective Castellan turned to watch the coroner, Wendy Martinez, and her team as they worked over and around the body. Dressed in white protective equipment, including hairnets, gloves, face masks, booties, and jumpsuits, they looked like ghosts who had materialized to carry the deceased's spirit into the brightening sky.

"Not sure of the cause of death." Castellan studied his notebook, looked up. "You ladies need to come to my office when we're finished here. I'll let you know what time."

"I'm going back to the house," Claire said after Castellan stepped out of earshot.

"Claire, Stop!" Avery caught up with her sister on the bridge. Yellow crime scene tape stretched across the handrail like a Christmas tinsel garland. It gave her the creeps. "What do you think about Jay?"

"I don't," Claire said.

"I mean, do you think he's hot?"

"Really? Is that what's on your mind right now?" Claire crossed her arms.

"I think he likes me. If I'm not misreading the signs. He said I didn't look as old as I am."

"Well then, he must be hot for you. Any guy who would say something like that—"

"Okay, okay, I get the message. But I can't help it if I get nervous when he's around. I'm not dead yet."

"No, but the guy in our creek is."

"Don't know if I'd take advantage of an opportunity with Jay, even if I could. Not sure I'm confident enough to expose my naked body parts to a man like him."

"Avery," Claire said in her disapproving big-sister voice. "There's more at stake here than your sex life. Like a dead hunter on our property. And we… especially me, could be a suspect in his death."

"A 67-year-old retired legal assistant? I'm having trouble picturing that threat being taken seriously."

Claire harrumphed, ducked under the crime scene tape, and stalked away.

Avery decided they could talk later. A distance away, Jay and Detective Castellan stood together, listening intently to the coroner. Avery snuck behind the nearest tree, then the next, until she drew within earshot of the trio.

"Based on the contents of his wallet, I've confirmed the deceased as Thorne Mondae." Even with her hazmat outfit covering her severe suit, Wendy Martinez looked like a woman who took her job seriously. It couldn't have been easy for a young Latina to secure such an important position in an East Texas city. "We've booked his wallet and cellphone into evidence. We'll get a warrant for his call records. My assistants are photographing the scene. And looking for footprints—his or anyone else's—weapons, you know the drill."

"Could you get into the phone?" Detective Castellan asked.

"No. It was turned off and password protected. Guess he didn't want to scare the deer with a ringing phone."

"Time of death?"

"Just an estimate." Wendy surveyed the few vultures who still roosted in trees. "Sometime before noon, day before yesterday, based on how long it took the birds to find him. A dead body starts to smell 24 to 36 hours after death, depending on the weather. The hotter the temperature, the faster the corpse decomposes, releasing chemicals that attract insects and animals. It's been cool, so it might have taken a little longer. Vultures detect bodies principally by their odor. They can smell a body a mile away and find it within minutes."

More about vultures than she needed to know, but the information fascinated Avery.

"What about the cause of death?" Castellan asked.

"Cause of death appears to be an arrow through the heart. Couldn't see it at first because he fell face down. When we turned him over, it became obvious. There are footprints down the embankment, sort of like he was stumbling. I'm guessing he got shot some yards from here, then staggered until he fell into the creek. A living being doesn't necessarily die the second an arrow pierces them. It can take a few minutes." Martinez coaxed a strand of black hair back into her bun.

Avery glanced at the body. The shaft of an arrow jutted from his chest like a flagpole. She shuddered, wondering how an arrow tearing through one's heart might feel. Then she remembered that was exactly what the dead man intended to do to an unsuspecting deer.

"Homicide, then?" Detective Castellan asked.

"Unless it was an accident and the culprit ran, or the victim did it to himself."

Avery leaned against the scrub oak, resting her exhausted body for a few seconds. The morning's events had sapped her energy which had been at low tide the last few months. When she rubbed against the tree's rough bark, a big chunk broke away and clunked to the ground. The trio turned to stare at her.

"You can stop pretending you're not listening," Jay said.

Avery felt her face flush. She stepped from behind the tree.

5

Detective Castellan stared at Avery through contracted brows. Before he had a chance to speak, a commotion at the bridge distracted him. A woman Avery identified as Bitty Binaila, the Wildlife Chairperson, was attempting to approach and being prevented by the assigned officers. After directing the crime scene technicians to carry Mondae's body across the bridge and into the waiting van, Castellan told the officers to allow Bitty to cross over.

"Somebody must have killed him on purpose!" She rushed upon the crime scene in a tizzy.

A second-generation Indian immigrant, Bitty had inherited a small fortune from her parents. They made their money in the restaurant business and, as their only child, she reaped the benefits. After their deaths, Bitty sold the chain of restaurants that specialized in authentic Indian food and retired to Rancho Exotica. Claire and Avery had become her instant friends because she cooked delicious vegetarian curries for the development's potlucks, and they bonded based on their meat-free dietary preferences.

Detective Castellan, who seemed to have forgotten that Avery still hovered near her protective tree, stood quietly while Bitty flapped about in her blue cotton kurti over white leggings and slip-on sneakers, her gray-streaked hair plaited into a thick braid down her back. A solemn owl watching a twittering sandpiper.

"You oversee the hunters," Castellan said when Bitty settled down.

Remaining still, keeping her face neutral, Avery remained near her tree to blend into or hide behind, whichever became necessary. She attempted to merge into the background so the detective wouldn't make her leave. So far, so good.

Age did have its advantages. Most young people held an idea about senior citizens that might not be entirely accurate. And the detective, young by her standards, looked to be early 40s. The under-50 crowd seemed to think anyone older had to be harmless, slightly forgetful, somewhat incapacitated, and therefore incapable of interfering with a murder investigation. If being misjudged as an innocuous old lady allowed her to stick around, Avery was more than willing to take advantage.

"What makes you think it was murder?" Castellan asked Bitty.

"Murder?" Bitty's face contorted. "Did I use the word murder?"

"Let's start with when you last saw the victim."

"He was supposed to be hunting with his son, Isaac." Bitty took a deep breath. "But I haven't seen Thorne... Mr. Mondae... since Thursday morning at six-thirty. He and Isaac were assigned to the property adjacent to the sisters' acreage." She pointed across the bordering creek. "The property that butts into theirs from Gazelle Street. That's probably where he parked."

Detective Castellan motioned for the uniformed officer stationed at the bridge. "Have someone go to the bordering street, it's called..." He looked at Bitty.

"Gazelle, like the animal," she said. "Parallel to the road that runs in front of this forest, but a block east."

Castellan pulled a piece of paper from his pocket. "Here's a map the front gate attendant gave me." He handed it to the officer. "It's a UTV, and if it's there, have it taken to the yard for forensic examination." Castellan turned back to Bitty. "Was Thorne Mondae supposed to sign out?"

"Well, yes." Bitty's bird eyes darted about the forest. "But his son signed out for him."

"Is that standard procedure?"

"It's pretty informal. No set rules about signing in and out. I just need a general idea of where the hunters will be. And we keep harvest records. But Isaac called me to say they were checking out early. He said neither he nor his father had shot anything that day. Said they were going their separate ways, and Thorne didn't want to take the time to come back to the barn."

Bitty had retained the slight lilt to her speech picked up from her native Indian parents.

"The barn is where everyone signs in and out," Jay said.

"What time did Isaac sign both of them out?" Castellan asked Bitty.

"Must have been after 12:00 p.m., because I remember being in the middle of a bowl of coconut chickpea curry when Isaac called. I always eat my lunch at noon. But I'd have to check the books to be sure."

"Why are you so sure someone did this on purpose?"

"Our hunters are expert marksmen. Their skills are tested before they are allowed to bow hunt the Rancho Exotica deer. Seems unlikely he could have been shot by accident. We take every precaution."

"Would anyone else be assigned to this area besides Mr. Mondae and his son?"

"No, just them."

"What about an accident? Do you know of any way he could have shot himself?"

"I don't know much about bow hunting or any other kind of hunting, for that matter."

Detective Castellan turned to Jay. "What about you? Do you bow hunt? Could it have been an accident?"

Jay cast a quick look at Avery. "I haven't hunted in years and never with a crossbow."

Did he want her to know he no longer hunted? Avery didn't like feeling so off balance around a man, but just in case he cared, she gave him a subtle nod of approval.

Castellan answered a call on his cellphone. "No vehicle parked on Gazelle," he announced, jamming his phone into a pocket. "So, as far as we know," Castellan closed his notebook and shoved it next to the phone, "Mr. Mondae's son, Isaac, was the last person to see him alive."

It didn't sound like a question to Avery, but Bitty supplied the answer that lurked in all their minds.

"Except whoever killed him," she said.

6

A collective hum rose from the crowd in front of the sisters' house. They reminded Avery of the wake of vultures covering the body in their forest. The onlookers fluttered around a tall, thin woman wearing a flowy white dress with an abstract flower design and pristine white boots. She carried a wide-brimmed hat and waved it about as if fanning flies off the picnic table at a garden party. Accompanying the woman, a hip young man in skinny jeans sported a hooded sweatshirt and bomber jacket. Two uniformed police officers stood among them and appeared to be asking questions. Detective Castellan joined the crowd, then led the newcomers to the front door. As Claire pulled it open, Avery let Jay in through the back door.

"May we use your home for a few minutes?" Detective Castellan said. "This is Adrianna Mondae, Thorne's wife, and Isaac, his son. We'll save time not driving to the station."

Claire steered them to the open concept dining area. The sisters had hand-built the upholstered banquet that accommodated five or six comfortably, eight in a pinch. Since Avery's sitting area opened next to the banquet, she and Jay settled on Claire's side to give Castellan the illusion of privacy.

"I want to see my husband." Adrianna Mondae tossed the sun hat onto the glass tabletop and sat next to her stepson. Her being a former fashion model was common knowledge in the neighborhood, and her demeanor shouted it. Sitting stiff and straight, she did not deign to acknowledge anyone else.

Bodhi, clueless to the unspoken rules of class distinction, immediately laid on her feet. She jerked them from beneath the dog. He looked perplexed but moved away and promptly settled on Jay's feet.

"He loves to lay on visitors' feet," Avery said.

"I'm flattered," Jay said.

"I'm sorry, Mrs. Mondae," Butler Castellan said. "But Mr. Mondae's remains have been removed from the crime scene. You can visit him at the coroner's office when we finish. You want to find out what happened to your husband. The sooner you cooperate, the sooner we can solve this."

A ten-foot island separated the dining alcove and Claire's sitting area. Avery stretched her neck trying to see what was going on but could barely hear the visitors. She only caught snippets of the conversation. She hoped Claire and Jay would be able to decipher some of it as well. Soon, restless and curious, she moseyed toward the table where the Detective and the victim's family sat.

"Avery," Claire whispered. "What are you doing?"

Avery pretended not to hear.

"Would you like something to drink? Coffee, tea, a soft drink?" she asked the trio gathered around the banquet. "Do we have any lemonade left over, Claire? Probably not. My sister felt it necessary to serve refreshments to the mob outside."

"Tea," Adrianna said, as if she spoke to an invisible servant. Detective Castellan declined, pulled out his worn and ragged notebook.

"A coke, if you have it," Isaac said. When he swiveled to glance at her, his wide-set eyes flashed with a resentment that mystified Avery.

"Mrs. Mondae," Detective Castellan said. "Why didn't you report your husband missing two days ago?"

Avery placed a glass of iced tea in front of Adrianna and a Coke for Isaac.

"I wanted hot tea." Adrianna still did not acknowledge Avery.

"Oh, pardon me, Madam. Let me fix that for you right away."

Detective Castellan looked as if he just now noticed Avery. "I'll take her iced tea," he said.

Isaac knitted his eyebrows and glowered beneath them.

"I left home Thursday before noon," Adrianna said. "Spent the night in our—mine and Thorne's—Turtle Creek condo in Dallas. Attended a charity event for the German-Russian Heritage Society on Friday evening. The Society's a non-profit that connects people interested in the common history unique to Germanic-Russian ethnics and to preserve their heritage."

A pack of wealthy Highland Park matrons with too much time on their hands, Avery speculated.

"Not familiar with it," Castellan said.

"It's incorporated under the laws of the State of North Dakota. That's where I'm from."

"That accounts for the absence of a Texas accent."

Adrianna had a way of not looking at the person she addressed. Made her appear suspicious to Avery. She'd been a fashion model before she married Thorne. Surely, she'd been able to look into a camera.

"And what accounts for your accent? It's definitely not Texan." Adrianna picked at the flowers in her hatband, gave Castellan a whimsical smile. "I'm guessing your heritage is a continent away from Germany or Russia."

"Yes, a continent or two. Trinidad, to be specific." Castellan seemed to emphasize his slight accent to counteract Adrianna's fastidious pronunciations. "So, you left before noon on Thursday…"

"My stepson spent the time at my house here, although I assumed Thorne would be with him. He can tell you I wasn't there." She used manicured, red-tipped fingers to dunk the teabag hung over her mug in the hot water.

"Sugar, Splenda, Stevia?" Avery lingered near the 10-foot granite-topped island rubbing a dishtowel across its already spotless surface.

"No thanks." When Adrianna sipped the tea, her upper lip wrinkled. "Plenty of people saw me at the charity event."

"You drove back this morning?"

"After having breakfast with a friend."

"I'll need names—from the charity event and your friend."

"I'll make a list. My personal trainer is my friend. She was with me the whole time."

"Your personal trainer?" Castellan looked like he'd never heard of such a thing.

Avery wondered why she hung out at charity events and breakfasts with her personal trainer. Who did that?

"We're friends. She met me at the condo, slept over, and attended the charity event with me. After we woke up the next morning, we had a training session. I don't like to miss my scheduled days even when I'm busy. Then we went to breakfast, after which I drove back to the Ranch. I found out from Isaac what had happened. We came directly here." Nary a tear nor a sniffle that Avery could detect.

When Detective Castellan turned dark eyes on Isaac, he began to shuffle his feet, and a bead of sweat trickled down his jaw. He slugged down a shot of cola.

"You may have been the last person to see your father alive," the detective said. "Tell me about it, starting with when you signed in to hunt. The wildlife lady said it was 6:30 a.m. day before yesterday, Thursday."

"We drove Dad's BMS Beast to the hunting site." Isaac's Adam's apple bobbed when he swallowed. "We'd been hanging out for an hour or so. We got separated when I moved to a different location hoping for some action. After a while, I got tired and bored, so decided to leave. I looked for my dad, but he wasn't where I'd left him. He hadn't checked out at the barn. I didn't realize he hadn't come home until this morning."

"You didn't call him, and he didn't call you? No texts or emails?"

"No."

"You either?" The detective looked pointedly at Adrianna.

"No."

"And you two didn't communicate?"

The interviewees avoided each other eyes, as well as Castellan's. The son sweated while the wife studied her manicure.

"Three days, and no communication among immediate family members."

"Close-knit family." Claire lowered her voice.

"Definitely phono-phobic." Avery whispered, following her sister's example. Although the others were close to 20 feet away, the concrete floors and modern sparsity of furnishings created an echo in the open concept common area.

Castellan shook his head as though wondering at the lack of familial communication. "Where did you go after you signed out at the barn?"

Avery noticed the detective did not mention what Bitty told him. That Isaac had also signed out for his father.

"It was around 12:30 p.m. I remember because that's what I wrote in the harvest record." Isaac hesitated, wringing his hands, and cast a nervous look in Adrianna's direction. "I took the Beast and drove to my girlfriend's place. She lives in an apartment in town, in Sweetgum. Spent the weekend and didn't come back until this morning. When I heard the news from a neighbor, I waited for Adrianna, and we came directly here."

A much taller Adrianna looked down on her stepson with a withering gaze.

"Why did you leave your father alone? And then sign out for him at the barn?" Castellan wrote something in his notebook while he talked.

Isaac was really sweating now, getting disapproving looks from both his stepmother and the detective. He shifted in his chair and gawped over his shoulder at Avery and Claire, a look menacing enough to make them wary.

"I thought Dad was going to town to have lunch with Scopes Redfield—"

"Who's that?" Castellan furrowed his brow and flipped through the notebook.

"He's my husband's best friend and business partner," Adrianna said.

"They often met at a local diner. I remembered him mentioning something like that. I wasn't worried about him. He can take care of himself." Isaac defiant, challenging.

Avery exchanged a glance with Claire that said apparently not.

"Thorne and Scopes like to frequent the Thunderbird Café," Adrianna said. "It reminds them of their early life in Chicago. When they were boys and first met."

"How would he have gotten to the restaurant without a vehicle?"

"Scopes could have picked him up?" Isaac squirmed in his chair. Another over-the-shoulder glance at the sisters.

On the sofa, Jay edged forward, tensing. Bodhi rose and raised his hackles.

"The victim was in camouflage from head to toe. Would he have gone to a restaurant wearing hunting clothes?"

"The Thunderbird's a dive. Bikers, dirt farmers, cops, all go there. No one would have noticed an old man wearing camo."

"But you wouldn't have known if he came home, because you weren't there."

Isaac clinched his fists, leaped up, his chair crashing to the floor. He darted across the room toward Claire and Avery.

"Why aren't you questioning those two—those sisters!" Isaac shouted.

Jay sprang from the sectional and caught him by the hood of his shirt. He jerked back, choking, his face turning crimson. Claire and Avery leaped up. Scuttled away from the fracas.

"They're the most obvious killers! Why aren't you putting them on the hot seat?"

"Get ahold of yourself Mr. Mondae," Castellan said in a tight voice, "or I'll put you in handcuffs."

"Don't you know anything? That older one harassed my dad when he was hunting a couple weeks ago. When he called the game warden, she got reprimanded. Interfering with a legitimate hunt. They found his body on their property. And they hate hunters! Everybody knows that."

"Mr. Mondae—"

Avery stood up to Isaac and said: "Texas has a 'stand your ground' law. Not only was Thorne on our property, but he brandished a lethal weapon. Claire would have been perfectly within her legal rights to shoot him."

7

You're making it sound like I did it! Claire's words from yesterday, when Isaac Mondae accused the sisters of murdering his father, rang in Avery's head. She had reminded him of the Castle Doctrine, also known as Texas's "stand your ground" law, intimating that if Claire had killed him, it must have been in self-defense.

Her sister sat in Detective Castellan's office at this very moment being grilled as a "person of interest." Castellan hadn't exactly called her that, but Avery deduced it based on every true crime program she had seen. They streamed through her brain like a YouTube video. The sisters had only lived here a few months, and they were in trouble with the law. Not the new life Avery had envisioned.

After an hour waiting in the police department's reception area, her only companion a young African American woman, Avery overheard the duty officer say:

"You can go home now, Mr. Redfield."

Avery's ears pricked up. She remembered Adrianna Mondae mentioning him as the victim, Thorne's, best friend. The one Isaac thought he could have been having lunch with instead of being murdered in their forest. The officer was dismissing him from the police station. Avery had better act now.

He stopped next to the only other occupant of the reception area, and they stood in conversation for a few minutes. Whatever their relationship, when the woman saw Scopes Redfield, a white-toothed smile spread across her wide face framed by short, curly hair. She sported an athletic build in a severely cut crimson suit, her ebony skin in sharp contrast. She was no older than 30, and her sapphire eyes shone above the peaks of high cheekbones, two flashlight beams in a darkened room. Avery could not stop looking at her.

"Hi, Mr. Redfield," Avery said as they breezed by. "Sorry about your friend, Thorne Mondae."

When they stopped, Scopes gave her a measured look, and she returned it with her widest smile.

Avery had never seen anyone so average. Even though they were close to the same height, he stood in stark contrast to the young woman. A rough-hewn driftwood statue beside an ebony carved Cleopatra. There was nothing special about Scopes, and the white Henley shirt with pleated khaki pants made him fade into the background even more. He rubbed fingerprint powder off his fingers into the palm of his hand, then slid aviator sunglasses over the rim of his golf-shoe-logo brimmed hat.

"I'm Avery Halverson. My sister and I live at Rancho Exotica. Mr. Mondae was murdered in our forest. I'm so sorry." She looked at his hands. "I'm here to be questioned too. I'm nervous about the process. I've never been part of a murder investigation before." She widened her eyes into what she hoped was an innocent-but-frightened expression.

"It's not so bad." His wary stance softened. "They just take your fingerprints. Do a DNA swab. A few questions about where you were and when."

"You must be feeling overwhelmed. I mean, being his best friend and all."

"Thanks, but I'm okay. Just tired."

She indicated the vacant upholstered chairs next to her. "Would you care to sit for a minute? You and your—"

"Niece," Scopes said, "and my assistant. She works for me at my office in Sweetgum."

"Onia Redfield," the woman said.

"Please, both of you. I could use the company. As a distraction."

Scopes glanced briefly at the revolving glass door, then at his niece. Her face remained impassive as they settled themselves next to Avery.

"That's a lovely name," Avery said to the woman. "Does it have a special meaning, a family name or something?" Her two new friends fidgeted.

"It's native. From the Andaman Islands." Onia spoke in a flat voice, her gaze unfocused, as if she had explained her existence one too many times. "I'm adopted. Obviously."

Scopes had been studying the room, but looked at Onia after she finished speaking.

"She's always been family to me," he said.

After a brief, awkward silence, Avery decided to change a subject that appeared to make them both uneasy.

"Mr. Redfield," she began. "Did you see Mr. Mondae the day he passed? His son seemed to think the two of you had a lunch date." She threw off the question as if it were an afterthought.

"Isaac is mistaken," Scopes said. "I did not see Thorne on Thursday. We didn't have an engagement." He paused as if expecting her to contradict him. "When I spoke with him by phone the day before, he talked about taking the weekend off to go hunting. He invited me, but I declined."

"Isaac seemed to think you like to frequent the Thunderbird Café because it reminded you of your early years in Chicago."

Scopes looked up at the ceiling as if imagining those bygone days. "To be honest, that's the last thing I want. To be reminded of Chicago and what happened there. My misspent youth, if you will. Thorne and I were involved in a lot of things I'm not proud of…"

"You were?" This was news to Avery. "Like, illegal things?" From the look on Scopes's face, she calculated she might have landed too close to the truth and overstepped her bounds.

Scopes sighed like a heavy weight sat on his chest. "Some of it. I've spent my adult years trying to make up for the things we did back then."

Onia placed a consoling hand on his shoulder, and he covered it with his own.

"And Thorne? Has he spent this time making up for it? Maybe something that happened in his past is the reason he's dead now. Could that be the case?" *Careful, Avery, don't scare him off.*

Scopes tightened his shoulders. He exchanged a look with Onia, who sat with her arms crossed, her lips pressed into a thin line. Avery had the impression she had hit upon something significant.

"I can't speak for a dead man," Scopes said. "I have no idea what happened to him or if his past had anything to do with it." A vein pulsed in his temple. "Thorne and I go… *went* to the Thunderbird Café because it's informal and the food's good. That's about all you can say for it."

"All that needs to be said for a local eatery, I guess."

Scopes nodded, then stood. The door to Detective Castellan's office opened. Claire, looking as if she'd been waterboarded, emerged followed by the detective. Castellan stared at Avery and Scopes.

"Are you two acquainted?" he asked.

"We are now," Avery said.

"We're leaving." Scopes extended a beckoning hand to Onia.

As she passed by Avery, Claire rolled her eyes and took a deep breath. "I need a nap," she said. "I'll wait for you in the car." She pushed through the revolving doors without looking back.

"Nice to meet you, Onia." Avery hoped she pronounced the name correctly.

"Likewise." Scopes left followed by his niece.

"Your turn," Castellan said.

Avery wished she could find a rock to hide under.

* * *

A technician entered Castellan's office, took Avery's fingerprints, and swabbed her jaw for a DNA sample. She sat in a stiff chair facing the detective. Dark circles beneath his eyes telegraphed the sleepless night he'd spent since the suspicious death.

"Do your worst." Avery realized her defiant tone probably revealed her nervousness more than it showed any real bravery.

"Are you comfortable, Ms. Halverson? It's not too chilly in here?"

"No, I'm fine. I just want this over with."

"I'll make it as quick and painless as possible. I'm sure you're ready to go home and get some rest."

What old lady wouldn't be? Avery felt sure that was what he was thinking. Glad he didn't know her sister reclined in the minivan taking a much-needed nap after being grilled by the detective.

"Where were you between the hours of 7:30 a.m. and 12:30 p.m. on Thursday?" His deep voice and matter of fact manner made her want to cringe in his intimidating presence, but she was determined to keep up the brave façade.

"In bed, asleep, just like my sister, at least until 9:00 or 9:30. Then we had coffee." Avery tried to take the defensive tone out of her voice. He didn't seem like the kind of man who would appreciate an attitude. But he had asked that question when they were in the forest.

"You need to answer for yourself. Not your sister." Chastised, like a disobedient child. "Do you normally sleep late? Until 9:30 in the morning."

"Ever since daylight savings time. Takes us a while to get used to it. Besides, we're retired. After we quit working for others, my sister and I established a new rule for our lives. *There are no rules.* We can sleep as late as we want, eat anything for breakfast we want, whether it's considered a breakfast food or not, go to bed as late as we want, or stay up all night reading. Eat chocolate pie for lunch or cereal for dinner. Work in the yard or clean house or binge-watch Netflix instead. No rules." *Have indiscriminate sex with a variety of men.* Of course, neither of them had done that yet.

"You're still speaking for your sister."

"Oh, sorry."

"This new code of no rules... that doesn't apply to murder, does it?" He leaned back in his big leather chair and stared at her beneath dark brows. A move calculated to intimidate a little old lady. It was working.

"We said 'no rules,' not values. You can't compare murder with breakfast food." An intimidated but defiant Avery knew from the ID channel that it was wrong to stare unflinchingly into the interrogator's eyes, a sure sign you were telling a lie. But it was equally wrong to avoid eye contact entirely. Her heart thumped in her chest as she struggled between the two extremes.

"Do you have any idea who might have killed Thorne Mondae?"

"Not a clue."

"And you didn't go near the crime scene before you heard the vultures on your roof?"

"Correct."

"Has your sister ever expressed any animosity toward Mr. Mondae after their confrontation over the hunter harassment accusation?"

Avery thought for a moment. "You told me not to speak for my sister."

A slight frown indented Castellan's forehead. "You can answer the question."

"Well... she did call him 'dickhead' a couple of times. But that's hardly a death threat. You can't really believe my sister had anything to do with this. She wouldn't hurt a fly. Of course, that's what people always say about serial killers. But Claire is totally nonviolent. Definitely not a psychopath or a sociopath." Avery clamped her mouth shut. Her jittery nerves were making her overshare again.

Nothing from the detective, his face a smooth blank.

"Did you notice that neither the wife nor the son shed any tears?" Avery couldn't resist. Pregnant silences made her uncomfortable. "Not one. Neither of them appeared all that upset that their loved one was dead. *Murdered*, no less. I'd be hysterical, bawling all over the place if something happened to my sister. That didn't look normal to me, them not acting the least bit upset. Yeah, I know 'everybody reacts differently to grief.' I hear that all the time on true crime TV, but the person who reacts differently always ends up being the killer. They acted more like they were setting up alibis. Making sure you knew they were nowhere near the crime scene." Avery stopped to catch her breath.

"Thank you," Castellan said. "No more questions. You can go now."

"I hope I didn't say anything to make you think my sister might be—"

Castellan gave her a strained smile, then rose and showed her to the door.

Avery felt like things had been left hanging. Like maybe getting the detective to admit he didn't think Claire would commit a murder. But he wasn't going to do that. Detectives didn't show their cards to witnesses or persons of interest.

"Don't take any out-of-town trips," Castellan said as she sucked in a deep breath and walked out of the police station.

8

The morning after their interviews with Detective Castellan, Avery sat on the patio drinking coffee with her sister and Bodhi. Except the dog merely licked his privates and was not having coffee.

"I can't believe that detective told us not to leave town," Claire said.

"Yeah, that means we'd have to miss the class reunion." Avery nudged Bodhi, who stared at her as if he had no idea his self-ministrations were unacceptable. "I'm not missing that. We haven't been to one in years. We swore we'd start participating in things when we retired and had more time."

Gold and red leaves drifted from the buckeye tree in their back yard. Beyond, the yellow crime scene tape that cordoned off the woods lifted and fell with the breeze, never letting them forget what had happened in their enchanted forest. Now, it loomed sinister and unapproachable.

"Can't believe I'm saying this, but maybe we… or at least me… should talk to a lawyer."

Avery noticed her sister's slumped shoulders and the exhausted look on her face. Claire must be more worried about the murder investigation than she thought.

"We both worked for corporate lawyers. Who would we call?"

"My boss worked in law enforcement before she got her law license. She'll help for free."

"Good. Just because we were employed by attorneys doesn't mean we can afford their fees."

When Claire reached Mary Mayberry on her cellphone, she put her on speaker. Claire had worked for Mary for 15 years before retirement. It had been a mutually beneficial relationship but had not necessarily developed into a friendship. Still, Claire convinced Avery that the loyalty between them made her feel comfortable enough to ask Mary for a favor. After greetings all around, and Claire filling her former boss in on the situation, Mary said:

"This isn't the wild west anymore. While a cop, I can't think of a single time I told a witness not to leave town. People have free will. Even those who committed a crime still elect to flee. But they probably don't think once they run, every second of every day could be the day the police show up to arrest them. That's why we have a court system, to determine if the suspect is a flight risk."

"We're not a flight risk," Avery said. "Were going to a reunion in our hometown. No chance of us staying there."

"I wouldn't worry about it," Mary said. "If either of you gets charged with something, let me know. I'll hook you up with a criminal lawyer. Otherwise, I think you're fine going to the reunion. Have fun."

* * *

Common belief dictated that growing up in a small town had to be a Norman Rockwell experience—all pastoral and Pleasantville. But neither sister had ever felt comfortable in the Little Mountain ranching community and could not wait to leave for college. Their attendance at a religious private school in Abilene, to please their widowed mother, proved no different. Independent and rebellious, they remained a degree removed from the conventional and the expected. After the death of their mother years ago, their only connection to the Hill Country town, they had never ventured back to Little Mountain.

Time, however, had softened their resentment, and their Facebook connections created a desire to revisit the past. They entered the high school gym, decorated for the All-School Reunion, feeling both excited and anxious. Their tiny town required only one schoolhouse and one reunion to accommodate all the alumni—the ones who bothered to show up anyway.

Claire had another motive for her attendance. She had spent 12 years in the same small schoolhouse with Tom Wellman, an accomplished athlete and homecoming king. While a massive crush on the elusive Tom threatened to overwhelm her, he never noticed his shy classmate. Since learning he was now a widower, she wished upon every visible star—of which there were many in the Rancho Exotica night sky—that he would attend the reunion. No longer a shy and awkward teenager, she made plans to hook up with him no matter how much of an old coot he might have turned into.

Not long after entering the gym and seeking out their respective classmates, a breathless Claire returned to Avery's side, her cheeks flushed. "Guess who's here."

"A handsome high school athlete resurrected from your distant past?"

"Tom Wellman!"

Tom looked good for a man in his late 60s. He still hit close to six feet, even if the gravity of old age—no pun intended—had shaved off an inch or two, and he maintained a trim body by hard work on his cattle ranch.

"And?" Avery said.

After untold years of celibacy, Claire was determined to bed the man she had never forgotten. She only had one requirement—that he not be "hideous."

"And he's definitely not hideous!"

Avery couldn't argue; she would have done the same thing if given the opportunity. Although her celibacy record had not reached the same heights as her sister's, it would become the new benchmark if Claire succeeded in her seduction plans.

As good as her word, Claire holed up with Tom in a far corner of the gym, and they only had eyes for each other. A display of overhead lights had been strung across the room, and the couple glowed beneath them. Avery gazed at the scene with pleasure, happy that her sister seemed on the verge of achieving one of her greatest desires.

She turned to survey the sparsely decorated gym. The very one where they had played basketball, volleyball, the despised dodgeball, and every other kind of ball when they were schoolgirls. The memories it aroused were not great ones. She still remembered feeling different from her classmates, and that anxiousness rose inside her again. Reminding herself she was now a grown woman—an *old* woman—she refused to validate those child-hood insecurities.

"Hey, Avery." Harry Mendelson, a guy from the class below her, saun-tered up and glued himself to her side.

She had read about Harry online, how he had formed his own software company and acquired a net worth of well over $100 million. In the classmate update bulletin, he listed his occupation as "unemployed and unemployable" as a gag. Avery thought it funny because she knew the multimillionaire had taken early retirement.

He had followed Avery around in grade school, wanting her to be his girlfriend. Trying to give her his ID bracelet. That's what kids did then. She'd never been interested, and he stopped following her in high school, although that soulful longing never left his face when he looked at her.

"Harry, good to see you."

Apparently, the hang-dog expression had frozen on his face. "You were my dream girl, you know."

"That's nice of you to say." In a corner, she noticed an extremely tipsy woman in a lowcut dress ladling punch from a plastic bowl. Avery knew it had been spiked. "Isn't that lady in the sparkly black dress your wife?"

Harry glanced at the woman. "What lady?"

Right on cue, Kenneth Kaufmann, the ubiquitous gay who remained closeted during high school, but popped gleeful from his shell when freed by his college attendance, materialized beside them.

"Hey Avery. Hey Harry," Kenneth said. "Long time, no see."

"Avery looks as beautiful as she always did," Harry said.

"I was a gawky kid," Avery said.

"I must have been looking through the eyes of love."

Avery fought off her gag reflex.

Kenneth looked from Harry to Avery and back, apparently choosing to ignore the lovefest between them.

"Harry," he said, "sorry to hear about your unemployment troubles. I know a guy who knows a guy that might be able to help. Give you some tips on your resume. Point you toward some job opportunities."

Avery sighed and rolled her eyes, searching the room for some means of escape.

"Appreciate it, buddy," Harry said.

"That was just a joke, Kenneth," Avery said. "Harry being funny—"

"I know you all thought I was a loser in high school." Kenneth raised his voice loud enough to draw the attention of several nearby groups. "But look at this!" He jerked a rectangular piece of paper from his shirt pocket and waved it around. "Now do you think I'm a loser? Don't believe how much I make? Check this out!"

Avery realized he had pulled out his paycheck. The surrounding groups twittered, and some laughed outright as Kenneth ran around brandishing the check under their noses. Had the guy never heard of electronic deposit?

"Harry, stop him," Avery said. "He's making a fool of himself."

Harry dutifully trotted off at his queen's command and followed Kenneth, attempting to take the check from him, with Kenneth eluding him to trip off to another table to show them the money.

Alone at last, Avery wandered to a table lit with candles bearing a card label that read "In Memoriam." Several of her classmates had passed away in the last 50 years. Each one stared back at her from a framed photograph sitting on a black satin tablecloth with a tea candle burning beside it. She had heard about six of them, but the seventh one caught her by surprise. Avery picked up the photo, looked at it closely. Betty Rosing had been quiet and shy to the point of disappearing in a boisterous high school. And she hadn't friended anyone on social media to Avery's knowledge. But she had no idea the woman had passed away.

"I can't believe she's dead," Megan Benson said as she sidled up next to Avery. Megan had been one of the popular girls in school, a group Avery had not been a part of but had no particular enmity towards.

"Yeah, me neither." Avery could barely remember Betty but tried to appear sympathetic. "Were you good friends?"

Megan looked at her as if she'd peed in the punch. "Not really. I'm just a sentimental person, I suppose. I miss high school so much. Loved growing up in a small town where everybody knew each other. I married Marty McGregor, my high school sweetheart. We still live here."

"How romantic." Avery recalled Marty as a big bully and misogynist. She replaced Betty's photo on the table.

"I remember you and your sister. Is she here? You were always so close." Megan followed Avery's eyes as she glanced at Claire and Tom huddled in the corner. "Ah, with Tom Wellman, I see. Didn't his wife die recently?"

"It's been several years."

"Claire was such a good student. Valedictorian of her class. Right?"

"Yeah, my sister the intellectual scholar."

"And quite the athlete as well."

"She was?" Claire had never been particularly athletic.

"Come here." Megan led her to the yearbook table and selected Claire's senior year. She thumbed through the pages until she stopped at a photo. "Look at this."

Avery stared at an incredibly young, big-eyed Claire holding a silver trophy. *Uh oh.*

"A crack archer! She was the best in school in archery class and won second place in district. Can't believe you don't remember that!"

Avery grabbed the yearbook out of Megan's hand and ran toward the side of the room where her sister had been. But the corner was deserted. She collapsed into the chair abandoned by her sister, plopped the yearbook onto the table, and rubbed her throbbing temple with trembling fingers. Was it possible her illness had caused more memory loss than she imagined? How else could she have forgotten Claire was a perfect shot with a bow and arrow? A vision of Thorne Mondae's body with an arrow buried deep in his chest arose in living color in her mind. The horror of the murder might have caused her to suppress the memory, but that didn't sound like something she would do. More importantly, did Detective Castellan know about Claire's archery expertise? How could he unless she told him?

"Did you miss me?" Harry the stalker was back.

"There's your wife, Harry," Avery said, snapping back to reality. "She's pretty tipsy."

As they watched, Mrs. Mendelson tripped and fell face-first, a full-body crash onto a table where many of their old classmates sat. The table broke; food and drinks flew everywhere. The reunion cake, with the words

"Welcome to the Little Mountain Reunion" emblazoned across the butter-cream icing in the school colors of maroon and gold, skidded across the hardwood floor. It landed at Avery's feet. No loss there. She hated white supermarket cake.

"You need to take her home."

"I'm not leaving with her," Harry said, "I'm leaving with you."

"Then go get your car and pick me up out front."

After he left, looking exhilarated, Avery hustled over to where his dazed wife had landed on the floor and scooped her up. Plucking a clean napkin off the table, she helped wipe white icing off Mrs. Mendelson's black dress. She looked as if she were about to cry.

"I'm sorry," she said. "I took a Xanax before coming. I was so afraid of meeting Harry's friends. And now I've made a complete fool of myself."

"It's okay. Everyone is half-sloshed. They won't remember a thing. Let's go. Harry's waiting for you outside."

With Avery's assistance, Mrs. Mendelson staggered out the front door. A late model Mercedes pulled up to the curb and left its engine running. Avery helped her into the passenger side and looked at a forlorn Harry over her head.

"Yep, that's how this day is going to end," Avery said.

Harry squealed off in his fancy car with his sad wife.

Back inside, Avery looked everywhere for Claire. When she didn't find her, she texted.

Where the hell are you?

Megan stood at the podium talking about the classmates who had passed.

"By the time you reach your 50-year reunion," Megan said, "it's only natural that some of your classmates will have passed away. But they live on in our memories and in our hearts. Let's take a minute and say a silent prayer for all who have gone before us. And for whom we dedicated this beautiful table." Avery noticed that the candle next to Betty Rosing's photo had gone out. Seemed appropriate. "Shall we pray?"

Avery hated prayer being forced on people in group situations. She never knew where to look. Down at the floor and people figured you were praying too. Up at the ceiling and she got a crick in her neck. She stared straight ahead at Betty's photo until a shadowy figure strode up to the In Memoriam table. With hair a tad grayer than the photograph and a few more wrinkles, it was the very much alive Betty Rosing.

"I'm not dead," Betty announced.

The room resounded with gasps coming from the audience. A few shrieks and moans, and one woman started wailing.

"Oh my God, Betty!" Megan cried. "It's a miracle; you're really alive."

"It's not a freaking miracle. I never died. I don't know where you got the idea that I had."

"No one had heard from you. Or knew where you were. I wrote to your last known address, but—"

"How would you feel if everyone thought you were dead? Did anyone think to Google me?"

The room grew quiet; the only sound was Megan trying to catch her breath. Her face turned red. Replaced with a blank look. Avery thought she might be having a seizure. Megan dropped to the floor.

Screams filled the room. A cacophony of fear and panic.

From the back, Claire made her way to the front. Tom Wellman followed.

"Step aside," Claire said. "He knows CPR." Tom and Claire positioned Megan so he could administer life-saving techniques.

"I'm calling 9-1-1," Avery said.

They learned later that Megan had suffered a brain aneurysm. She was dead before she hit the floor. If that was the way class reunions normally went, Avery had attended her first and last.

During the commotion, and after the ambulance had carried away Megan's lifeless body, Claire disappeared again. Avery texted to meet her outside in the parking lot. By the time she got there, all she saw was Claire driving away with Tom in his Suburban, whipping up a cloud of caliche dust in his wake.

Her sister riding into the sunset with her cowboy.

9

Claire texted her sister from Tom Wellman's midnight blue metallic Suburban. With the gigantic console and rocket-ship-like control panel between them, she couldn't get near him if she'd wanted to.

> *Claire:*   *Staying with Tom for the weekend. Be careful driving home by yourself.*
> *Avery:*   *Okay, have fun.*
> *Claire:*   *Did you enjoy the reunion?*
> *Avery:*   *Aside from the dead woman who was actually alive and the live woman who dropped dead? Sure, typical high school reunion. It was a blast. We need to have a talk when you return.*

That last sentence sounded ominous, but Claire shoved aside any other thoughts except the fact that she was really with Tom Wellman… at last! He drove her to the ranch-style house he'd built for his parents in the 70s and updated in the 80s. Although well-maintained, Claire noted with chagrin that the décor hadn't been upgraded since then, but she soon learned that was just Tom being himself. He wasn't interested in his surroundings as long as they were functional. She found comfort and familiarity in his arms, surprised that this was the same boy who had seemed so out of reach as a teenager. Just a much older version.

When she woke the next morning, she felt as comfortable as if she'd known him all her life, which, of course, she had.

"I love Rancho Exotica'" Claire nestled her head against Tom's chest. "But this murder has really put me off. Avery and I thought everything would be perfect when we retired, but it's not turning out that way. I might as well have stayed where I was. Working for the world's biggest asshole."

He responded with his hardy laugh. "That's a big asshole. What did he or she do?"

"How long you got?"

"All day." Tom removed his arm from around Claire. "Let me fix some coffee first. Sounds like this might take a while. Cream and sugar?"

"Stevia and nondairy creamer." She gave him a sly smile. The night before, they had visited the local grocery store where, he purchased a number of items she felt sure had never been on his list before, including the condiments.

* * *

While working for lawyers, Claire had developed the habit of checking her inbox as soon as she sat down at her desk. That day, she had immediately known something was wrong. She picked up and studied the official draft that had lain there like a scorpion ready to strike. Merritt Bank, the payor, had sent a check in the amount of $250,000 to her boss, Charles, a senior partner in the law firm where she had worked for many years. It had been drawn on the trust fund of the Dickens children, and an attached sticky note instructed Claire to deposit it into Charles's account. He had endorsed the back with his full name, account number, and the words "for deposit only."

Two years earlier, the four little Dickens girls had lost both parents in a car crash. Charles Milton stepped in and did what any good public servant would do, especially one expecting a percentage of the settlement. He sued the parties responsible for the tragic accident, a tire manufacturer and an automaker, and secured the girls an agreement that would make any major law firm proud. After deducting expenses from the original multi-million-dollar settlement, the attorneys had taken another 35%, which was collected by the firm. They doled out the money in varying amounts among the partners, including her boss, who received the lion's share because he generated the client.

Problem was, Charles had already received his portion, and this new check was not a part of that. Claire wondered where it came from and why. Her boss had a gambling problem he managed to hide from his colleagues but had been unable to fool his clever and resourceful assistant. Claire, being discreet and valuing her employment with the prestigious firm, looked past Charles's weaknesses. They did not directly affect her and, as far as she knew, had not bent toward the illegal.

"About this check…" Claire waved the offending paper in the air when Charles sauntered into the office. "I thought we had been paid for everything in the Dickens case."

Charles stopped and stared at her. He had returned from a court hearing wearing a dark blue suit that had been tailored to broaden his shoulders and slenderize his gut. He sheared his hair on the sides and wore more length on the side-parted top. The young guy's style looked ridiculous on a chunky middle-aged man. She felt embarrassed for him.

"I have a court order," he said. "It's in the file."

He slinked into his office before she could ask him anything else. Claire pulled the Dickens orphans' file. Most of their information would be online as well, but a signed copy of the court order should have been placed in the file folder. And there it was duly signed by Judge Mildred Betancourt.

The other attorney Claire supported, Mary Mayberry, came out of her office with a marked-up document she needed Claire to edit.

"Hey, Claire," Mary said. "I'd do these myself, except I have to leave early to pick up my kids from school. The nanny usually does it, but she's in Mexico for a week."

"No problem," Claire said. The younger attorneys such as Mary rarely gave her edits since their Microsoft Word fluency equaled or exceeded hers. While Mary pulled her trench coat over her pantsuit, Claire asked: "Mary, look at this court order. It's signed by Judge Betancourt. Does it look right to you?"

Mary studied the paper. "Looks fine. We have lots of signed orders from her. Is there some problem?"

Claire shook her head. "Not that I know of. I just wanted someone else to see it." After Mary left, a distracted Claire shoved the order back into the folder.

The day passed slowly. Friday meant that many of the firm personnel, especially the senior attorneys, left early to get a head start on the weekend. When Charles finally emerged from his office, he gave Claire permission to leave whenever she wanted.

"Thanks!" After he left, Claire pulled out the Dickens order and photocopied it. She checked her client files, picked a few whose cases had been tried before Judge Betancourt, and compared them to the Dickens order.

"I'm an idiot!" she announced.

"And we hoped you'd never find out." A secretary, stationed on the other side of the half-wall that had been placed between bays to create the illusion of privacy, stuck her head around the corner, laughing.

"Jackie, come here," Claire said.

Jackie stumbled around the partition as if her feet hurt. Which they probably did since she wore 4-inch bright yellow stilettos.

"See this order signed by Judge Betancourt?" Claire presented the Dickens order. "Do you see any difference compared to this one?" She held parallel an order extracted from another client file. "Specifically, the Judge's signature."

Jackie pulled on the cat-eye, rhinestone encrusted glasses hanging from a chain around her neck and studied both documents. "Looks the same to me. What's wrong with it?"

"On both of them, her name is typed 'Judge Mildred Betancourt' below the line. And she signed on the line "Mildred Betancourt.""

"Yeah, so?"

"On the first one, the Dickens Order, she actually signs on the line 'Ms. Mildred Betancourt.' Why would she put the 'Ms.' title in front of her name on a legal document when she's signing as Judge? Just seems odd to me. I have several court orders signed by her, and she didn't do that on any of the others."

"So, she changed it up one day. What's the big deal?"

"Just strange, that's all. Thanks, Jackie." Claire replaced the documents in their file jackets. "I'm leaving for the weekend. Have a good one."

"You too." Jackie tottered off in her heels.

Over the weekend, Claire had discussed the situation with Avery. The following Monday, she clipped the bank check to the copy of the court order and carried it to her supervisor.

* * *

"What happened?" Tom sat across the breakfast table watching Claire finish off an English muffin filled with almond butter and pineapple preserves. They had moved from bed to dining table during Claire's extended story.

"The firm returned the money to the bank because Judge Betancourt had no record of ever signing the order. Charles had forged it. He resigned from the firm effective immediately, but as far as I know he never suffered any repercussions. I received the cold shoulder from most firm attorneys because I snitched, and none of them wanted to work with me. Which was fine by me because I'd had enough of the legal business by then. I transferred to the Marketing Department to work on a client-sharing database that nobody used or cared about. That's when Avery and I decided to start building our house. When I quit, they never bothered to replace me. And the database sunk into oblivion."

"What happened to the attorney, Charles?"

"As my dear sister, Avery, described it: 'He laughed maniacally all the way to his secret lair, alternately wringing his hands and stroking an unamused hairless cat.'"

Tom smiled but didn't laugh out loud. *Tough crowd.*

"In private practice, he embezzled from the trust account of a boy injured in an automobile accident. Apparently, champagne tastes sweeter when it's purchased with money soaked in a child's tears. I'm pretty sure he's in Club Fed now, serving time for fraud and tax evasion."

Tom nodded his approval. "I can see why you retired. I love what I do, so I'm not planning on retiring." Claire decided now was not the time to engage Tom in a discussion about the ecological disaster that was cattle ranching, not to mention the animal cruelty.

After they dressed, Tom drove her around his acreage in his Kawasaki Mule. While they checked fences and filled water troughs, Claire tried not to pay too much attention to the cows. She wanted to avoid making any personal connection if that was even possible. Tom seemed to want to show her that he took good care of his animals. That their welfare was important to him. But he grew wary and silent when she said:

"But their lives become a nightmare when you sell them for slaughter."

The following tense silence broke only after Tom parked the Mule to check his trail camera. "Need to make sure this thing is still functioning." He flipped open the camouflage-colored plastic box and resorted the batteries. He looked at Claire in a conciliatory way as if to say he did not want to argue. Neither did she. "My parents' old ranch house is empty, so I post the camera to protect the building from intruders." He wrapped and buckled the strap high on a porch post and out of eyesight. "This property is leased to deer hunters, and I've had some stuff stolen a couple of times."

That's when Claire had one of those *Uh oh* moments. She jerked her cellphone from her hoodie pocket and frantically ticked off a text to Avery.

10

Avery waited for Bodhi to jump onto the golf cart, then slid into the driver's seat. Claire remained in Little Mountain with Tom, and Avery had dismissed the pet sitter. The sitter hadn't taken Bodhi out for his ritual evening ride, and he danced on the faux-leather upholstered seat, anxious to take his scenic tour around the neighborhood.

The sisters had never envisioned themselves as retired senior citizens whose greatest entertainment consisted of tooling around the property in their golf cart, sporting a good-sized dog and a sun-visor, searching for the exotic animals who made their home on the ranch. Yet here Avery sat, giddy as a kid at an amusement park. The house had been a little lonely without Claire, but Bodhi provided the best company one could hope for in a critter who couldn't talk.

Claire had wanted to leave him at the animal shelter because she dubbed him "too cute."

"Someone is bound to adopt him," she said. "He's just too cute. We need to adopt one that nobody else is going to want."

"You know I'm all for adopting a dog missing a leg, or blind and deaf, or a senior. We've had our share of special needs animals in the past, both dogs and cats, and several 'plain brown dogs.' But look at him."

Bodhi—named "Pepper" at the time—stretched across both their laps, his long merle coat hanging in knots. He looked directly into their eyes, his brown orbs sad and listless, begging them to take him out of this dungeon. She could see Claire wavering.

"What if we take him and that senior black lab mix in the pen next to him? It's hard to get a black dog adopted. Especially an old one. We'd be balancing our cute dog with a plain one."

"Well, okay. I guess so."

As it turned out, the workers at the shelter had already processed the adoption of the senior black lab mix. Scheduled to become the house dog at the local retirement home, she would have many people who understood and loved her. They only made it home with Bodhi, the world's most perfect dog, as he came to be known by the sisters. Avery figured the whole world probably felt the same way about their canine companions.

Avery drove down a sidewalk that bordered one of the small lagoons, one of the three connecting lakes in Rancho Exotica. When she stopped, Bodhi leaped off the cart to take care of business. Together they strode down the pathway, the dog occasionally chasing black crows soaring overhead. Okay, so maybe he wasn't the world's *smartest* dog, thinking he could catch a flying bird. But who was she to tell him differently? A sociable group of vultures perched in a giant dead tree next to one of the several picnic tables located along the walkway.

After a short half-mile hike, she shooed Bodhi onto the cart. They crossed a dam that divided two of the lakes, and a gray heron flew across their path croaking his disgruntlement. Past the cul-de-sac named "Stripers Inlet," and redubbed by Avery as "*Strippers* Inlet," they turned onto the road that led into the development's RV park. Property owners could live in the park, hooking their motorhomes up to water and electric in one of the concrete spaces, while their permanent dwelling was being built. If a homeowner had visitors who arrived in their own RVs, they could also utilize Rancho Exotica's facilities.

Avery knew Jay Vidocq lived in one of the vehicles parked at the site but wasn't sure which one. Driving Bodhi around the roads that interlaced the grounds meant she ran the risk of Jay spotting them, but decided she didn't care. She had every right to be there and often took Bodhi to the adjacent pond to wade when the summer weather grew hot and humid.

As fate would have it, he stood outside his gray Winnebago, the vehicle adorned with what looked like a boomerang in sunflower yellow. Jay shoved boxes into its storage hold. He waved her over. She complied, albeit with a slight blush that warmed her face.

"Hey," Jay said, petting Bodhi, who stared at him with loving eyes. Avery hoped she didn't have the same puppy dog look on her face.

"Hi, Jay," she said. "Just taking Bodhi out for his daily walk and golf cart ride. I've been out of town, and the pet sitter doesn't know how to get him onto the cart. Although with a treat he would jump on by himself. We even offered to pay her extra if she took him out, but…" Avery gulped and swallowed. *Shut up. You don't have to justify yourself to him.*

He waited, as if expecting her to continue, then said: "I'd be happy to sit with him when you leave town. Bet I could get him on the cart."

"Looks like you could get him to run into a burning building if you asked him real nice."

Jay's deep laugh sent a thrill through Avery.

"Want to come in for a beer? Dos Equis? I also have a California Riesling." Avery hesitated, looking at Bodhi.

"Bring the dog inside. I'll give him some Fiji water."

"He wouldn't expect anything less."

After Jay had shown her around the late model Forza, she duly admired all its accoutrements while wondering how he could afford such a nice motorhome on a cop's salary. They settled down with their drinks. Bodhi lapped loudly from the bowl Jay had given him, spilling water over the wood-look luxury vinyl plank flooring.

"Did you go on a vacation?" Jay asked. "You said you were out of town."

"My sister and I went to our class reunion. We're from a small town in the Hill Country. It was for all the classes since it was such a small school."

"Never been to one." He didn't sound like he regretted it.

As the setting sun dipped behind the pine trees, they sat across from each other at the dinette table. The red light glowing between the tree trunks cast a warm light across their faces. Avery felt a sense of comfort and well-being she had rarely experienced while in the presence of a man.

"Nice motorhome." Avery took a sip of the dry wine from a bar glass Jay provided.

Jay's mood turned solemn. "A hand-me-down from my wife's parents. It's only a few years old, but they bought a bigger, better one. Like they do everything."

"Your wife comes from money."

"You could say that. I could never satisfy her…" He slanted a glance at Avery. "…*moneywise*. She wanted me to get a better job, with more prestige, even within the police department. I loved what I did, but I didn't want to tell other officers what to do. Just being a homicide detective was enough. When we moved here, she thought I'd at least have more time for her, go to fancy balls and charity events, black tie parties, boring crap like that."

"Doesn't sound like you… being somebody's boy toy." He winced at the boy toy comment. "I mean, what little I know of you."

"When I became so involved with the community, volunteering to be the head of security and other committees, I was gone from home as much as when I was working. She kicked my ass out a couple of months ago." He chuckled, swigged his beer straight from the bottle. "I feel as comfortable here as I did in our new house. More comfortable." The daylight outside had disappeared. The RV stood in a deep darkness. "I'll turn on the lamps."

Avery had been lulled into a sense of ease while he talked. She roused herself, wary of becoming too comfortable around him. Or having any expectations other than just being friends.

"We should go," she said. Bodhi had fallen asleep on Jay's feet but woke when he moved to switch on the lights. Avery shifted toward the door.

"Don't go." He put a hand on her arm. "Stay awhile. It's nice having someone to talk to. Tell me about you… your life… before you moved here."

"It's boring…" It hadn't really been that boring, but she felt disinclined to share too many details with him at such short acquaintance. "I'm sure yours was much more eventful."

"We might know some of the same people. You worked at a law firm. I'm in law enforcement. Our paths may have crossed."

"Not likely. I worked for corporate lawyers."

"Why did you leave?"

Avery sighed. "Are you sure you want to hear this?"

"I'm sure."

She settled back into the dinette booth. *Just remember you asked for it.*

* * *

Flu season had bedridden a dearth of secretaries, and their attorneys were on the prowl for warm bodies to replace them. Avery helped as much as she could, but the constant ringing of her phone lines had limited her usefulness. Clients kept calling, asking silly questions like, "How long will he be on there?" when she told them her boss, Larry Edenborough, was on the phone. Was she psychic or something?

In Conference Room A, Larry sat with another partner, MC Carton. MC had agreed to help Larry with discovery, and the mountains of documents delivered by Federal Express dwarfed the attorneys. MC had a reputation among the law firm's employees as being difficult. Avery had never had any direct dealings with him, but she knew he hung several deadheads on his walls. Every time she passed his office, she apologized to the deer, elk, and bighorn sheep who looked down at her in stoic silence.

"I'm so sorry that happened to you," she said to the unhearing, unseeing animals. "Someday, I hope you get justice."

Larry called Avery into the conference room, handed her a stack of papers, and asked her to make copies.

"I have this thumb drive from the client." MC passed her a small plastic drive that did indeed look like a thumb with a silver USB connector attached. "I need to know what documents are on it."

When Avery glanced at Larry, he nodded, and she said: "If there's an index, I'll print it out for you."

MC did not acknowledge her. She left the room, placing the thumb drive beside her computer to check after she'd made the copies. After leaving the copy room, she decided to see if the drive had an index so she could take it to MC at the same time she took Larry's copies. When she wedged it into her computer, it brought up five documents, but no index. She opened and visually scanned them when they appeared on her computer monitor. She carried the copies into the conference room and laid them on the table beside Larry. MC didn't look up.

"There's no index on the thumb drive," she said, "but the documents on it are—"

"Could you do that without talking?" MC said.

Avery stared at the lawyer to see if he had intentionally insulted her, but his face was as impassive as if he'd been speaking to an automaton. Her open mouth hung suspended in mid-sentence, dangling there for several seconds. When she looked at Larry, he ducked his head.

"Sorry," she said, "but I don't know sign language."

"You're still talking," MC said.

"I could send up smoke signals, but I don't think security would approve of me starting a fire."

"You're still talking." A vein in MC's temple bulged like a water balloon filled to the breaking point.

A quick glance at Larry showed his attention focused on a stack of papers, but she could see his jaw muscle clench. Avery waited.

"Just print out the first page of each document!" MC's face turned the color of eggplant.

Avery walked to the door, muttering under her breath: "Could you die without me killing you?" She pictured his head exploding. She wouldn't even mind if a bit of brain matter splattered onto her dress.

"What did you say?" MC asked.

"I think we've reached the end of this conversation."

Avery stalked to her desk, jerked the thumb drive out of her computer, and laid it in her out basket. She went straight to the Personnel Director's office, told her she quit, and went back to her desk to collect her things.

* * *

The ending hadn't exactly happened that way, but Avery decided Jay did not need to know everything about her.

"I've had dealings with lawyers that made me want to punch them in the face." Jay's grin softened the effect of his words.

"I've worked for some bad, some good, and some great. But my departure was an accumulation of things. I was tired of working, tired of being told what to do, tired of driving to downtown Dallas." That was just part of the story, but he needn't know that. She wanted to avoid leaving the impression of being a sickly old lady.

"Is that attorney still with your firm?" Jay asked.

"He died of colon cancer about six months later. I wouldn't wish cancer on anyone, but I didn't shed any tears when I heard the news. Neither did the dead animals on his walls. But enough about the past. Have you learned anything new about Thorne Mondae's murder?"

"Not much," Jay said. "You already know the cause of death. Shot with a bow and arrow straight through the heart. Based on the insects and vultures, the time of death was somewhere between 9:30 a.m. and 12:30 p.m. Thursday. Detective Castellan believes the killer must be either someone who lives in Rancho Exotica or has easy access to it."

"Like a friend or relative on the permanent list?" Some property owners placed frequent visitors on a permanent access list so they wouldn't have to call the front gate every time that person visited.

"Or a vendor, someone on a construction crew, deliveries—lots of possibilities."

"What about footprints? It was muddy right around the creek embankment where he fell."

"Just the prints made by Mondae's boots when he staggered into the creek. No others were found." Jay paused. "Except mine, of course, when I went down the embankment to identify the body. But Wendy already knew about those because her and Butler saw me when I was still standing next to the victim."

"I'm pretty sure Detective Castellan suspects Claire. Maybe even me. But especially her because of her confrontation with Mondae."

"He's never verbalized that to me. But he's keeping me at a distance from the investigation since I live here. Technically, I could be a suspect, too."

Bodhi strode to the RV door and whined.

"We'd better go," Avery said. "It's dark out there. Without any streetlights, this community goes pitch black. Kinda scary."

"Want me to drive you?"

"No, thank you. I'm sure everyone in Rancho Exotica knows by now that my golf cart is parked in front of your RV."

"You don't have to worry about my reputation."

"I'm not, but I'm not feeding the rumor mill any more by letting you drive me home and leaving my golf cart here overnight." Not that she particularly cared what people thought, but she did have to live here, probably for the rest of her life.

He opened the door to let them out. When she turned to say goodbye, he dipped his head close to hers, and he smelled as if a fresh sea breeze had drifted by. She thought he might be about to kiss her. Instinct made her pull back, creating an awkward moment. She quickly followed Bodhi out the door and urged him onto the cart.

"Thanks for the wine." Before starting the cart, she clicked on a message from Claire. "*Uh oh.*"

"What's wrong?" Jay looked concerned.

"Oh, nothing. A text from my sister. See you."

Avery read Claire's message.

Go immediately into the forest and retrieve the trail camera we left attached to the tree in front of the shed. Do not tell anyone you have it! We'll talk when I get back. DO IT NOW!

* * *

After leaving Jay's Winnebago, Avery drove the five minutes to her house, parked the golf cart in the garage, and slipped Bodhi through the connecting door into the mudroom. She promised him his supper just as soon as she returned from her mission. Retrieving the giant flashlight from the laundry room, she crept down the hill and across the bridge into the dark woods, the beams throwing eerie shadows across the thick accumulation of trees. Instead of being silent, as one would expect, the forest twittered, buzzed, and hummed with insects and birds. A hoot owl penetrated the blackness with the ghostly question "*who?*" The shed loomed in the distance, its metal roof glinting off the torchlight. Inside, the sisters maintained extra gardening tools, a couple of wooden feral cat shelters, and a small tiller and weed eater. They were among the few residents in the development who had space for their two automobiles in their garage. Most of their neighbors were packed full of junk they forgot they had and would never use.

Avery had strapped the trail camera to one of the holly trees that grew wild in the forest. It faced the shed to record the comings and goings of the woodland wildlife, including feral cats. With the oppressive darkness closing around her, she quickly unstrapped the camera and scrambled back to the trail. She wanted to run but feared tripping over a branch or rock in the blackness. A sudden rustling behind a wax myrtle stopped her. With a shaking hand, she flicked the light toward the sound. A white-tailed deer froze in her tracks and stared back. After a brief stare-down, the doe stomped her hoof, snorted, and with a leaping hop darted into the darkness.

Whew! It could have been a bobcat, coyote, copperhead, or some other carnivorous creature. She'd even heard an alligator lived in one of the community's lakes. The things she did to accommodate her big sister! Whatever was on that trail camera had better be photos of a bare-chested Chris Hemsworth, or Claire was in big trouble. She stumbled hurriedly across the bridge to the welcome lights of home and the wagging tail of a very hungry dog.

11

The next day, Avery sat on the sofa next to Bodhi staring at the trail camera pictures on her laptop. When Claire walked into the house, Avery gritted her teeth, prepared to give her sister a long-overdue lecture. Claire had been holding out on her, which wasn't like her. The sisters didn't keep secrets from each other. She waited until Claire had rolled her suitcase into her bedroom and returned.

"I'm very angry with you," Avery said.

"Sorry I stayed in Little Mountain, but you knew I was going to hook up with Tom if I could." Faint shadows beneath Claire's eyes meant she probably had a good time.

"That's not the reason." Avery turned the laptop screen toward her. "You lied to me."

Claire scooted Bodhi into the corner of the sofa, sat next to Avery, and scanned the computer photos. "Oh, that. I intended to tell you—"

"You were in the forest the day Thorne Mondae was murdered! Why didn't you tell me? Look at the pictures. First, Thorne passes by activating the camera, and a few minutes later you appear. Acting as if nothing happened."

"Nothing did happen. I never saw him." Claire examined the field camera Avery had laid atop her Noguchi knock-off coffee table. "Can't believe CSI missed this thing. Guess the camouflage and being tied to a tree trunk hid it too well. What a lucky break for us!"

"For *you*, you mean. I wasn't meandering around the forest at the same time as the murder victim. What if Detective Castellan finds out? You're already in his crosshairs. With these photos, he'd have enough to arrest you. Especially with what I learned at the reunion."

Claire cocked an eyebrow at her sister. "Castellan won't find out unless you tell him. What did you learn at the reunion?"

"You failed to mention your high school prize-winning archery skills. Megan Benson reminded me of your second-place district win. Showed me your yearbook photo holding up your trophy. Cute pic, by the way."

"Thanks." Claire avoided looking at her but stared at the laptop as if it were a cobra ready to strike. "I assume that was before Megan collapsed and died of a brain aneurysm."

"Don't think the two events were related." Avery eyed her sister from beneath furrowed brows. "I get why you didn't mention that or your picture on the trail camera to the detective. But why not tell me? Don't you trust me?"

"Well… maybe I forgot which day it was. They run together when you're retired. As for the archery thing—can't believe you didn't remember. It was a pretty significant event in my life."

Avery had been wondering the same thing and supplied the only explanation she could come up with: "You won that award when you were 17. We placed that trail camera in the forest a mere three weeks ago, and *neither one of us remembered it*! Is it a surprise I didn't remember something that happened to you 50 years ago?"

"Okay, good point."

"Why were you in the forest in the first place?"

"Thought I heard a cat howling. I went to check the traps."

The sisters had placed a couple of live animal traps trying to catch feral cats. They intended to neuter them, release them back into the forest, and continue to provide food and housing for the released cats. The trail camera would photograph them to confirm they were not sick or injured.

Still miffed, Avery moved closer to her sister on the tuxedo sofa so they could review the trail camera photos together. A date and time identified each black and white shot. The camera, which would not take photos unless it detected movement, faced their storage shed where the cat condos had been housed. The boxes provided a place for the ferals to hide and get warm. So far, they had not discovered any feral cats.

The snapshots' subjects glowed with the ethereal light of other-worldly creatures. A blurry shot of a white-tailed deer and one of a ringed racoon appeared before they saw Thorne Mondae. In a hunched position with what looked like a long stick protruding from his chest, he tottered past the lens. Then he must have stumbled down the creek bank, crossed the stream, and fell on the other side, his torso resting face down in the embankment.

"This photo says he activated the camera at 10:57 a.m. Thursday morning," Claire said.

The next photo showed Claire skulking out of the forest mist five minutes after Thorne and from the same direction. The time stamp showed 11:02 a.m.

"That's not good." Claire stared at the next photo. As Avery watched closely for her reaction, her sister's body stiffened and her eyes widened.

From behind the shed, a shadowy figure popped up. The time stamp read 11:06 a.m. The person wore full camouflage, top to bottom, including his or her shirt, pants, boots, billed cap with sunglasses pushed above the brim, and a dark ski mask obscuring the face. Impossible to tell whether it was male or female or much else.

Claire sucked in a deep breath. "Could that be—?"

"—the killer?" Avery said. "That's what I think."

"What are we going to do?" Claire asked.

"If we turn this sim card over to Detective Castellan, he'll have even more proof that you're the most likely murderer. Coupled with the expert archer thing and your confrontation with Thorne, you're bound to be the prime suspect." Avery felt like crying. She was glad to see her sister looked more composed than she felt, even facing a possible death sentence and ultimate lethal injection.

"What about that mystery figure behind the shed?" Claire's hopeful face made Avery feel even worse. "Wouldn't the detective agree with us it's the killer?"

"I doubt it, not with everything he has on you. You showed up right behind Mondae, like you'd been stalking him. The person behind the shed might be a witness. But they turned up after you did. Cops can get tunnel vision. Once they have a suspect in their sights, especially one with as much evidence against them as you, they don't need to look elsewhere."

"But if the Shadowy Figure is a witness, he can testify that I didn't do it!"

"Not if he's the killer. He'll let you take the blame. And we're assuming it's a male. It could just as easily be a female. Regardless, even if Castellan tries to find them, are you willing to trust your freedom to those odds?"

"I'll call Mary Mayberry, the lawyer." Claire dashed to the other side of the kitchen to retrieve her cellphone. Rarely had Avery seen her sister move so fast.

"Wait!" She ran after Claire. "Technically, we're withholding evidence. A lawyer might have to tell the police since she's an officer of the court."

"Or have you been watching too much crime TV?" Claire gripped the phone until her knuckles turned white but didn't move to dial it.

"We can't ask anybody without telling them the reason we want to know." Avery scratched her head. "Maybe I could ask Jay—"

"No! Absolutely not." Claire's face tightened into a resolute grimace.

"I trust him. He wouldn't tell anyone if I asked him not to."

"No, I mean it. *Do. Not. Tell. Jay.*"

"But…"

"Avery. Do you know the real reason I didn't tell you about being in the forest the day of the murder?"

Avery did not like the hardness of Claire's expression. "No, why?" She had a feeling she wasn't going to like the answer.

"Because you have a big mouth and can't keep a freaking secret!"

Avery huffed out an offended snort. She retreated to her side of the great room and flopped into her favorite chair. Bodhi collapsed on her feet as if he meant to console her.

"Your other momma is a mean old witch, Bodhi," she whispered to the dog. "I wish we'd never moved here." Bodhi whined. "Sorry, fella. I didn't mean that. We wouldn't have you if we hadn't moved to Rancho Exotica."

After a short time, Claire moseyed over to Avery's sitting area and pretended to be looking for a snack in the walk-in pantry. Her usual way of saying *sorry*. Not saying it, letting a little cooldown time pass, then acting as if nothing had happened. That there had been no cross words between sisters. Avery sighed. She couldn't stay mad at Claire for long. She had a point. Avery did have a compulsion to confess, but she knew in her heart this was a secret she would keep for as long as necessary. Because nothing and no one meant more to her than Claire.

"We need to find out who murdered Thorne Mondae," Claire said in a soft but firm voice. "We have to prove I'm innocent. We have information no one else has—we've seen the killer. We're the only ones who can."

12

Leaving a whining Bodhi behind, Avery and Claire climbed onto their golf cart. A dog would be unwelcome at their neighbor's Bunco party.

"Guess who invited me into his RV for a glass of wine while you were having geezer sex with Tom Wellman," Avery said.

Claire ignored her, feigning indifference.

"Jay Vidocq! I think he tried to kiss me. Not positive, but it sure looked that way."

"I don't really need the details."

"Why do you get negative every time I talk about Jay? He's a nice guy." Avery hadn't quite gotten over her sister saying she had a big mouth. "I'm happy for you. Finding Tom. Why can't just this once you be happy for me? You've never approved of my boyfriends."

"I don't disapprove of Jay. I like him." Claire cleared her throat like those words had been hard to get out of her mouth.

"But…"

"But he's technically still a married man. And his wife lives here, in Rancho Exotica. I don't want you to get the reputation as a husband-stealing floozy."

The sisters stared at each other, their lips twitching, then burst into laughter.

"A senior citizen femme fatale, that's me!" Avery said.

"Besides, we have more important things to do." Claire pushed a strand of curly hair out of her face.

"Really? What's more important than me having sex for the first time in a number of years I've successfully repressed?"

"Keeping me from being arrested for murder and confined to life in a maximum-security prison," Claire said.

"Good point. The only sex you'd get there would be a heavily tattooed inmate with pierced nipples having their way with you in the shower."

The sisters pulled into the driveway of a Texas traditional house. Both sisters preferred contemporary style, and Avery often railed at the similarity among the homes in the community. Claire agreed but reminded her of something a former friend had said many years ago.

"Not everybody wants to be different!" the friend insisted. A concept totally foreign to the sisters.

If the house was standard fare, it perfectly matched its owner. Penelope Viktor opened the heavy wooden door to let the sisters inside. She was one of three resident ladies who looked and acted so much alike, the sisters could hardly tell them apart. Penelope had set up several different open areas of her home with six card tables, each surrounded by four chairs. Some guests gathered around the kitchen peninsula eating snacks while others visited in small groups.

Claire and Avery chose separate tables with Avery sitting the first round with two members of PAM. Along with Penelope, Angela Sheldon Hickson and Mabel Sheldon Tobias, who were sisters in real life, formed the group Avery referred to as "PAM." Their first names spelled the moniker. Angela sat on her left with Mabel on her right. Or maybe it was the other way around.

"It must have been frightening," Mabel said, "finding that body in your forest." Mabel's salt-and-pepper hair had been cut into a short do that gave her un-made-up face a manly plainness. She shook the dice in hands with fingernails that appeared to have never been touched by a manicurist before flinging them across the table.

"I heard his son Isaac was hunting with him. The last person to see him alive." Angela resembled her sister, except a more feminine version. Her short bob and feathery bangs framed a thin face that had received a dab of makeup here and there but with no obvious plan to complete the job.

"Yes, it was unnerving," Avery said. "I don't know much about it, though." *Not anything I'm telling you anyway.*

"That son of his," Angela said. "Have you ever seen him? Dresses real fancy. My grandson went to high school with him. Said he wore suits and starched white shirts to class and real gold watches. Not interested in sports. His heroes were billionaires, and he tacked their pictures up in his locker. Bought girls expensive gifts."

Avery rolled a Bunco and wrote down the 21 points on her scorecard.

"Lucky you!" Mabel shouted. A startled Avery rolled again and turned up diddly-squat. "I hear Thorne Mondae banished Isaac from Dallas to the Sweetgum office because he kept pestering him to give him a higher-paying position."

"But this is where he met Shania, so that worked out for him." Angela threw the dice and rolled three of a kind. She kept rolling.

"Who's Shania?" Avery never averted her gaze from the game table. No one ever took their eyes off the rolling dice during a Bunco round.

"His girlfriend. They're engaged. Thorne didn't approve of her. Too much of a country hick." It impressed Avery that Angela could talk and roll dice at the same time. "Heard they're getting married now that Thorne's dead. Throwing a big wedding at his father's house. Inviting the whole neighborhood. I'll bet Thorne's turning over in his grave while his son frivols away all his hard-earned money."

"He's still at the coroner's office," her sister corrected. "Hasn't been buried yet."

"I was speaking figuratively," Angela said.

"If he's turning over, it's on a slab in the coroner's vault," Mabel said.

"It was just a figure of speech, for goodness sakes. No one thought a dead man would turn over. Quit making a federal case out of it."

"Are you sure Thorne's wealth was earned?" The sisterly bickering made Avery uncomfortable. Maybe a little too close to home. "Heard a rumor that he and his business partner, Scopes Redfield, may have done things in the past which weren't exactly legal. Just speculating. Maybe they became wealthy using ill-gotten gains."

"People have been spinning stories like that about Thorne ever since he and Adrianna moved here." Angela swiped her bangs out of her eyes before taking her last roll. "Sounds possible to me. Where there's smoke there's fire."

Her sister huffed. "Don't believe everything you hear."

"Just repeating what others told me. Never said it was a fact."

After the bell rang indicating the end of the game, a relieved Avery gathered with the other ladies around the snack table and exchanged pleasantries. No one else brought up the murder, not while the entire group listened. However, Penelope did blurt out, "Saw your golf cart parked by Jay Vidocq's Winnebago in the RV park. Did your batteries run down?"

Avery hoped the heat she felt in her face did not manifest itself in her cheeks. Into the thundering silence, she muttered, "Are you sure it was mine?"

"A turquoise six-seater with white upholstery? Who else could it be?"

"It's Caribbean blue," Avery said. "I just stopped to use his bathroom." She tried to ignore the skeptical faces surrounding her.

"Bet he goes back to his wife any day now," Angela said. "She's young and beautiful and rich."

All the things I'm not.

"Most men aren't going to let that get away, if they can help it," Mabel said.

Avery wanted to protest, to insist that she had many wonderful qualities to offer Jay, but she had no reason to lay claim to him. He had been kind and friendly, but that was all. What was there to say? Any attempt to create a list of her appealing attributes came up short.

Soon after, she and Claire beat a hasty retreat. Back in their tell-tale Caribbean blue golf cart, Avery asked her sister, "What are some of my qualities that would appeal to a man?"

"Don't let those old biddies get to you, Avery," Claire said. "They've got nothing going on in their lives, and they don't want you to either."

"You didn't answer my question," Avery said.

"Well, let me see. You're pretty and kind and funny." Claire shot her a sidelong glance. "How many do I need to list before you start feeling better?"

That drew a smile from Avery. "That's enough for now. I'll give you a little more time to think about it."

"Okay, thanks." When Claire grinned at her sister, the deep dimples in her cheeks indented, and her dark blue eyes sparkled. "I learned a bit about Thorne Mondae's son, Isaac, while I was sitting at the table with Penelope. She told me he was living above his means and had gambling debts. That he shared his lavish lifestyle with his fiancé whom his father did not approve of. That's a motive right there."

Avery told her sister about the wedding plans which were scheduled to be held the next month.

"They haven't even buried him yet," Claire protested.

"Angela and Mabel have already beat that cliché to death," Avery said. "No pun intended."

Claire cocked her head but didn't ask for details. "Isaac needs to go to the top of our suspect list."

"Yeah, right after you," Avery said. "We don't have any real evidence against him, unless you count the fact that he was the last known person to be with his father when he was alive."

"We have to find out a lot more."

"PAM may be boring and interchangeable, but they are a rich source of information."

"Just because Penelope, Angela, and Mabel don't have sparkling, outgoing personalities like you doesn't mean they don't have one." Claire hit her with a direct shot. "Not everyone needs to be an extrovert."

"Does being a gossip mean you have personality?" Avery retaliated.

"When a person keeps their personality on the inside, people think it doesn't exist."

"A dilemma for the ages: When a tree falls in the forest, does it make a sound if nobody's there to hear it? Ergo, is it possible to have a personality if you don't let anyone see it?"

"And the tyranny of the extrovert persists."

13

In the Peaceful Meadow Funeral Home's parking lot, Avery and Claire parked their 15-year-old Honda Accord among the plethora of new SUVs. Based on a childhood that provided necessities but few luxuries, the sisters had developed a frugal policy when it came to vehicles. They refused to go into debt for a depreciating asset. Consequently, their two low-maintenance, highly reliable automobiles had been bought used and for cash. Avery suspected Claire secretly longed to drive a brand-new vehicle out of the dealership showroom even if it did depreciate in value by 30% the minute it left the lot. To be honest, so did Avery.

Inside, they recognized several residents of Rancho Exotica. Among them stood PAM—Pamela, Angela and Mabel. They herded together with their husbands who looked as much alike as their wives.

In line to go inside the chapel, Jay Vidocq looked like a wet dream in a well-cut black suit and starched white shirt, no tie. Avery did a doubletake when she noticed his hand on the waist of a petite woman with long dark hair curled into loose ringlets. He appeared to be guiding her into the chapel. He looked around quickly, saw Avery, and gave her a brief wave behind the woman's back.

"Is that Jay's wife?" Avery whispered to Claire.

"Don't know. I've never seen her."

"He looks so handsome."

"He's okay for a *married* old cop guy."

"He's better looking and younger than Tom Wellman!"

"Younger, maybe. Beauty is in the eye of the beholder."

"It's hard to argue with someone who speaks in cliches."

"Cliches become cliches because they are universally true."

When PAM gathered around the plate glass window that looked out onto a portico, Avery followed them. A white stretch limo pulled beneath the porch roof.

"Who could that be?" Penelope asked. "His wife is already here."

"It's his son, Isaac!" Angela said in a voice that, although meant to be a whisper, reverberated around the room.

When the chauffeur opened the limousine door, out stepped Isaac Mondae. He wore a suit that had been tailored to fit his slender torso to perfection. Next out, a woman who appeared to be a number of years older grasped his extended hand, her flouncy mini skirt more appropriate to a cocktail party than a funeral. She had covered the glittering top with a white fur jacket Avery guessed was real. The couple exhibited more jewels than a Hollywood power couple walking the red carpet.

"PAM said he was squandering his inheritance before Thorne Mondae died." Avery whispered to Claire who had followed her to the window.

"Looks like he's amped up the spending now that he knows he's getting the money soon."

"I don't know, Claire. Maybe the limo is just part of Peaceful Meadow's luxury funeral service package."

"Maybe, but that doesn't explain the clothes and furs and jewels."

"I can't believe people still wear fur. That industry should have gone out of business years ago."

"Maybe it's fake."

"Much like the bimbo wearing it."

Inside the chapel, which looked as if it would hold several hundred people, most of the seats were filled. Near the roped-off family section stood the deceased's wife, Adrianna Mondae, looking like she just stepped off the cover of *Vogue*. She confronted Onia Redfield, shaking her red-lacquered index finger in the young woman's face.

"I have as much right to be here as you do!" Onia's voice quavered with anger.

"If you don't stop spreading those wild rumors about my husband, I'm going to sue you!" Adrianna used her superior height to put up an imposing front. A smaller Onia looked like David facing the giant Goliath having forgotten his sling and stones.

"Then you'll find out it's the truth." Her belief in the righteousness of her cause seemed to give Onia courage. "He's my father as much as he is Isaac's. I'm entitled to mourn his loss as much as you and his son do."

"Which isn't saying much," Avery whispered to Claire. They stood in the aisle watching the embarrassing outbreak as it unfolded before them like a one-act play on a bright stage.

"Did you hear what she said?" Claire whispered. "Who is she? She couldn't possibly be Thorne Mondae's daughter."

"She was at the police department with Scopes Redfield. He told me she was his niece. You saw them when you came out of Detective Castellan's office."

"Guess I was too traumatized to notice."

The sisters retreated to the hallway while Avery explained what little she knew about Onia. They could still hear the loud confrontation at the front of the chapel, and Avery could glimpse the body language through the open doors.

"I'm having security escort you out!" Adrianna shouted. "This service is by invitation only, and your name isn't on the list."

"I came with my uncle, as his guest." Onia's voice had toned down a decibel or two, as if she knew she wasn't going to win this one.

"I don't remember including guests. Now, either leave, or I am calling security." Adrianna stared at her adversary who returned the intense gaze. A hush fell over the crowd as neither woman appeared close to retreating.

Finally, a red-faced Onia whirled and tramped out the door toward the parking lot.

Adrianna slumped in the pew like a collapsed marionette.

"I'm going after Onia," Claire said to Avery.

"You don't even know her. She won't talk to a complete stranger."

"I'll tell her you're my sister. You've met her. And I saw her at the police station with Scopes. She needs someone to support her right now. Be her friend."

"Okay but be subtle. She just landed on the suspect list with the rest of us." Avery watched her sister rush out, trying to catch Onia before she drove off in a huff. She wondered why Scopes Redfield had not followed his niece but discovered the reason when she walked back into the chapel.

The service was already in progress, and he sat on the podium with a couple of others who were either speakers or song leaders. While the pastor droned in a narcoleptic monotone, Avery searched the room for familiar faces. Specifically, Jay Vidocq. She caught him sitting next to the woman he had escorted inside. They sat stiffly, not touching, her with a frown between her brows, him with a neutral face. Avery's stomach drew into a knot.

A woman in the family section stood out from the others. She looked well-put-together and almost as glamourous as Adrianna, although a decade older. She wore all black, and a wide-brimmed hat decorated with black and white feathers swept across her face in a dramatic fashion. Based on accounts she had heard from PAM, Avery guessed her to be the dead man's ex-wife. Her calm, emotionless demeanor mimicked most of the other unmoved faces in the room. It seemed as if hysterically distraught friends or relatives who had been devasted by the death of Thorne Mondae either chose not to attend or did not exist.

The minister finished with the traditional deep-South biblical warning calculated to scare the nonbeliever into changing that condition before the same thing happened to them that happened to the deceased. Avery had yet to see anyone take the opportunity at a funeral to correct that situation.

He then announced that Scopes Redfield wished to speak about his life-long friend. Scopes displayed the poker face common to the room. He pulled a small piece of notepaper from his suit pocket and cleared his throat.

"I'd like to read from the poem 'Remember Me,' by Margaret Mead." He glanced down at his paper, paused for effect.

"…[A]s you stand upon a shore, gazing at a beautiful sea—
remember me.

As you look in awe at a mighty forest and its grand majesty—
remember me.

As you look upon a flower and admire its simplicity—
remember me.

...

For if you always think of me, I will never be gone.

"Thorne Mondae will never be forgotten. A man who accomplished
big things in his life, yet appreciated the simpler ones—family, friends, the
beauty of nature. Even in death, he reposed in a lovely forest, one which
brings back fond memories of the Jarawa Reserve in the Andaman Islands.
A place both he and I visited and appreciated for its natural beauty and unaffected primitive peoples. If my friend had to die, I'm glad it was in such a
happy place doing what he loved. R-I-P, Thorne."

The choir sang several hymns, and the minister presented another brief
message which basically amounted to: *If you don't repent and be baptized right
now you will go to hell*.

14

The visions of a flaming hell promulgated by the funeral preacher did not put Avery off her lunch. What did were the platters of carcasses that dominated the buffet table. She rummaged around and found a salad with nothing dead on it except maybe an insect or two and a dinner roll with a little pat of margarine. The dessert table looked more promising. She cornered a brownie and a slice of carrot cake. Not vegan, but she was desperate. She joined a table where PAM, along with their interchangeable husbands, sat scarfing down the fatty meats.

"Who was that woman sitting in the family section?" Avery washed down a bite of cake with a swig of iced tea. "The one in the big hat." PAM lit up like a flash of lightning against a dark stormy sky.

"Oh, that's Thorne's ex-wife. Isaac's mother," Mabel said. "Lianne Rhinehart. I don't think she goes by Mondae anymore. Kicked him to the curb as soon as she got what she wanted—a child and a fortune."

"Are you going to eat that mac and cheese?" Mabel's husband asked. Avery assumed he belonged to her because he sat beside her.

"You can have it, honey." Mabel scrapped the uneaten food onto her husband's empty plate.

"She won't be inheriting anything from Thorne?"

"Got all she needed when they divorced."

"All she needed, maybe, but not all she wanted." A tall man in a blue button-down shirt and dark pants had spoken from the next table. "Sorry. I couldn't help overhearing your conversation. I've known both Thorne and

Lianne for a long time. Name's Bud Tengle. I'm one of their tenants. My business is, anyway."

"Would you care to join me, Mr. Tengle?" Avery scraped back her chair and drew her purse over her shoulder. "I was just about to grab something from the dessert table." She needed to get him away from PAM and husbands to grill him more effectively.

"You already had a brownie and a big piece of carrot cake," Angela said. "Maybe Mr. Tengle would like to sit with us while you get more food."

Avery slid her hand beneath Bud Tengle's arm and pulled him up with a hard jerk. "Mr. Tengle's had lunch. He's going with me. Aren't you?" She drew a vise grip around his arm.

"Looks like it," he said.

They wandered around the dessert table for a few minutes, and Avery resisted the urge to seize a miniature pecan pie. Mr. Tengle selected a piece of chocolate cake, and they sat down at an empty table. She noticed Jay glancing in their direction and wondered if he suspected some sort of romantic liaison. When their eyes met, he looked away. She regarded Bud Tengle and realized no one could suspect them of being a couple because he was 30 years younger than her.

The weird thing about being old was that she didn't feel old. She still thought of herself as that 30–40-something who could be appealing to anyone of almost any age. Most senior citizens admitted they didn't feel any different now than they had when they were young. But a quick look in a mirror reminded her that she no longer possessed that unlined youthful face and lithe figure. No sense dwelling on it. After what had happened to her before she moved to Rancho Exotica, she should be happy just to be alive and well.

"Mr. Tengle—

"Please, call me Bud."

"Of course. I'm Avery Halverson. I live in Rancho Exotica with my sister. That's the gated community where Thorne Mondae lives... lived." She decided honesty would be the best approach. "My sister is a prime suspect in his death. I'm trying to prove she had nothing to do with it. Is there anything you can tell me about him or his family that might help?"

He squinted at her through narrowed eyes. "You're retired? You look a little young for that."

"Thank you. I'm older than I look."

"Good for you." His whole face contracted when he smiled. "Know what I said when I heard Thorne was dead?"

"My sincerest condolences…"

"Dammit, somebody beat me to it!"

Avery laughed a bit self-consciously. "You said that to the cops?"

"Sure did. They looked as surprised as you do. I don't have anything to hide, so why should I hold back? I've had trouble with both Thorne and Lianne. And I'm not the only one. They could be hard-nosed when dealing with tenants, especially her. In their bad cop/worse cop routine, he let her be the grand executioner. Never did anything to stop her bullying. They've racked up dozens of lawsuits by refusing to keep properties in good repair."

"Have you filed a lawsuit against them?" When he looked dubious, she said: "I could look it up, but it would be easier if you shared the information."

"Course I have. I lease one of their commercial properties, but my wife and I live above the warehouse in an apartment with our two children. The whole place fell into disrepair and became dangerous. I was concerned for my family. The Mondaes refused to fix anything, including the air conditioning units, storm doors, safety locks, landscaping. Lianne told me it was my responsibility. Since when is the air conditioning in a rented building the tenant's responsibility?" His face contorted with an anger that went deeper than concern for himself. "When I refused to pay the rent, they threatened me with inventory seizure and eviction. I beat them to the punch, though. I claimed $1,000,000 in damages and danger to my family."

"Sorry to hear that, Bud." Avery understood the distress for his home and family. "You said it was mainly her that caused your troubles. That she was the one in charge?"

"All the tenants called her 'The Enforcer,' but we blamed Thorne because he didn't try to stop her. As landlords, they knew how to run a business, get ahold of their money, and how to keep it. Once they had it, they didn't want to let go." Bud had picked at his cake during the conversation but pushed it aside.

Avery tried to think of anything else she should ask. She made a mental note to read "How to be a Private Investigator" on *wikiHow* the minute she got home.

"I was on the other side of the country when Thorne was killed," Bud volunteered. "I told the police that. Not sure they believed me."

"Thank you for sharing." Avery stood, shook hands with Bud. Across the room, she saw Adrianna Mondae exit after eating at the table with Isaac and his girlfriend, Shania. Maybe she'd had enough familial closeness.

"To tell you the truth," Bud Tengle said, "I'm glad Thorne's dead. I'm just sorry they didn't get Lianne as well."

"Uh, okay." Avery thought her new friend might be a little too forthcoming. "Nice meeting you. Good luck with your lawsuit."

Avery headed toward the exit Adrianna had taken hanging back just enough not be seen. The hallway opened into a casket showroom. Various rectangular boxes ranging from pine to mahogany and from steel to bronze lay atop daises with their open tops exposing plush satin linings. Beyond, a small office with picture windows faced onto the showroom. Inside, Adrianna spoke animatedly with Jay. Avery wondered what those two had to discuss.

As she moved closer, they shifted positions so that if either of them looked her way, they would be able to spot Avery. She searched for a place to hide. Without thinking, she grabbed a nearby stepstool and used it to struggle into a lovely mahogany coffin lined in creamy white satin. Just as she scrunched her legs into the bottom half, Jay glanced her way. Startled, she grabbed the coffin lid and pulled it down after her. The suffocating darkness sent a trill of fear down her spine. She panicked, ramming the palms of her hands hard against the lid.

The casket had locked from the outside and wouldn't budge.

15

Claire followed as Onia Redfield stomped out of the funeral home and dived into her white SUV. She lowered her head onto the steering wheel, and her shoulders shook with sobs. Claire ducked behind a column, deciding to wait a few minutes until the woman composed herself. Good thing she was a patient person; it took a while. When Onia at last raised her head, pulled a tissue from her purse, and wiped her eyes, Claire approached the open window.

"Hi, Onia. I'm Claire Browning. Avery Halverson is my sister. You met her at the Sweetgum Police Station with your Uncle Scopes."

The young woman stared at her through electric blue eyes swollen with tears. "Can I help you?"

Claire thought about what to say to gain her confidence. Onia probably needed a friend, someone on her side, more than anything else. "I wanted to tell you I'm sorry about what happened in there. How Adrianna treated you. Sounds to me like you have as much right to be at the funeral as anyone. I mean, with Thorne Mondae being your biological father and all." She hoped she hadn't gone too far.

"Really?" Onia eyed her suspiciously, then her face relaxed, apparently assuming an elderly lady in a conservative black sheath and white cable knit cardigan did not present much of a threat. "I remember you and your sister. From the police station."

Claire wiped beads of sweat from her upper lip. Even in October, the relentless Texas sun sucked the perspiration right out of a person, especially if they were standing in its direct rays and wearing a sweater.

"Get in," Onia said. "I'll turn on the air conditioner."

A surprised Claire settled herself into the passenger side of the SUV. Onia exhibited the trusting traits of a young woman who had grown up with all the comforts and security an American upper-middle-class upbringing could provide. After starting the engine, she hit the AC full blast. It might have been a bit of overkill. Maybe she was still upset over her confrontation with Adrianna. Claire buttoned up her sweater.

"My name was originally Rebecca," she began. "But I changed it to 'Onia' about a year ago. It's a native Jarawa name." She pronounced it *huh RAH wah*. "Which means 'outsider' in Great Andamanese, the language of an indigenous tribe located in the Andaman Islands. An Indian archipelago in the Bay of Bengal."

"The Bay of Bengal… that's off the coast of—"

"East coast of India. The Andaman and Nicobar Islands are bordered by the Bay on one side and the Andaman Sea and Thailand on the other. I always knew I was different, and the moniker 'outsider' seemed appropriate. When Uncle Scopes told me about the circumstances of my birth, it was quite a shock."

"I can imagine." This young woman seemed starved for a confidant. As if she had suppressed the facts of her past for a hundred years, and it could no longer be contained. "I'd like to hear more about it." Claire hoped she sounded sincere, because she was.

When Onia opened her mouth, the words burst from inside her like a fissure in the earth belches forth black lava after centuries of keeping it confined.

* * *

It had been close to a year ago when Rebecca Redfield slammed into her office and dropped into her swivel desk chair. When she pulled out her computer keyboard tray, it banged against her knees. "Ouch, dammit!" No one heard her cry because her closed office door made the room virtually soundproof. She pounded her password into her computer and tapped her foot waiting for it to pull up her daily schedule. "Oh crap, I don't have time for this BS!"

She punched a number into her desk phone and waited for someone to pick up. When they didn't, she jerked her cellphone from her purse and typed a text message.

Mom, too busy to meet for lunch. Have to reschedule. Am still pissed at you and Dad. We'll talk later.

Last night's fierce argument with her parents had left her frustrated and exhausted. She couldn't understand what the big mystery was. Wouldn't any adopted child want to know about their biological father and mother? Previously, she had never asked, being perfectly happy with the parents fate dealt her. But that was before. She floated through undergraduate school making the honor roll, excelling in sports, winning popularity contests, and even a beauty pageant. The beauty thing held little interest for her, since she had bigger and better plans to succeed in the world of business.

In the top 15% of her class, she had earned a Master of Science Degree in Finance from Southern Methodist University's Cox School of Business in University Park, a wealthy enclave in the heart of Dallas. Through the years, she had worked with Uncle Scopes at various jobs in the investment business he managed for himself and Thorne Mondae.

When she graduated, Uncle Scopes had given her the full-time job as his assistant and promised to tutor her in the practical aspects of finance that school couldn't teach her. Like how to keep your head when the stock market takes a drastic plunge, and everyone around you is losing theirs. He had bought during the 2008 stock market crash and reaped the rewards when the market recovered.

After several years in Dallas, they moved to the boonies of East Texas. The pandemic, the nightmare of commuting to downtown, and advanced computer technology had made working from home both desirable and safer.

He opened a small office in Sweetgum which mainly housed him, Rebecca, and a secretary.

When Uncle Scopes decided to cut back his work schedule, and the burden would have been too much for Rebecca alone, he hired a young man to assist. Rafael Valencia had grown up in South Texas but graduated with a marketing degree from Baylor University in Waco. The move had proved serendipitous because Rebecca and Rafael, a handsome Hispanic man whose family had immigrated from Mexico long before he was born, became immediately attracted to one another.

Love was a wonderful thing, and her parents approved of Rafe. For Rebecca, neglected questions about her heritage came roaring to the surface. Rafe knew everything about his family and had often visited the ancestral home in Mexico City where his elderly grandmother still lived. But Rebecca could share nothing about her culture and customs. Like a jigsaw puzzle with pieces dropped on the floor and chewed up by the dog, her ancestry was a picture impossible to complete.

Just last Saturday, with both their parents and Uncle Scopes present, Rafe had proposed to her at a dinner he surreptitiously arranged at the Sweetgum Country Club. His family laughed and chattered with hers, but she never felt like the connection was equal. James and Myrna were not her parents. Even Uncle Scopes was not her uncle. She free floated in a world where she had no roots.

What if she and Rafe wanted to have children? What if she had genetic problems that would affect the health of their babies? How would they know? No way to plan for such an event with her DNA a complete mystery.

She had a social security number, obtained when she was a child, so there must be documentation somewhere. Rebecca hounded her parents mercilessly, while they thwarted her at every turn. Until last night, when she screamed and yelled, threatened to move to a foreign country and never contact them again, and separate them from their grandbabies forever. Faced with the prospect of their worst nightmare, her parents relented.

Uncle Scopes had saved her from being drowned by a Jarawa tribal elder because she was a half-white baby, and he wanted to keep the tribe pure. Who were the Jarawa, and where were the Andaman Islands? Her parents showed her on Google maps and described the tribe as one of the world's most primitive. Uncle Scopes had brought her to the United States using forged documents. And they had used her fake birth certificate to officially, if not legally, adopt her and obtain a social security number. Nothing was impossible if you knew the right people. Apparently, Uncle Scopes was the right people. They denied knowing any more details.

When she decided to confront Uncle Scopes, they begged her not to. It had been a difficult time for him, they said. She cared not at all. She had the right to know everything about herself, didn't she? And the ultimate question: Exactly who were her biological father and mother?

She opened her office door so she would hear the second Scopes entered the office. Ten minutes later, she heard the secretary greet him, and he walked past, giving her a little wave.

"I want to talk to you," she said in a strained voice.

He stopped. "Of course. Can it wait until I put my things up?" He indicated his briefcase and suit jacket. "Maybe get some coffee?"

"Put your stuff away," she said. "I'll bring your coffee. I know how you like it." She hadn't brought him coffee since working part-time as a college student, trying to win his favor in any way possible. He had to know something unusual was up.

"I talked to James this morning," Scopes said after Rebecca handed across a steaming mug of black coffee. "I know you're upset. I get that. But your parents love you. They want whatever is best for you. They... *we*... didn't think it necessary to tell you about your heritage until it became an issue." He sighed, blew across the coffee to cool it, took a sip. "Which I guess we all knew it eventually would."

"It felt like they were withholding something. And I want to know what. Is there something wrong with me? Am I flawed in some unspeakable way? That's the way they're making me feel." Rebecca clutched the arms of her chair as if she might shoot out at any second.

"There's nothing wrong with you!" Scopes walked around the desk, sat in the guest chair next to her, took her hand. "You are perfect. Always have been."

"Then tell me everything you know. The truth. Promise."

"I promise." Scopes told her that he and Thorne landed on the Andaman Islands to enlist the Jarawa tribesmen to help them poach fish. That they intended to sell them on the mainland for a profit.

"You mean you stole from them?" Rebecca recognized an unfamiliar side to her uncle. He never talked about his past, even though she knew he and Thorne had been friends for many years. His pained expression saddened her, but she had to know.

"Yes, we stole their fish, and we did it with their help." Scopes let go of her hand and reached for his coffee. He stared into the black abyss as though looking into a past that caused him great discomfort. "But even worse," he finally looked up, "we stole your mother's innocence."

"What do you mean?"

"She was very young, a virgin. Her name was Anjale. Thorne got her drunk, lured her away from her people. Took advantage of her."

"What?" Rebecca leaped up and stood behind her chair, arms crossed. "What are you saying? That—"

"—Thorne Mondae is your biological father." Scopes's skin had turned pale, and he wiped sweat from his forehead.

"No, no, no! It's impossible. That little toad of a man is my father? My flesh and blood?" A vein throbbed in her forehead. She felt sick and crumpled into her chair, not trying to hold back the tears.

"I'm so sorry, sweetheart. I should have stopped him, but he had this strange hold over me. I was never able to thwart his baser instincts. And what if I had? The best thing that ever happened to me… you… would never have been born. You're a beautiful, precious gift to both your parents and me. We are eternally grateful that you were born, that you exist. It doesn't matter who your biological father was. James is your real father. Myrna is your real mother. I hope you can forgive me and remember the good things. You've had a wonderful life, and it will continue as long as we live."

Rebecca wiped her wet eyes. "Does he know?"

"I never told him. The nurse, Riya Singh, who was there when you were born and took care of your mother, contacted me back in the states. Told me you were in danger. I returned in time to save you from being drowned by a tribesman. The Jarawa are quite insulated and don't want any-one from outside fraternizing with their women. Because their way of life is protected by the Indian government, they pretty much do whatever they want."

"Like murdering babies."

"Yes, if they are born to widows, or if they have light skin or, in your case, blue eyes. Obviously not pure blood Jarawa."

And my mother… Anjale? What happened to her? Does she know I'm alive?"

"I don't think so." His chin trembled. "I brought you to this country to save your life. Returning you to her would have put you back in the same situation." He rubbed his temple where the hair had begun to recede. "I sent Nurse Singh money to take care of Anjale. Have been all these years."

"Would she know where my mother is now?"

"Probably."

"How do I get in touch with her?"

"Rebecca, please." He moved behind his desk, his face sagging like a defeated man. "Think about this. Are you going to be okay with whatever you discover? Some things just need to be left in the past."

"No, I want to know. Doesn't matter what I learn. There's nothing worse than not knowing."

Uncle Scopes sighed.

Two weeks later Rebecca boarded an airplane headed for Port Blair, Andaman Islands.

16

A feeling of impending doom enveloped Avery. She began to hyperventilate, her heart raced, and she broke into a sweat. Pressure gathered in her chest, and she couldn't catch her breath. The casket felt hot, cramped, like a vise gripping and squeezing her. She grew lightheaded, and her body shook to its core. If she hadn't known she was having a panic attack, she would have thought it was another seizure. Her mind leaped back to that fateful day she and Claire decided to retire. A day her sister described to her, since she remembered nothing, when she finally awoke in the hospital.

* * *

Claire had ridden shotgun while Avery drove them out of downtown and pulled into the high occupancy vehicle lane. She agreed with her younger sister that their current jobs weren't bringing them much happiness for individual reasons, but primarily they just felt exhausted. They had been driving to downtown from one suburb or another since they graduated from college. Although both had education degrees, neither of them had taken the teaching route. Once established in the legal groove, they were unable to find a way out. Although far from rich, they made a respectable middle-class income, and their upbringing had not taught them to expect more. They did have the resolve and drive not to end up like their widowed mother and spend their retirement existing on nothing but a social security check from the federal government.

The big question, and the one that most concerned Claire was, where would they live? With no living parents, no children, and few relatives, they could pick from anywhere in the United States. They loved Oregon, but the cost of living proved beyond their means. Since they had been born and raised in Texas, most of their friends and relatives lived here, and the cost of living was reasonable, Texas won by default.

In the middle of this discussion and five o'clock traffic, Avery suddenly looked confused. She seemed to stare at something that wasn't there. Her body seized up, and she let go of the steering wheel. Her foot smashed into the gas pedal, and they slammed into the car ahead. The seatbelts jerked into their middles as the airbags deployed. The smell of chemicals and burning filled their nostrils. Avery's forehead bounced against the steering wheel.

"Avery!" Claire screamed. Behind them, tires screeched, and brakes squealed as a pile of cars tried to avoid smashing into them. All Claire could do was hold on until the crashing stopped. "Are you okay? Can you talk?" Avery looked as if she were in a trance. Her forehead swelled from the bump. The vehicles surrounding them erupted with exiting drivers and passengers. "Help me!" she cried. "It's my sister. She's hurt." She dialed 9-1-1.

Amid the honking horns and screeching tires, Claire pushed out of her airbag. She rushed to the driver's side door and jerked it open. Avery had collapsed to the right side of the steering wheel. While Claire pulled at her arm, a man in a business suit pulled from Avery's waist and together they lifted her onto the tarmac.

"I know CPR," he said. Claire gazed at her sister's clenched teeth and staring eyes. Her chest heaved.

"What's happening to her?" Claire heard a shaky voice that sounded as if it came from someone on the verge of hysteria.

"Looks like she's still breathing," he said. "May be a stroke. She needs to be hospitalized as soon as possible."

"They're coming," Claire said. "Is there anything I can do in the meantime?" She wanted to scream but knew that wouldn't help her sister.

"No, not really. I'm sorry." The kind man stood beside her while Claire sat on the rough concrete next to Avery. She brushed the hair from her eyes, speaking softly: "I'm here, Avery. Stay with me. Everything's going to be alright." Finally, the paramedics arrived and loaded her into the ambulance.

"Where are you taking her?" Claire asked.

"Parkland, ma'am," the EMT said.

"Can I come with you? My car is unavailable." They both turned to looked at the crushed vehicle from which she had emerged. The smell of burned rubber, exhaust fumes, and chemicals filled Claire's nose, and a sick knot formed in her gut.

"Okay," the EMT said, "but we need to get her out of here right now." The urgency in his voice terrified Claire.

* * *

Don't fight it. It'll just make it worse. Avery had been taught by her therapist to take a deep breath. Focus on just letting it happen, letting the anxiety attack run its course. She closed her eyes. Pretended she was in bed, getting ready for a good night's sleep. Unable to pull a deep breath from her lungs, Avery focused on breathing from her diaphragm. As each labored breath came more evenly, her heart slowed, and the panic attack gradually receded.

The problem of being locked in a casket remained, but right now she had other issues to deal with. Specifically, eavesdropping on the conversation between Jay Vidocq and Adrianna Mondae. She swiped sweat from her forehead, regulated her breathing, and lay still to listen.

"Mr. Vidocq," Adrianna was saying in low-pitched girlish tones. Avery thought she was either trying to be sexy or prevent being overhead. Either way, the affectation made it more difficult for Avery to hear.

"Call me Jay." Avery would have huffed in disapproval if she hadn't been locked in a coffin with a limited air supply.

"Jay. I wanted you to understand what happened between me and Onia. She's been threatening me, and I need her put on the list of people banned from Rancho Exotica. I fear for my safety."

"Who is she? I heard her say she was Thorne's daughter. Can that be true?"

"We knew her as Scopes's niece. Adopted by his brother and sister-in-law when she was a baby. They named her Rebecca. She's worked for the investment company as Scopes's assistant since she graduated from SMU. Since Thorne is based in Dallas and heads the real estate business, we haven't seen much of her over the years. But last year, she took a trip to the Andaman Islands and found her birth mother—an indigenous woman who is a member of the Jarawa tribe. That's when she changed her name, in honor of her ancestry, she claimed. Her mother said Thorne was her real father. I don't know the whole story, but she tried to extort money from Thorne by threatening to tell me of her existence."

"She must have done it, since you obviously know about her."

"Yes, but he's the one who told me. He swore he'd never touched her mother. He said he'd met her among other tribespeople when he and Scopes visited the Island. But he denies they had intimate relations."

"And you believed him?"

"Of course, I believed him." There was an awkward pause. "Look, Jay, my husband could be a real ass and was most of the time, but I didn't know him to be a liar. Threatening to tell me or anybody else was a hollow threat where Thorne was concerned. He never gave a fig about his reputation. If you had something to say about him, go ahead. He didn't care." She hesitated, took a deep breath. "It's bad luck to speak ill of the dead, but I often had the feeling he reveled in the nasty things people said about him. He thrived on the contempt of others."

"Did she have any proof she was his daughter? DNA, for example?"

"Not that I know of."

"She threatened Thorne with exposure. Is it possible his refusal to acknowledge her made her snap? She appears to be a volatile personality."

"It's possible, I suppose."

"Mrs. Mondae," Jay said in an authoritative tone, "as soon as you get home, call the gatehouse and have Onia's name put on the banned list. Tell them I said so. Then, call Detective Castellan at the Sweetgum Police Department and tell him everything you've told me. Okay?"

"I promise. Thank you so much. You've been a big help. I feel so much safer with you on security."

An annoyed and overheated Avery heaved a disgusted, but silent and shallow, sigh in her tomb. *Would these two ever quit talking?* Finally, it sounded as if Jay and Adrianna were leaving. Avery counted to one hundred, then began banging on the lid of her prison.

"Help, somebody. I've been buried alive. Get me out of here. Help!"

She punched and kicked the lid as hard as her cramped space would allow. It only took a minute—the longest minute of her life. The lid raised and a rush of fresh air filled her nostrils. The face of Jay Vidocq appeared above. *Uh oh.*

"What are you doing in here?" Jay looked both amused and incredulous.

"Casket shopping?" Avery struggled to sit. "Just wanted to make sure it fit and was comfortable."

Jay positively guffawed. He looked cute, but it irritated Avery. Then she saw a crowd had gathered behind him, and numerous funeral attendees witnessed her humiliation. She tried to duck behind Jay noting his over-six-feet height served a useful purpose other than being merely attractive.

"Hey, Avery, you gonna buy that one?" Angela, one of the PAM ladies, hi-fived her sister, Mabel, and the other bystanders twittered.

"Maybe they'll give you a deal on the Deluxe Legacy Package," Mabel said, "especially now that it's used!"

"I believe it includes cremation and limo service," Penelope said.

Avery hunkered down wishing a Texas tornado would vacuum up a trio of old biddies and hurl them into oblivion.

"Why is that woman in a casket?" Adrianna Mondae's usually rigid exterior exuded shock and horror. Scopes Redfield stood beside her frowning his disapproval.

The funeral director, with his slicked-back hair and buffed fingernails, rushed onto the scene all aflutter. "This is most unconventional! She's going to have to pay for the merchandise if there's any damage!"

Could this get any worse? Avery's only relief lay in the fact that her sister wasn't there. A casket was the last place Claire needed to see her sister.

Jay!" she called in a loud whisper, tugging at his jacket. "Get those people out of here!" She wriggled in frustration and anger.

It took him several minutes to clear the room. She waited until he extended his hand to help her climb out. She forced her stiff limbs to function. After a couple of unsuccessful efforts and with the support of Jay's arm around her waist, she climbed out of the box. She stretched her knees several times since they had atrophied during her sojourn in the cramped space. The left one crackled when she flexed it. She flushed, hoping her sweaty armpits didn't smell.

"You were eavesdropping on my conversation with Adrianna Mondae." A frown split Jay's brow.

"No, really I—"

"Listen, Avery." Her name on his lips sent a thrill through her body, or it would have if she hadn't been so discomfited. "I know what you're doing. You're worried about your sister being a person of interest in a murder investigation. But playing private investigator is serious business. It's not like novels where it's all fun and games, and any nonprofessional can do it. It's lots of hard work and requires resources the average person can't access. Leave it to the professionals."

"But you don't understand."

"Yes, I do understand. I don't want you or Claire to get hurt. Murder is a dangerous business. Nice people don't murder other nice people. Let Detective Castellan handle it. He's perfectly capable."

"But—"

"And it would be nice if you had the good grace to be embarrassed." Jay pursed his lips in disapproval. "I did catch you hiding in a coffin. So did everybody else at the funeral."

A miffed Avery said, "I've been locked in that thing for an hour. I had a panic attack. I'm sweating like a prisoner escaped in the desert and pursued by a baying pack of dogs. I'm sorry you think I'm not ashamed enough. I'm scared, and tired, and humiliated. Does that satisfy you?"

"Nice analogy," he said. "The escaped prisoner thing."

"Thank God!" Claire cried from the open door. "I've been looking everywhere for you." She rushed to her sister and gave her a quick hug. She must have been really scared.

"I was uh… locked in that casket," Avery said, glancing at Jay and deciding she either had to tell the truth or he would. "Maybe by somebody who wanted to scare me. Or kill me."

"What the hell were you doing there in the first place?" Claire had passed the relieved-to-find-you stage and now worked on the you-scared-the-crap-out-of-me stage.

"Apparently," Jay said, "she was trying it on for size. I doubt if anyone locked you inside. There's a simple metal clasp on the outside that secured the lid from opening. All I had to do was lift the clasp and pull up."

"And I appreciate it." Although it didn't come out sounding exactly grateful. Avery motioned to her sister. "Let's get out of here." She hated to leave things between her and Jay in such an uncomfortable place, but she needed to talk to her sister.

Claire looked at her and then at Jay, as if she suspected there was more to this situation than what appeared on the surface. "I saw a group of people leaving this room. What happened?"

"I need some fresh air," Avery said. "I'll explain everything when we get home." Although unable to look him in the eye, she thanked Jay for rescuing her. She tried to put a little more gratitude into her tone, relieved that he didn't bring up the amateur detective thing in front of Claire. Or the fact that the biggest gossips in all of Rancho Exotica had witnessed her humiliation.

Together, the sisters walked into the clear evening air with Claire supporting her. Avery sucked in breath after breath and flexed her bad knees.

"I may have to have a knee replacement to reduce stress on my joints," she said. "Did you know that once a body is cremated, any of its spare medical parts or prosthetics are melted down and salvaged for road signs and car parts?"

"*All* of a dead body's medical parts would be spare, wouldn't they?"

"Good point," Avery said, "but—"

"I don't care!" Claire said. "Quit trying to distract me and tell me why you were really in the coffin."

17

Avery tempted Bodhi onto the cart by waving a jerky treat in front of his nose. Driving down their curvy extended driveway, she eyed the forest to her right. A feeling of dread spread over her when she remembered the gruesome death that had occurred there. Most of the trees' leaves had turned, and a good number of them had fallen to the ground. But the yellow sweetgum refused to give up until its competitors grew bare.

After Thorne Mondae's funeral, Claire had given her a brief description of what Onia told her. It consisted principally of the circumstances of her birth and adoption and how that culminated in what she overheard Adrianna tell Jay. That Onia had threatened Thorne if he did not acknowledge her as his daughter. Claire felt sorry for the young woman, learning that she'd known her father her whole life, yet he refused to accept her. Her intelligence impressed Claire, who felt she had a right to be angry. She didn't believe Onia had a compelling reason to kill Thorne.

Avery told Claire what she had discovered about Bud Tengle. He admitted to being happy that Thorne was dead but denied having anything to do with his murder. She didn't have a feel for Tengle's guilt or innocence. They needed more information, like a confirmation of his alibi that he'd been across the country.

The flashback in the coffin weighed on Avery's mind. After the rush hour seizure, she had spent three weeks in the hospital and another 10 days in rehab. She had been the only patient in her ward who could get out of bed without help. Because of so many strong drugs, she did not know where she was most of the time. Claire visited every day and admitted later that she doubted Avery would ever fully recover. With the help of a sympathetic nurse, Claire deduced that the doctors were overmedicating her. She demanded that they stop giving her anything other than medicine treating the seizure and insisted on a reduction of the anticonvulsants. When they complied, Avery began to get better. She owed her sister her life.

Avery told Jay Vidocq she quit her job the day the attorney told her to stop talking. The truth was, she had continued to push on because of her overwhelming fear of unemployment. She declined to tell Jay the truth because she didn't want him to know about the seizure and how ill she'd been.

She gratefully walked away from the legal business without a backward glance. Why spend the rest of her short life locked in an office building doing work she had never really liked? Claire told her dozens of times she'd never been close to dying, but Avery felt as if she had.

After being released from the rehab facility, she spent weeks working with a home nurse and physical therapist. Claire had taken an extended leave from her job, but when she discovered her boss was a thief and the firm protected him, she quit too. Both of them had never felt so relieved and free.

The sisters decided that all the stress they had been under caused Avery's seizure. They already owned the acreage in Rancho Exotica, and they moved into their new home designed by Claire as soon as it was completed. Their modern house's soaring angles and row-upon-row of windows set into 20-foot walls integrated beautifully with the surrounding forest of natural hardwoods and planted groves of pine trees.

Avery thought she might be having an epiphany. She surveyed the natural beauty surrounding her—gigantic trees, sparkling lakes, free-roaming wild animals, and the peace derived from stroking their beloved Bodhi's soft fur. She realized her fear of another seizure had passed. She had a few side effects from the anti-seizure medication she continued to take—diminished eyesight, slight hearing impairment, and occasionally dizziness—but otherwise she felt healthy and fearless enough to continue attempting to solve Thorne's murder. With the help of her sister, of course, as it had always been.

When she snapped out of her reverie, Avery realized she had driven in front of Thorne Mondae's house. Something had directed her there. Overcome with curiosity, she drove the golf cart a quarter mile past the mansion to a utility easement. She pulled into the woodsy area and drove the cart into a shallow creek bed. Hopefully, it wouldn't be seen unless someone specifically looked for it. She attached Bodhi to his leash, and they bobbed among the trees until close enough to see Thorne's back patio. She bore witness to a family barbecue.

Isaac Mondae, wearing khaki shorts and a Hawaiian shirt, swilled Budweiser while he flipped burgers over a smoking grill. Standing behind and nuzzling his neck stood his soon-to-be-wife Shania in a jean skirt and flower-embossed cowboy boots. Displayed across a white sectional, Adrianna Mondae modeled an ankle-length lounge dress and cuddled next to a svelte African American woman in sweatpants and sleeveless top. Judging by her ripped biceps, the woman must be Adrianna's personal trainer—her alibi for the time of the murder.

The relaxed and leisurely group seemed in perfect harmony with one another, which surprised Avery. Adrianna and Isaac had exhibited a cold disdain for each other when Detective Castellan interviewed them at the house. Maybe that was all an act to convince the detective they weren't in cahoots, that they hadn't planned Thorne's murder together. But she was getting ahead of herself.

Suddenly, she received a surprise more startling than Adrianna and Isaac's friendliness. A slight movement from Avery set off the garage's motion detector light. With its neon-like flash, the sudden brightness the women on the patio. When they saw her, they caterwauled like cats in heat. Isaac dashed across the patio toward Avery while dialing his cellphone and screaming: "I've got a gun! I'm calling security and the police!"

Dragging Bodhi behind her, Avery scrambled toward the golf cart as fast as she could across the rugged ground squishy with pine needles.

18

Avery ran for her Caribbean blue golf cart as fast as her arthritic knees and the uneven terrain would allow. Once she tugged Bodhi's leash, he had kept pace with her. The vehicle was within sight when a red golf cart pulled up in front of her and screeched to a halt.

"Jump on!" Jay shouted.

"What about my golf cart?"

"Leave it there. No one will see it. We'll come pick it up later. Now hurry!"

She and Bodhi jumped up next to Jay, and he sped off. A relative term considering his cart was lucky to reach 15 miles per hour. It was like fleeing a crime scene riding a tortoise.

"We should have used my cart," Avery complained. "At least it'll get up to 30."

"Maybe," Jay shot back, "if you're going downhill." He looked behind them. He didn't even have a rearview mirror. "Besides, your cart is instantly identifiable. You're the only one in this entire development who has a Caribbean blue six-seater with a matching top. They can see it coming in the next county."

Avery harrumphed and crossed her arms. Bodhi stuck his nose into the breeze, his eyelids fluttering at half-mast. Good to see somebody was enjoying this.

Jay dialed his cellphone.

"Adrianna," he said. "I caught the person hanging around your property. Yeah. They're really sorry. Out walking her dog and got lost. Swears it won't happen again." He paused, listening. "No need to be afraid. A resident just took a wrong turn. Tell Isaac to put his Glock back in the safe. Thanks, bye."

"You know what kind of gun he has?" Avery asked.

"I make it a priority to be informed about firearms in the community."

"Isn't it against the bylaws to discharge a weapon inside the development?"

"Texas law takes precedence over RE restrictions. You know that. You're the one who reminded Isaac of the 'stand your ground' laws."

"That was just bravado. Neither Claire nor I would shoot anyone. We don't own any guns. It's different when the laws are being used against me." She tried not to think about how many families in Rancho Exotica owned firearms, but since it was Texas, she suspected a great many.

In the RV park, Jay drove them to his Winnebago with the sunflower yellow boomerang. Inside, he handed Avery a glass of tea and poured out a bowl of water for Bodhi. He pulled out two boxes of Girl Scout cookies—a box of Thin Mints and another of Peanut Butter Sandwiches—and offered them to her. She picked the Thin Mints since she felt fairly certain they were vegan.

"Good choice," he said.

"I prefer them frozen," she said.

He cocked an eyebrow. "Sorry, didn't know you were coming, or I'd have stuck them in the freezer. Milk?"

"No thanks. I don't drink cow's milk."

He sighed but didn't pursue it. She was glad. She didn't feel like discussing her food choices. After settling himself in the captain's chair that doubled as the driver's seat, he munched a peanut butter cookie and gazed at her beneath hooded eyes. Jay impressed her as a man who liked to be in charge and positioned himself accordingly.

"Avery," he began in his stern lecture-mode voice.

"Jay?" She steeled herself, feeling like a naughty child and resenting it. Bodhi whined as if he too expected a scolding.

"Why do you keep putting yourself in these situations? Isaac Mondae was fully prepared to use that gun of his. Do you have a death wish or something?"

Avery dropped her head. She felt guilty not being honest with Jay, not telling him the truth about her seizure. But she just didn't want him thinking of her as a sick old lady. She knew the truth would come out some day, but today wasn't the day.

"Rancho Exotica is our refuge. Claire's and mine," she finally said. "A place we came to because we needed the peace and quiet. The absence of stress. When Thorne Mondae was murdered in our forest and we became suspects, our world turned upside down. We need to restore that world to its rightful position. That's why I want so much to discover who killed Mr. Mondae." Avery had been looking down during this speech, not wanting Jay to perceive that she wasn't telling him the whole truth—that her desperation rose primarily from fear for her sister. She raised her head to get a quick glance at his face. Checking to see if he bought her explanation. He wasn't a pushover, having worked with criminals all those years on the police force— meaning the perpetrators, of course, not the cops.

"Okay, I get that." His face wore a sincere expression. "But the police are in a much better position to do that than you are. Don't you see that?"

"No, they're not.

"How can you say that?"

"Because of PAM."

"Who's Pam?"

"P-A-M. Penelope, Angela and Mabel. A major cog in the churn that is the Rancho Exotica rumor mill. By living here, we're in a unique position to discover information the out-of-touch police could never learn. We're insiders, undercover operatives. People know things, especially in a mini-Peyton Place like RE. And they tell what they know to others who belong here, not to the police. Can't *you* see that?"

Jay's forehead crinkled as if he were considering it. "We? Does that mean you want me to participate in your amateur detective shenanigans?"

"You're not an amateur. Wouldn't it be better if we threw in our lot together and helped each other? You have access to information the police gather, and I have access to the mostly female rumor mill. We'd be a formidable team."

"I like the sound of that." Jay heaved a deep sigh. He studied her, his dark blue eyes probing the nooks and crannies of her psyche. That's the way it felt, anyway. Slowly, he rose from the captain's chair and slid into the dining banquet next to her. She couldn't look at him, but felt his hand draw a lock of hair away from her face. He ran his finger down her cheek. "I just don't want anything to happen to you," he said in a hoarse whisper.

Avery stiffened when he kissed her neck, and her breathing deepened. It had been so long since a man had touched her like that. A trail of kisses against bare skin followed. She stiffened, then willed her body to relax. He undid the top few buttons of her blouse with titillating slowness and drew it down over her shoulder. Bodhi whined. He sounded jealous.

"You… you're married," Avery stuttered.

"Separated."

His mouth covered hers as he pushed her down onto the banquette, his hard body insistent against her. Desires she had long suppressed rose to the surface. *This is really going to happen.* She felt both thrilled and frightened. She was too fat, too wrinkled, too old and sick. She couldn't satisfy him.

But I'm going to do it anyway! I'm going to have sex at least once more before I die.

"Turn off the lights," she whispered, hoping the dark would cover her physical flaws. When he pulled away, her insecurities came flooding back. She mentally swatted them away like annoying gnats. No time for that now. She had no intention of letting this rare opportunity get away. When Jay returned, the room's only light filtered through curtained windows from the glow of a harvest moon. Avery opened her arms and welcomed him. His lovemaking proved efficient while remaining personal and tender.

When it was over, to the mutual satisfaction of both, and she cuddled in his lap while he sat in the captain's chair, Jay said, "I can't do anything illegal to help you."

"I wouldn't expect you to."

"I assume you've told me everything."

Grasping the blanket he'd wrapped around her shoulders, Avery squirmed out of his arms and stood. She walked to the RV's window and watched the small herd of spotted Axis deer drink from the pond. The moon reflecting in the water created a dewy radiance.

"You look pretty in the moonlight," he said.

Later, she would claim that her brain had temporarily turned soft and mushy from the ambiance and the first-class sex. That her out-of-body state caused her to reveal the sworn secret.

"Well…" she began, "there is one tiny little thing… about the uh… about our trail camera."

19

"You told Jay about the trail camera?" Claire yelled across the expanse of their open concept living area.

Avery had always hated her penchant for needing to confess. And was she ever sorry now, admitting to Claire she told Jay about the images from the trail camera. The ones that clearly showed her sister in the forest within proximity of the victim when he was murdered. And that the Shadowy Figure who appeared wearing a ski mask might be the real killer. She dashed for the sliding patio door trying to escape her sister's wrath. Expecting a walk, an exultant Bodhi jumped around as if he straddled a pogo stick. He blocked her intended exit just as Claire stormed across the floor like a nitrous-injected drag racer. Hands on hips, she glared at Avery until she slunk back to her chair and hunkered down.

"Why did you do that?" Claire's angry voice echoed around the room. "What possible excuse could you have for blabbing something we both agreed to keep secret?"

"Afterglow?" Avery dropped her head trying to look repentant.

"You're going to get me arrested and sent to prison. Is that what you want?"

"No, of course not." Avery thought for a moment. "Don't take this the wrong way, but would you still get your Social Security checks if you're in prison?"

Claire flung around, stalked back to her side of the house, and flipped on her TV. She turned the volume up so loud, Bodhi slammed out the doggie door into the backyard. Avery imagined him lying on the patio with his wide front paws covering floppy ears.

Avery sat in silence, waiting until enough time had passed for Claire to cool off. She tuned into an episode of *See No Evil* on the ID channel, grateful for the closed captions since she couldn't hear a thing with Claire's volume turned to an ear-splitting level. After the first half of the program, Claire finally dialed back the sound to a dull roar. Bodhi must have decided it was safe to come inside, and he clattered through the doggie door. As though torn between which of the sisters he should grace with his company, he hesitated. A sneaky Avery carried his bowl to the pantry and filled it with kibble, so he chose her by default. Nary a peep out of Claire.

A half-hour later, after the TV program ended, an impatient Avery could wait no longer. She crept to her sister's side of the common area and slid into an armchair. Claire cut her with a stony stare and tight-lipped silence.

"I'm sorry. Really, I am," Avery began. "But we need help. We can't find out who killed Thorne without Jay. He volunteers with the police. He can learn things we can't. And he was a homicide investigator with the Dallas PD. He knows stuff. You're worried, afraid. So am I. But I trust Jay. He's willing to help, and we need to let him. It's time we trusted somebody besides each other."

* * *

It took Claire a couple of days to come around. When she announced that Tom Wellman planned to visit, the anticipation banished her frown and brought a happy glow to her face. Avery welcomed the diversion hoping Tom would take the heat off her.

When he arrived, the three of them went to dinner at the Rancho Exotica Clubhouse. Although the community had to go to the Sweetgum Country Club to play golf or swim in a heated pool, the RE Clubhouse did offer a small restaurant and dining room, and the upstairs provided a banquet hall where the annual Christmas Dinner-Dance was held. Built in the Texas Hill Country style, the dining room sported a set of tall windows overlooking one of the RE lakes, a giant limestone-covered fireplace, and cathedral ceiling. The tables and dining chairs were rough-hewn logs which weren't very comfortable but looked appropriate for the setting.

The offerings of the restaurant consisted of typical Texas fare: burgers, steaks, fries, chicken. Avery opted for the food she often fell back on 30 years ago when she first became vegetarian. A salad and a baked potato. If you called iceberg lettuce, a chunk of tomato, and a slice of cucumber a salad. She brought her own dressing in a small plastic container and plant butter for the potato. The restaurant never complained about her condiments, and she never complained about their lack of vegetarian options. What would be the point?

When Jay texted, she told him about Tom visiting and their plans to catch dinner at the clubhouse. He said he'd meet them there, which made her happy because she didn't have to put her ego on the line and invite him. He arrived looking dapper in pressed jeans and a fresh white shirt. Claire introduced Tom, who wore jeans and an army green shirt. Claire told Avery he rarely ventured into bright colors, which was sad since his coloring would look great in contrast to bright red or blue.

Claire seemed quite smitten with Tom. He displayed a polite and generous nature, endearing himself to the others when he paid for their dinners. Meanwhile, Avery tried to ignore the chicken dish with heaps of cheese her date, Jay, ordered. Not the time or place to start criticizing his food choices. That could come later when the glow of new intimacy wore off a bit.

While Jay and Tom chatted about the University of Texas football team, Avery searched the restaurant for familiar faces. She spotted Bart Downs, Rancho Exotica's only bachelor, sitting at the bar sipping a sudsy draft beer. RE did have a couple of widowers whose wives had died while living in the community. There were widows as well, but that single situation didn't seem to last long. They hooked up with a new man faster than a toupee in a tornado. Bless the digital age and online dating.

A slightly tipsy Bart lurched to their table. "Ladies." He tipped his John Deere gimme cap. Claire introduced him to Tom, but he said he already knew Jay. They had worked together at the Dallas PD where Bart had been an investigator.

"Can I buy you a beer?" Tom asked. Avery felt pretty sure Claire kicked his shin beneath the table, but it came too late.

"Thanks!" Bart grabbed a chair from an empty table and tucked it at the end of the booth. The waitress delivered the draft beer Tom had ordered.

After tossing a bit of small talk back and forth, Bart said, "I hear you sisters are trying to find out who killed Thorne Mondae."

"Sounds like the RE rumor mill is a runaway train," Avery said. "Unstoppable." Nervous little twitters passed around the table. "Any ideas?"

"I'm sure Bart has no idea who murdered Mr. Mondae," Claire said.

"I'm not accusing him. But he was an investigator. Maybe he could head us in the right direction." Rancho Exotica had its fair share of ex-cops, it seemed.

Using his index finger, Bart skimmed the foam off the top of his beer.

"I do have a theory," he said.

Everyone looked at him as if he had confessed.

"Really?" Looks like he had piqued Claire's interest. "We'd love to hear it."

After a big swig from his mug, Bart began. "I think it's possible Thorne could have been depressed over something and committed suicide."

"Suicide?" Jay looked incredulous. "He had an arrow straight through his heart. How could he have done that to himself?"

"Besides," Avery said, "what did he have to be despondent about? He had everything he could possibly desire." She thought for a second. "Well, there may have been a couple of things…" She stopped when she saw the subtle shake of Claire's head. Her sister was right. Not a good idea to share anything with Bart.

"I didn't know him," Bart said, "but I do know he wasn't going to win a popularity contest. I also heard he and his ex-wife had lots of lawsuits filed against them and their real estate business."

"To the point of losing the business?" Tom asked. "That could make a man suicidal."

Avery noted that Tom had just exploded Claire's dream of persuading him to turn his profitable cattle ranch into a nonprofit animal rescue and sanctuary.

"I don't know about that," Bart said. "It's possible."

"Still doesn't explain how he managed to shoot himself with an arrow." Jay tapped his spoon against the table in an impatient gesture. Avery wondered if he and Bart had worked together in Dallas and if it possibly hadn't gone well.

"In order to kill himself," Bart said, "he'd have to shoot the arrow straight up into the air, lie down on the ground, and wait for it to fall and spear him through the chest."

A disbelieving silence followed, until Avery burst out laughing. The nearby restaurant patrons turned to stare, but she couldn't help herself. She'd never heard anything more preposterous. Tom squirmed uncomfortably, Jay tapped faster, and Claire hid an amused smile behind her hand. Bart kept his face composed if a bit pouty.

"Wouldn't that take some physical machinations almost impossible to calculate?" Avery asked. "He'd have to shoot it perfectly straight, then be sure to lie down in exactly the right place that guaranteed the arrow came down fast enough and accurate enough to pierce a major organ."

"Even if he's a strong, straight shooter," Tom began, "and he's able to place himself in a prime position, I'm wondering whether the terminal velocity would be lethal or just incredibly painful."

"The trick would be *finding* it on the way down," Claire said. "When it dropped, it wouldn't be easy to see, and a decent bow would throw it up a long way."

"Claire knows what she's talking about," Tom said. "She was an expert marksman… or should I say *marksperson*… when we were in high school."

Oops. Probably shouldn't have told that Tom old boy.

"She was?" Jay and Bart said in unison. They favored Claire with open-mouthed stares.

"It was a long time ago," she threw in hastily.

"Good news," Jay said after searching through his cellphone. "Google says 'MythBusters' did an episode on what happens when you shoot an arrow straight up into the air. When it inevitably came back down, would it still be moving fast enough to kill you?"

"And?" Avery asked.

"After skimming over all the physics calculations which I don't under-stand, the final conclusion is that the arrow speed would be potentially lethal. Depends where it hits you."

Bart's face settled into justified smugness. Tom nodded his head. Claire and Avery exchanged dubious looks. Jay stared across the room with wary surprise and not a little panic. Avery spotted the woman she had seen with him at the funeral and deduced to be his wife. She saw them, shoved her chair back with a loud scrape, and marched over. The men, all polite gentle-men, stood up. Avery tried to dive below the table.

"Sounds like ya'll are having a good time." A petite woman with long dark hair, her eyes shot out sparks of anger when she looked at Avery. "Didn't realize my husband had started dating."

"Macy," Jay began. "It's not—"

"Not a date? What is it then? You, a strange woman. Eating dinner together."

I'm not that strange.

"We're just… hanging out."

Avery frowned. Hanging out? Probably the most noncommittal phrase he could have used. He could be doing that with anyone, including the home-less guy "hanging out" in the alleyway next to the county courthouse.

"Hello, Macy," Bart said. "Nice to see you."

"Hi Bart. Doesn't this look like a date to you? I mean, if you and I had agreed to meet here, you buy my dinner, and we eat together. Wouldn't that be a date?" Bart looked as if he wished he'd kept his mouth shut. "Guess I could be dating too."

"I can see you're in pain," Avery said, "and I'm sorry for that. But remember that you kicked Jay out of his home. Not the other way around." Avery couldn't believe something so confrontational came out of her mouth.

"That's none of your business!" Avery felt bad when Macy swiped a tear from her cheek. She'd been in a similar situation herself and understood Macy's pain.

Bart jumped from his chair. "I'll buy you a drink." He took her elbow and directed her toward the bar. Men did not like catfights, and Bart seemed to be trying to head this one off before it started.

"Sure." Macy looked at Jay. "I'm throwing the rest of your stuff out of the house and setting fire to it if you don't come get it tomorrow." She stalked off with Bart.

Although glad Bart had taken Macy off, hopefully to offer consolation, Avery strongly felt the awkward silence that replaced them. To fill the void, she said: "Claire, we need to add Bart to the suspect list. Anybody who would come up with that cockamamie theory about the murder must be trying to steer attention away from himself."

"Apparently," Claire said, "it had the opposite effect on you."

20

At her request, Avery's cohorts—Claire, Tom, and Jay, grumbling under their breaths—dragged the barstools from the kitchen island into the entry hall outside the office. The sisters had confiscated a small bedroom with a Murphy bed, furnished it with a desk, printer and shelving, and called it an office. Even if Avery hadn't placed a corkboard in front of the only window, the room wouldn't have been large enough for all of them to gather. Although it blocked out the light, the board would be the source of enlightenment for solving the murder of Thorne Mondae. She opened the French doors that separated the office from the hall.

"Now what?" Claire demanded.

Avery began: "I consulted *wikiHow* to learn to become a citizen, also known as an *amateur*, detective." She ignored the snickers from the trio. "The information wasn't too helpful, as it turns out. Not specific enough. But, as Claire knows, I do watch a lot of shows on the Investigation Discovery channel."

"And she means a *lot*," Claire said.

"I really like that Joe Kenda guy," Tom said. "*Homicide Hunter*, I think it's called."

Avery gave him a disapproving frown. *Butt out, cowboy. This is my rodeo.*

"Please turn your attention to this board." She stepped aside to reveal the corkboard where she had pinned photos of the people she now thought of as suspects, plus a description typed below their pictures cataloging the reasons they should be on the list. Avery explained this to the group.

Slipping on her reading glasses, Claire stepped up to the board. She studied her picture, the first one in the lineup, and the paragraph printed beneath it.

"Do you think you could have found a more unflattering picture of me?" she asked Avery.

"Probably. But I think this one's representational without being a mugshot."

"You could have used one taken from my better side."

"Which is…?"

"'Claire Halverson Browning,'" Claire read. "'A suspect because the victim's body was found in her forest, she had threatened him while hunting, and she is an award-winning archer.' Guess that about covers it."

"*Ah hem*," Jay cleared his throat and searched the room as if hoping someone else would fill in the gap.

In the growing silence, the sisters exchanged glances, neither one willing to reveal the big secret to the one clueless person in the room.

"What?" Tom said. "What's going on? I feel like the idiot in a horror movie who doesn't know the monster is standing behind him."

Nervous laughter from the others. More dead silence.

"Oh, good grief!" Claire gave in first. "I'll tell you. I'm the one it affects. We found our trail camera in the forest. The forensics team overlooked it. When we downloaded the photos, they showed me in the forest at the same time Thorne Mondae was murdered."

"What?" Tom's eyes widened. "But you didn't—"

"Of course, I didn't kill him! I was checking the feral cat traps. I never even saw Thorne."

"But that's not all," Avery said. "A shadowy figure wearing a ski mask appeared from behind the storage shed a few minutes after Thorne activated the camera. Covered head to toe in camouflage. It could have been another hunter or anybody, really."

"Have you seen the photos?" Tom asked Jay.

"Not yet."

"That trail camera and the photos are evidence." Tom frowned at Claire. "Why didn't you give them to the police?"

"Isn't it obvious?" Claire's voice rose an octave. "I'm in the forest at the same time a man is murdered. It practically proves I'm guilty. Especially with all the other things working against me."

"You don't know that. Besides, the… what did you call him…"

"Shadowy Figure," Avery supplied.

"The Shadowy Figure could be the killer, couldn't he?"

"Or *she*."

"Or a witness," Jay said.

"A witness could tell the police what he or she saw." Tom fidgeted with excitement. "They could testify that Claire didn't shoot Mr. Mondae and clear her of any wrongdoing!"

"We discussed that," Avery said. "If it's a witness, wouldn't they have come forward already? I believe it's the killer. They would leave Claire to take the blame."

"Maybe they're afraid of repercussions," Jay said. "If the killer did it once, they probably won't have any qualms about doing it again."

"We need to see the pictures." Tom declared with Jay nodding his agreement.

"We're getting off the subject," Avery said. "We're here to discuss the names on the suspect board to decide if any of them can be eliminated. We'll show the trail camera pictures later."

Jay counted the number of photos on the corkboard. "Nine suspects!" he said. "We'll be here all night."

"Ten," Avery said, "counting the Shadowy Figure on the trail camera." She read the crowd and could tell she was losing them. "Oh, alright! It just so happens I've saved each of the wanted posters on my computer—"

"Wanted posters?" Jay said. "You're funny."

"My sister, the amateur… oh, excuse me… the *citizen* detective. She always did enjoy playing dress up."

Avery scrunched her face, irritated that her posse was not taking her seriously.

"Finish what you were saying, Avery," Tom said.

She gave him a grateful nod. "I've printed out a copy for each of you." She pulled the preprinted and stapled pages out of a desk drawer and passed them around.

After rifling through the pages, Jay said, "The fashion model wife, the ne'er-do-well son, the illegitimate aboriginal daughter—"

"The illegitimate aboriginal daughter?" Tom said. "There's got to be a story there."

"I'll catch you up later," Claire said.

"—the resentful ex-wife, the spendthrift daughter-in-law, the wife's lesbian lover, and a disgruntled employee."

"Sounds like central casting for an episode of *Murder, She Wrote*," Claire said.

"You forgot 'senior citizen spinster with grudge against victim,'" Avery said. Claire shot her a frowny face.

"Doesn't a citizen detective need a special talent, something they're experts at?" Claire asked Avery. "All the cozy novels have amateur sleuths who are former FBI agents, grow rare orchids, win blue ribbons for pie baking or quilt making, or have clue-detecting dogs and cats. What's your special talent?"

Avery stiffened into a defensive posture.

"Based on these 'wanted posters,'" Jay said, flipping through the suspect lists Avery had given them, "I'd say she's a really good typist."

Everyone but Avery laughed.

After an uncomfortable silence, Claire said: "Don't be upset, Avery. You do have a special talent. Your willingness to put your ego on the line, do things that might not put you in the best light, maybe even make you appear stupid or silly to others. But you doggedly persist despite the naysayers. That's a rare talent, and one that serves a citizen detective well." Claire gave her a reassuring pat on the shoulder.

"Like locking yourself in a casket to eavesdrop on my conversation with Adrianna Mondae," Jay said without a note of detectable mockery.

"And being witnessed inside said casket by the entire Rancho Exotica community," Claire added.

"I feel like a bastard at a family reunion," Tom said. "I haven't heard about half of this stuff!"

"Details to follow," Claire said to Tom.

Avery frowned and pursed her lips. She couldn't tell whether they were making fun of her, or if they were sincere in their praise—such as it was.

"Well… thanks… I think," she said, deciding not to make a fuss. The task at hand was more important.

"Too many people with too many motives." Jay tactfully changed the subject. "We need to work on narrowing it down."

"You can take me off," Claire suggested.

"No one here thinks you killed him," Tom received an affectionate smile from Claire.

"In addition to the *well-typed* suspect list," Avery said, "I need to give out some assignments. First, Claire, we need to check out Bart's theory that Thorne could have committed suicide using a bow and arrow on himself."

"We already confirmed it was possible," Jay said. "Is there really any need to waste time on him?"

"Don't think it's necessary," Claire said.

"I agree," Tom said. "The guy was found face-down. If he shot himself, he would have been lying on his back. Which means he would've had to get back up, stagger across the creek, fall face first, and die. A lot of action for a guy with an arrow through his heart. Not likely."

"Fine, then." Avery hated it when the unwashed masses rose up against her. "The rest of you can ride around in your golf carts, drive into town for a Tex-Mex dinner, play mahjong or put jigsaw puzzles together. Whatever it is retired people are supposed to do. Meanwhile, I'll be out trying to solve a murder."

21

After the members of her posse had soothed Avery's ruffled feathers, she agreed to go on a picnic at one of the three lakes in Rancho Exotica. Tom drove the golf cart with Claire riding shotgun. Avery and Jay took the seats behind, with Avery placing Bodhi strategically between them. She hadn't completely unthawed and wanted him to know it.

The sweetgum leaves had begun to turn neon yellow and glowed against the evergreen pines. On many of the platted lots, groves of Loblolly pine shot a hundred feet into the sky. When passing by on the paved road, Avery could see the neatly laid out trees planted in wide, straight rows. Space between the trees, expansive enough for several people to walk abreast, opened up like a verdant bride marching down the aisle of a living cathedral. The pine rows mesmerized Avery as the golf cart sped past them. Bodhi broke her concentration when he began barking at the herd of Père David's deer who grazed on an unbuilt lot.

During the late 19th century, German troops had hunted Père David's to annihilation in their native China. The Europeans carried specimens back to their zoos and successfully bred them in captivity. In the early 20th century, when the 11th Duke of Bedford acquired a few animals, he created a large herd on his estate. The duke's great-grandson donated several dozen to the Chinese government in the '80s, and they successfully reintroduced them into the wild. All Père David's deer alive today descended from the duke's herd. Avery assumed that's where the Rancho Exotica herd came from, but had no idea how they ended up here.

Some residents made fun of the odd-looking creatures, but Avery admired them. Their informal Chinese name meant "four not alike," because they were described as having "the hooves of a cow but not a cow, the neck of a horse but not a horse, the antlers of a deer but not a deer, the tail of a donkey but not a donkey."

Avery hugged Bodhi close to stop his barking and prevent him jumping off the golf cart. The deer didn't like dogs, but as the cart slowly passed, the big creatures barely noted their presence. Anyone not bearing food fell beneath their interest.

The group unloaded their provisions and placed them on a table next to the lake. In a nearby dead tree, a dozen vultures perched in companionable silence. They eyed the humans below with disdain. When the group began to unpack, the big black birds flapped off in a huff, leaving behind gifts that had to be cleaned off the table with wet-wipes.

Avery had made her "Not Tuna" with pickles, onion, apples and pecans, but instead of tuna, she substituted finely chopped chickpeas and Vegenaise. When the guys grumbled, Avery said they were welcome to drive to the deli in town and buy their own sandwiches. Both men agreed to try the Not Tuna. She served it on crusty bread with chips, and the men ate every bite without complaint.

One of the few bald eagles who resided in Rancho Exotica paid them a visit, soaring across the azure lake and above the treetops of the bald cypresses that lined the water. Seeing the majestic creature improved Avery's attitude considerably.

"Why are eagles and cypresses called 'bald,' when they obviously are not?" She threw the query out to the group.

"The eagles have white heads in contrast to their dark bodies. Makes them look bald." Of course, Tom knew the answer. He was a walking *Wikipedia* of trivial information.

"Lots of conifers are evergreen, but bald cypress trees are deciduous and lose their leaves in the fall." Claire, the flora expert.

The group watched the eagle swoop out of sight.

After they tidied the picnic area, Avery removed her laptop from the cart and popped it open. She located the trail camera's sim card photos, then placed the computer in the middle of the picnic table.

"Here are the photos from the day Thorne Mondae was murdered. You guys said you wanted to see them."

Both men slid onto the bench and studied the pictures. Jay used the pointer to move down the rows until he and Tom had seen them all.

"Just like we told you," Claire said. "Thorne comes into view first, then I appear right after. Pretty incriminating, don't you think?"

"I don't know about that," Tom said. "You may have appeared too late after Thorne to have been his killer."

"Appreciate the vote of confidence," Claire said with a slight touch of sarcasm, "but how do you figure that?"

"I'm assuming the time on these photos is correct."

"As far as we know," Avery said.

"Let's assume that the killer is an average shot with a bow and arrow—"

"They make the hunters take prowess tests," Jay said. "They're probably better than average."

"But the shooter wouldn't necessarily have been one of our hunters," Avery said. "It could have been somebody who just dressed like one."

"Okay, but they would still have to be an average shot to pull off the murder." As if preparing for a lengthy speech, Tom swung his long legs over the bench and stood. "An expert shot with a bow and arrow could hit a deer at around 50 yards. Which means they could not have been much farther away from the victim than that. Thorne triggers the camera at…" He looked at Avery for confirmation since she had taken his place in front of the computer.

"This photo shows he activated the camera at 10:57 a.m. Thursday morning."

"And Claire?"

"Time stamp shows 11:02 a.m."

"This is pure speculation, you understand," Tom said. "But I'm esti-mating someone would be able to cover the distance, depending on the terrain, in approximately one to two minutes. Claire crosses the camera's view five minutes after Thorne."

"Then she couldn't have done it!" Avery said.

"Did you have any doubts?" Claire asked.

"Well…"

"Well, what?" Claire shot Tom her fearsome indented forehead frown.

"It's not positive proof," Tom said. "You might have been traveling over rough terrain, or become delayed if you stumbled or fell, or if anything happened to impede you. I'm just trying to think like the cops would. Maybe Jay can help with that."

"He's right about the evidence not being hard proof of innocence." Jay stared at the computer for a moment. "But what about this figure who's seen in the photo after the victim? He clocks in at 11:06, four minutes after Claire and nine minutes after Thorne. On the other hand, since he pops up from behind the shed, he could have been there all along. Correct me if I'm wrong, Tom, but couldn't he have shot the victim from behind the shed assuming the distance wasn't more than 50 yards?"

"Maybe he stayed hidden until he was sure Thorne was dead," Avery suggested, "and Claire had gone back to the house."

"Possible." Tom watched Claire with wary eyes.

"What do you think these photos mean?" Avery asked. "Here's a picture taken in the space where the Shadowy Figure eventually appears timed at 10:54 a.m., before either Thorne or Avery passed the camera. There's nothing visible that might have been in motion. What activated the camera if nothing moving was photographed?"

"Maybe a breeze moved a branch or a leaf fell." Tom sighed. "Yeah, I know that's a long-shot. Unlikely that would have been enough to get the motion detector to turn on the camera."

"Maybe a deer activated it," Claire said.

"No, because the camera took several deer and other mammal photos that caught the animals, are parts of them, quite clearly," Jay said.

"What if…" Avery whirled on the bench in excitement. "…what if the empty photos of the shed, the ones before Thorne and Claire appeared, were Shadowy Figure shooting the bow from behind the cover of the shed. The arrow flying by was visible enough to set off the motion detector but too fast for the camera to capture its picture?"

"That would have given Thorne three minutes to pass by the camera after being shot," Claire said. "It took him longer than the one- or two-minutes Tom suggested because he was injured, stumbling along at a slower pace… maybe even fell and got back up again."

The four friends stared at each other for several seconds before they all started talking at once. After the chatter quieted down, Avery said:

"Now that Claire can more or less be cleared, do we still need to try to solve the murder?"

No one spoke for a few moments.

"I can't answer for you," Jay finally said, "but I can suggest, under penalty of law, that you turn the trail camera and the sim card over to Detective Castellan immediately. You have been withholding crucial evidence in a homicide investigation for a month. The sooner you give it up, the better for us all."

"I second that motion," Tom said.

22

Avery didn't feel a bit guilty when she and Jay sneaked away from Claire and Tom after the wedding of Isaac Mondae and his fiancé, Shania. The formal affair had taken place in a vast white tent erected on the sprawling lawn behind the two-story colonial Thorne had built during his lifetime. Claire and Tom looked perfectly happy to be alone with their cocktails which were being served inside the house because the tent had to be completely reset from the nuptials to the dinner service.

After wandering around the house and dodging a plethora of other guests, Avery and Jay ended up standing beneath an elk head hung on the wall of Thorne Mondae's trophy room. They had happened onto the grotesque museum of needlessly murdered animals while searching for a private place to do a little necking—did they call it that anymore? Jay laughed when she named the room the "Dead Zone." He had a wonderful laugh, and she felt compelled to stand on her tiptoes and kiss him on the lips. He wrapped her in strong arms and kissed back. A rush of affection warmed her from head to toe. After a few minutes of this deliciously teenage behavior, they parted with both of them smiling. He wandered to the other side of the room to riffle through a desk drawer. A habit from his investigator days, she supposed.

"This deadhead reminds me of that line from *Arthur*," Avery said, "when an inebriated Dudley Moore is talking to his fiancé's father, the rich, gun-loving, animal-murdering nut job." She stopped to consider whether

Jay was old enough to be familiar with the movie since it had been released in the early 80s. Yeah, he probably caught it on American Movie Classics.

"What'd he say?" Jay moved next to her, and they gazed at the elk head.

"'You must have really hated that moose.'"

"That's an elk, not a moose."

"That's not the point." Avery rolled her eyes. "The point being, why else would you murder a totally innocent creature unless you deeply hated him? What other reason can you have for taking away someone's life?"

"I guess they believe they admire them. That it's somehow a way of honoring the animal."

"I admire my sister, but I don't cut off her head and hang it over the fireplace."

"Photographs are much tidier." Jay looked around, taking in the gazelles, deer, big horn sheep, and other hooved exotics, and shook his head. "It seems a terrible waste." His gaze returned to her; he cocked his head. "I wonder why you get so angry about things you have no control over."

It wasn't like him to ask philosophical questions.

"I feel it's my calling to try to change them."

After studying her for a moment, his gaze averted to a display of archery gear hanging in a dimly lit corner. "Come check this out."

Avery sighed, relieved she didn't have to discuss her anger issues with Jay. They weren't something she wanted to talk about.

She joined him, and they studied the mounted rack. Several different types of arrows hung in eight rows down a wooden board. Four bows created a frame around them. Next to the board hung an old photo of three men: an early-twenties Thorne Mondae, easily recognizable since even then he had been prematurely balding and sporting a middle-aged paunch; a black man in native dress, what little there was of it, holding a bow and arrow similar to those displayed on the board; and Scopes Redfield, a good guess based on him claiming to have been friends with Mondae during their Andaman Island trip.

Beneath the mounted rack stood an ancient credenza with heavy drawers. Jay pulled open the top drawer, but it was empty. He unceremoniously opened the next two. In the bottom one lay a square box with a dusty lid that looked as if it hadn't been opened in years. Avery couldn't resist. She jerked it out of the drawer and blew dust off the top.

"Avery!" Jay said. "You can't look through their private stuff."

"You opened the drawers." Ignoring Jay's disapproving look, Avery drew off the box top and set it on the credenza. Inside lay several pieces of yellowed paper that appeared to be old newspaper clippings. She flipped through reading the headlines: "Chicago Gangbangers with Vehicles Profit from New Handgun Ban," "North Sea Oil Rig Disaster Blamed on Production Company," "Baby Killing Tests India's Protection of Aboriginal Culture."

"You need to put those back, Avery, before somebody finds us."

"They look like clippings Thorne kept from his and Scopes's youthful travels. That last one refers to the Andaman Islands. These might give us some clues about Thorne's past. Which might have had something to do with his murder."

"There you two are!" Claire swept in with Tom following.

Avery turned, hiding the newspaper clippings behind her.

"What are you doing in here? What's that behind your back?" Couldn't put one over on Claire, who looked lovely and stylish in a burgundy and black color-blocked sheath.

Avery sighed and handed the articles to her sister. After studying them for a moment, Claire looked up with a questioning expression.

"Check out this wall hanging," Jay said.

The couples gazed at the wall.

"We found the newspaper clippings in a box inside this credenza," Avery said. "Beneath the bow and arrow display."

"*You* found them," Jay said.

"Couldn't someone have used these arrows to kill Thorne?" Avery ignored Jay's correction.

"I don't know why not," Tom said. "I wonder if this is all of them, or if there are any missing." He took the clippings from Claire and studied them.

"Claire, do you have your phone?" Avery hadn't bothered to bring hers into the wedding, but her sister carried an evening purse that would accommodate her cell.

Claire snapped a couple of shots of the bow and arrow display.

"What about these?" Tom held up the clippings. He spread them across the credenza top, and Claire photographed each article individually.

"Do you think they're significant? Claire asked.

"Possibly." Avery returned them to the box and slid it back into the bottom drawer. "Scopes did say they had a shady past. Maybe the articles will tell us something about it."

"These bows and arrows would have been accessible to just about anybody who knew Thorne." Jay sighed. "Doesn't limit the suspect pool much." He stepped away from the display, and the others followed.

"Before we rejoin the other wedding guests," Avery announced, "I'd like to apologize to you three. I acted like a tyrant trying to tell you what to do. Giving orders about the murder investigation."

The others shook their heads as if saying no big deal.

"Jay has the most experience, so I'm relying on him to guide us. Claire is a bulldog when she gets her teeth into something, obsessive-compulsive but in a good way. And Tom seems to have his brain library filled with miscellaneous information none of us knew we needed, but we did. We all have our strengths and weaknesses, and we are equal partners in this quest."

"What's your strength, Avery?" Tom asked with a mischievous grin.

Avery didn't want to repeat the storyboard meeting incident, so she said: "Persistence in the face of impossible odds?" A bit iffy but it sounded good.

"Being such an annoying pain in the ass that a person would do anything to get you off their back," Claire said.

They all laughed, even Avery, although she'd preferred it if her sister had said something complimentary instead of making a joke. That was a joke, wasn't it?

"Let's get a drink!" Jay said.

"One second." Avery moved in front of the door to stop their exit. "If no one objects, I'd like to ask you to do me a favor. All we have to do is look around the room," she gestured toward the dead heads on the walls, "and it becomes quite clear what an evil asshole Thorne Mondae was. But it's important that we find out who murdered him because Claire is still not cleared, nor are any of us who live at Rancho Exotica. Our lives are never going to return to normal until we solve this crime. A lot of the other suspects are at this wedding. I'm going to take Adrianna Mondae, the wife, as my assignment. Claire has already met Onia Redfield, so she could take her." Her sister nodded.

"Is she here?" Jay asked. "Don't think Adrianna would allow that. She banned her from Rancho Exotica."

"She's here," Claire said. "She came as Scopes Redfield's guest. Besides, she is Scopes's assistant and an employee of his and Thorne's investment company. Maybe Isaac had a good reason for persuading Adrianna to let her show up at his wedding."

"Jay could sniff that out," Avery said. "Take Scopes Redfield as his assignment. And any other possible suspects we don't know about, like disgruntled employees, business acquaintances, etcetera. And Tom, you could turn that country charm on Lianne, Thorne's ex-wife and Isaac's mother, see if she had any reason to kill him."

"Don't want to get involved in your murder suspect interrogations," Tom said. "That's best left to the police."

"I'm only asking you to talk to her if the opportunity arises." Avery tried to temper her irritation, to remember she was supposed to be playing nice. "Do it for Claire, if for no other reason. She needs your help."

"It's okay," Claire said. "No need for Tom to get involved. He's not a member of the community. We can do it ourselves." Claire shot Avery a look that said "lay off." She nodded an acknowledgment, not wanting her sister to feel uncomfortable.

"All righty, then," Avery said, "let's get this party started!"

23

Avery did not think the words "cowboy" and "wedding" should ever be uttered in the same sentence. And never paired in a real-life formal event where everyone, including family, friends, and business acquaintances could witness your lack of taste and style. Apparently, she comprised the minority opinion since cowboy weddings had become a mainstay of Texas wedding chic.

During the actual ceremony, the groom had stepped into character for the country theme by donning a bright white cowboy hat, a traditional bolo tie with white shirt, and paired them with his navy sport coat and sharply creased jeans. Avery never understood why cowboys wore too-long jeans that hung in folds until they met the arch of a boot stolen from a skinned reptile. Was it a style statement? Maybe she should ask Tom.

Avery sat next to a man who sported a similar outfit to the groom, only less formal.

"Them boots is genuine 'gator," the man said. He pronounced it *jin-u-wine*.

"You don't say," Avery said. "Are you a friend of Isaac's?"

"Nah, the bride. But I taught him about boot leather. Some online companies are advertising their stuff as quality caiman leather and passing the inferior stuff off to the consumer. Ain't no such critter as a caiman-crocodile or caiman-alligator. That's manufactured by them foreigners—he said *furners*—in China. I wouldn't let Isaac buy that. Especially now that he's come into some real money."

"You're a true friend."

Grateful when the bride began marching down the aisle, Avery hoped Shania could avoid tipping over the candles she had stuck into Mason jars and lined the walkway. Especially since the aisle had been formed by hay bales hauled inside and placed in rows as seating for the wedding guests. If ignited by a burning candle, the dry hay would go up like a torch.

She had no words to describe the bridal attire, but the image had seared itself on her brain for all eternity. All white from top to toe, Shania wore a cowboy hat with a sloping brim in front and waist-length tulle veil hanging behind. Her tea-length handkerchief-hemmed dress with long lace sleeves ended in a pair of high-heeled boots wrapped in white lace. She carried a bouquet of fake sunflowers.

Avery glanced past Tom at her sister. They exchanged wide-eyed stares and stifled giggles.

After the ceremony and cocktail hour—featuring the couples special drink, a Cowboy Margarita blended with limeade, tequila, raspberry liqueur, and beer—the sisters and their dates found a table far enough away from the DJ's speakers not to give Tom a headache, but close enough to the action to keep their prey in sight.

Plastic red and white checkered cloths covered the picnic tables with water and iced tea served in Mason jars. Either the bride had been hording Mason jars for quite some time, or there had been a big sale on Etsy. The centerpieces utilized masses of foliage and greenery paired with hydrangeas, baby's breath, and pheasant feathers connected by twine and shaped into wreaths around vintage outdoor lanterns.

When dinner came, Jay and Tom ate their Southern fried chicken, but the sisters made do with a vegetable salad, roll, and side of fruit. They had drunk a couple of Cowboy Margaritas during the cocktail hour, so didn't complain too much.

Not bothering to wait for their dates, the sisters had liquored up just enough to let go of their inhibitions and line up for the Electric Slide.

"Let's dance like no one is looking!" Claire verbalized their new life philosophy.

"When you're our age," Avery said, "no one *is* looking."

During the line dance, Avery noticed that the murder victim's wife, Adrianna, danced closely with another woman. The same woman she had cuddled with on her patio when Avery stalked them the night she slept with Jay. A memorable night for many reasons.

The woman contrasted Adrianna in every way—dark where she was light, medium where she was statuesque, muscular where she was slender, but it was an exquisite contrast. Every time they skipped, hopped, and turned, they glanced at each other and smiled. Avery thought she recognized what she called the "look of love" between them.

The song ended, and Avery spent a few seconds trying to catch her breath. Since her seizure, she became winded quickly, her body weak from overexertion. As soon as she recovered, she followed Adrianna to a drink station.

While standing behind her in a short line, she said, "Hi, Adrianna. Remember me? Avery Halverson. You were interrogated… I mean, you talked with Detective Castellan in my house over on Waterford Drive. I gave you some hot tea."

Adrianna squinted her heavily lined and mascaraed eyes and studied Avery like a bacteria specimen under a microscope. "Uh, yes, hello… Avery, is it?" She had a way of not looking at you when she looked at you.

"That woman dancing next to you, when you two were doing the Electric Slide, she's quite beautiful. She a friend of yours?" Forget the niceties and skip right to the chase.

"Yes, a friend." Adrianna looked as if she had diagnosed this older lady in a periwinkle cocktail jumpsuit as harmless. "And my health coach, Delia Adair." She studied the chunky roll around Avery's waist. The muffin-top had refused to be contained in spite of Avery fighting with a pair of Spanks until they surrendered around her hips. "Maybe you should meet her." She moved up a place in the drink line.

"Sure," Avery said, wondering if that was the same thing as a personal trainer. "I'd like to. Wasn't she the person you were with when Mr. Mondae… your husband was uh… killed? I didn't get a chance to say so at the funeral, but I'm very sorry for your loss."

Adrianna accepted a Cowboy Margarita from a bartender dressed like a wild west dance hall girl, like Miss Kitty in *Gunsmoke*. Adrianna took a delicate sip, blinked from the tart taste, then licked salt off her full lips. "Thank you, Avery, you're very kind." But it didn't sound sincere. "Aren't you the neighborhood Peeping Tom? The one Jay had to chase off my property?"

"Well, I—"

"If I catch you snooping around my home again, I'll shoot you." She slipped away before Avery had a chance to speak.

"Bugger!" She watched an irritated Adrianna escape her clutches before she had an opportunity to question her thoroughly. Maybe she needed to be more tactful when handling potential suspects.

"What's wrong, Avery?" One of the PAMs had been standing behind her in the drink line. She wasn't sure which one but upon closer scrutiny recognized Mabel, the one who wore no makeup but most needed it.

"Nothing's wrong," she said. "I'm fine."

"What would you ladies like to drink," Miss Kitty, the bartender, asked.

"Two Cowboy Margaritas," Mabel said. Avery wasn't going to argue with that. "Looks like our grieving widow, Adrianna, has made a love connection."

"What do you mean?"

"Her and that black woman are here together. Looks like a date to me."

"Her name's Delia, and she's Adrianna's personal trainer... I mean health coach." Avery wondered why she felt the need to defend a woman she didn't even like. It wasn't the woman she defended but her lifestyle choices. "They're friends."

"Okay, if you say so." Mabel accepted the proffered margaritas and passed one to Avery. They sipped for a few moments. "Did you hear what Thorne's son, Isaac, is trying to do to his stepmother?" Avery gave her a quizzical look, but Mabel continued before she could respond. "He and his new bride are trying to push Adrianna out of her and Thorne's house here in Rancho Exotica."

"How can he do that? It must be hers now that Thorne has passed."

"*Blackmail.*" Mabel let the ugly word dangle for a moment. "He's trying to ruin her reputation in the community. Shame her by claiming she has a lesbian lover."

"That's not exactly shocking news these days." Probably more shocking in a highly religious right-leaning enclave like Rancho Exotica than the rest of the world. On the other hand, Avery knew several same-sex couples lived together in RE that weren't brothers or sisters.

"Unless you're still a married woman. Can you guess who that might be?"

"You could just tell me."

"The very same person who is her alibi for the day Thorne was murdered and vice versa."

"Vice versa?"

"Well, sure. If Adrianna and Delia are lovers, and Delia is alibiing Adrianna, then Adrianna is alibiing Delia as well. Delia would have almost as much to gain by killing Thorne as Adrianna. The woman she loves is now one of the richest women in Texas."

Avery had never given Delia a serious thought as the possible killer.

"How's your new *friend*, Jay Vidocq?" Mabel smiled knowingly.

Avery puffed up, deciding not to dignify that with an answer.

"His wife's here. Everyone in the community got invited."

"She is?" Avery asked in spite of herself. "Where?"

"Over there." Mabel pointed with a stubby finger. "By the cake. Talking to her husband."

"*Estranged* husband." Avery excused herself and rushed back to their table to look for Claire. She needed to talk to her sister. But only Tom remained seated. He rubbed his head as if it ached despite the fact that they had picked a spot far from the DJ's booming speakers.

* * *

When Claire waved at Onia Redfield, the young woman beckoned her to the table where she ate dinner with her uncle, Scopes Redfield. Onia indicated an empty chair next to her and introduced Claire to her uncle.

Claire reminded Onia that she had seen him at the police station and the funeral as well.

"Pardon me for being nosy," Claire said, "but I'm surprised to see you here after that argument you had with Adrianna at Thorne's funeral. My condolences, by the way, Mr. Redfield. I understand he was a good friend of yours."

"Thank you," Scopes said. "Onia is here as my guest. But the dispute is between her and Adrianna. And this is Isaac's wedding. He has nothing against Onia."

"Does he know?" Claire hoped she hadn't overstepped her bounds, but she did have an assignment to complete. Her sojourn in Onia's vehicle while listening to her entire birth story entitled Claire to be a bit more personal than most. And the imminent possibility of a life sentence in a hardcore Texas prison hanging over her head.

Onia stiffened, as still as a piece of carved wood. Her strapless pewter dress sparkled in her sapphire eyes. Scopes proffered a blank expression, but the muscle in his right jaw twitched. He pushed his chair back slowly and rose. "May I offer you ladies some refreshment?"

An obviously relieved Onia ordered a glass of Chablis, and Claire asked for water. She'd already had three Cowboy Margaritas and needed to keep her head clear.

"Isaac knows I'm his half-sister," Onia said after Scopes left. She seemed more comfortable talking with him out of earshot. "I'm still avoiding Adrianna, but I think Isaac might be more accepting of me. I've asked nothing from him and expect nothing. All I wanted was for Thorne to acknowledge me as his daughter. When he refused…"

"You must have been terribly upset."

Fire flashed in those crystal eyes, then flared out. "Not enough to kill him, if that's what you're thinking."

Scopes returned with the drinks, and the conversation drifted to mundane remarks about the wedding. Claire observed that he treated his niece as if she were a porcelain doll, hovering about, asking if she were too hot or too cold, fetching drinks and snacks so she didn't have to move a muscle.

Overly protective, as if trying to replace something life had taken from her. Or from him.

After an appropriate period, Claire excused herself, saying she needed to check on her date. Not being much of a social butterfly, Tom might be by himself and lonely. Onia and Scopes didn't exactly jump for joy at her departure, but she did notice a collective sigh of relief.

* * *

Avery sat on the edge of a folding chair that had been covered with a burlap sack and tied with a lariat. She impatiently tapped her foot while shoveling cake into her mouth. When Claire walked up, she choked down the dry confection.

"Jay's hanging out with his wife," Avery pointed out to her sister. "Did you see him? Over by the cake." Avery felt betrayed even if she had no right to.

"No, but I'm sure he's just being nice. Is that your excuse for the cake binge?" Claire flopped into the chair next to Avery, who slapped her hand away when she tried to run her finger through the icing. "What flavor is it?"

"The top layers were vanilla decorated with buttercream boots and spurs on the sides. A cowboy and cowgirl riding a rearing white horse was the topper. As if either Isaac or Shania have ever been within a hundred yards of a horse." Avery wiped crumbs from her lips. "The bottom layer is decorated like a wooden log, and it's chocolate. It's edible but just barely."

"Where's Tom?"

"In the corner near the bar, lounging like a gigolo on the chaise next to Lianne Rhinehart Mondae. Goes by Rhinehart since she divorced Thorne 12 years ago. Looks like old Tom is really turning on the hillbilly charm, and she's lapping it up."

Tom sat with his arm on the back of a wicker sofa, while Lianne had insinuated herself beside him. When he spoke, she laughed and placed her hand on his knee. Lianne was one of those well-kept middle-aged women who, to the educated eye, employed a modest amount of cosmetic surgery and some occasional Botox. But in a subtle way that did not scream wind tunnel. She accented her low-cut black dress with a multi-layered beaded necklace and thick gold earrings.

"When did they pass around the bubbly?" Claire asked when Lianne sipped from a flute.

"Wait-people were bringing it around on trays. I passed since I've had a number of Cowboy Margaritas."

"Yeah, me too. I needed to complete my assignment."

"Glad to hear it," Avery said, still staring at Tom and Lianne. "Looks like your beau Tom couldn't resist the urge to go for the info I wanted, despite his initial protests."

"That's Tom. Too stubborn to do anything when it's somebody else's idea. But convince him he thought of it first, and he morphs into a stalking bloodhound."

"Can't wait to find out what he discovered. I'll be sure to pretend it was all his brilliant idea."

As the wedding reception wound down and before the couples headed home, Avery returned to Thorne's trophy room, removed the box of old newspaper clippings, and secreted them in the glovebox of Tom's Suburban.

24

Long before she had become Onia, Rebecca Redfield visited Europe. But this trip to Port Blair less than a year ago had been her first trip to an Asian country. The city proved to be more charming and less backward than she anticipated. Although Uncle Scopes had given her Nurse Singh's address and notified her that his niece intended to visit, he neglected to mention whether he'd informed the nurse of Rebecca's true identity. Uncle Scopes liked surprises, so he probably left it to her to break the news.

After landing at the Veer Savarkar International Airport, an exhausted Rebecca directed the taxi driver to deliver her to the Welcome Inn ten minutes away. Although a bit dated, the place overlooked the azure sea. She had specifically reserved a water view room, since it seemed ridiculous to come to an island and not be able to see the ocean. Without turning the bedcovers back, she lay down and fell immediately to sleep. When she woke, the sky had turned dark, and her stomach growled. She called Nurse Singh, who insisted she call her "Riya," and they agreed to meet in an hour at the hotel's Juniper Berry Restaurant.

Rebecca showered and dressed in a tropical midi-dress and sandals. She'd had her toenails painted a deep orange for her trip to the tropics. It coordinated with the flowers on her dress and the long scarf she tied around her unruly Afro in a fruitless attempt to tame it.

Displaying beautiful hardwood floors, the restaurant overlooked the pool and ultimately the Andaman Sea. From studying maps of the island, Rebecca knew Thailand lay on the other side of the bay. She ordered a champagne cocktail to await Riya. Since she had woken, a new and strange feeling of well-being had warmed her insides, and the drink added another layer of contentment. Surely, she could not already be adapting to this foreign land as if it were her home. But it felt nice, like a baby going back to the cocooning tenderness of her mother's womb. And in a way, that's exactly what she was doing. Shaking the fanciful ideas from her head, she ordered another drink.

An older lady, walking straight-backed but gracefully even though she used a cane, followed the hostess to her table. When they arrived, the woman said, "Rebecca Redfield?"

Rebecca stood, and they shook hands. Riya's felt soft against her cool one which had been holding the cocktail.

"Please sit," she said. "Can I get you a drink?"

"Whatever you're having."

After the waiter brought another champagne cocktail, Rebecca said: "Thank you for meeting me. I know it's a bit strange."

"Not at all. I'm thrilled to meet you." Riya tucked a lock of platinum hair behind her ear. The thick mane, parted simply on the side, fell halfway down her back. The nurse resembled one those women one sees from behind, thinking their long, luscious locks must belong to a young person. But when she turns, one's surprised to see a face lined with fine wrinkles.

They exchanged pleasantries until their fresh fish baked in banana leaves arrived. With no need for conversation, like women who had been best friends for years, they ate in silence for several minutes.

"Dessert?" Rebecca asked.

"I don't know. Are you having any?"

"Sure, why not. I'll take the mini tropical fruit pie with whipped cream."

"Me too!" Riya said.

Either they had the same culinary tastes, or Riya ordered the same things because she didn't know how much Rebecca could afford. If she ordered a dish, then Riya probably assumed it was affordable. Nice lady.

They moved to a booth in the bar area. Gradually Rebecca explained that she came to Port Blair to find her birth mother. Knowledge of her parentage had become so much more important now that she had marriage plans and the possibility of children. Riya nodded as if she totally understood.

"I was present when you were born," Riya said. "Such a beautiful baby, with those sapphire eyes against that dark skin." She stared into her drink, then at Rebecca. "You're a gorgeous young lady as well. You look so much like your mother."

"Glad I look like my mother and not my father!" Rebecca laughed but she meant every word.

Riya squirmed, as if she didn't quite know how to react. "The thing is… I mean, for your own good… and hers. Well, Rebecca, the truth is, your mother doesn't know you're alive. She thinks Tatehane, the tribal elder who kidnapped you, drowned you that same day. It's going to be a shock. It will probably be better if you let me talk to her first."

"Uncle Scopes told me."

"It was for the best. She would have wanted you back. Who could blame her? But Mr. Scopes wasn't putting you back into danger. As shameful as it seems, I've kept the secret all these years. Even seeing her often but never telling. I hope you can forgive us. I hope Anjale… your mother… can."

"Tell me about her," Rebecca said in a soft voice.

"Your Uncle Scopes continued to send money for Anjale and still does. To understand what happened, you need to know a little about the Jarawa. For generations, they shunned interaction with outsiders, but since the 1990s, contacts between them and outsiders have grown more frequent. The Trunk Road—"

"What's that?"

"The Great Andaman Trunk Road connects Port Blair to Diglipur, which means it runs from the north end of the island to the sound end for a distance of 360 kilometers. The Jarawa Reserve lies in a forested area smack in the middle."

"Oh yeah. I saw it on the map."

"Although discouraged by the Indian government, the road encourages the Jarawa to visit hospitals, marketplaces, even settlements on the edge of their reserve. It's controversial since such a primitive tribe is expected to remain untouched by civilization. It's not uncommon for children to show

up at mainstream schools and ask to be educated. After the... uh, the incident, Anjale's father brought her to Port Blair to send her to school. She still
lives here and worked for the hospital as a nurses' assistant until they let her
go during the Covid pandemic. They could only afford to keep essential personnel because of the financial strain on the hospital."

"Will she want to meet me?"

"I'm sure she will. We just have to break it to her gently. She never
married or had any other children and has little contact with her Jarawa
family. They live such different lives. She'll be ecstatic to discover you're alive."

Rebecca's head spun from the drinks. She hoped she hadn't made a
terrible mistake coming here and meeting her real mother. What would
Anjale think of her? "I'm feeling a little tipsy," she said to Riya. "Combination
of jetlag and the drinks. Probably need to go to my room and lie down." She
downed the water in the glass next to her half-full cocktail. "Can I call you
a taxi?"

"I brought my car." Riya stood, took up her cane, and hooked her purse
over her shoulder. "Don't worry. Everything will be alright." She patted
Rebecca's arm.

"Will you set up a meet-and-greet as soon as possible?" Rebecca caught
the back of the booth to steady herself.

"Yes, I'll call you."

Rebecca watched as Riya made her laborious way toward the exit, a
stranger who had become very important to her. Weird how that worked.
One day you didn't know someone existed, and the next day they held the
key to the rest of your life.

* * *

Rebecca assumed the basic square archery stance by positioning her
left foot in front of the shooting line, a spray-painted orange stripe created
by her 50 yards from the target. She turned sideways and placed her right
foot parallel with her left. Focusing her muscular energy, she nocked the
arrow by snapping its nock on the bowstring and placing it on the arrow rest.
While relaxing her hand and aligning the bow, she raised her arm a hair

above her nose and pointed. Maintaining proper form, she anchored her body, focused on the target, and released. The arrow fell short.

"Dammit!" She had failed to follow through by keeping her bow in hand and maintaining her position until sure she'd hit the target. Dropping the bow immediately after release was a common cause of steering the arrow in the wrong direction. Or so said her archery instructor.

For the past two weeks in Port Blair, she had been practicing her archery every day. From her mother, Anjale, she had obtained the primitive bow and arrows used by her native tribe, the Jarawa. She had taken lessons from a local professional she found at the athletic club.

When Riya first introduced mother and daughter, Rebecca felt as if she were gazing into her future. She looked so much like Anjale—the high cheekbones, athletic build, ebony skin—it was like looking into a mirror 20 years from now. The main difference was, of course, the eyes—Anjale's opaque brown compared to Rebecca's sapphire crystals.

Her mother had been shocked to see her, but a gradual acceptance grew between them, and Rebecca knew they had made a deep connection. Any niggling doubt about them being mother and daughter vanished, and she spent every day with Anjale. They visited beaches, took several touristy excursions including the Cellular Jail, the Natural Bridge at Neil Island, the Anthropological Museum, and snorkeled at Havelock Island using their handy full-face snorkel masks.

A trip to Anjale's native village deep in the Jarawa Reserve proved to be the most amazing event they shared. Riya had dropped them off a Tirur, near the edge of the reserve, and they walked the rest of the way. It had been quite some time since Anjale visited her ancestral home. She reacquainted herself with both relatives and other tribal friends while Rebecca surreptitiously snapped photos with her cellphone. Not wanting to be obtrusive in order to obtain more candid shots, she wanted to be accepted as one of them.

Although unwilling to go completely nude, she had opted for a dark midriff top near the color of her flesh and a tie-up skirt hoping she wouldn't look too American. Anjale wore a light-weight sarong. Compared to the Jarawa, they had grossly overdressed.

Anjale's father was still alive, as were other relatives, although Rebecca remained clueless as to how they were related. They stared at her eyes, mesmerized, but accepting since Anjale accompanied her. Could they guess who she really was—the baby threatened by Tatehane, the tribal elder who had tried to murder her? The bawling child a white man from across the ocean saved from drowning? She searched the faces of the old men, wondering if any of them could be Tatehane. She knew him to be beyond human law, but hoped he had been punished by some unknown universal entity seeking justice, if such a thing existed.

They gathered for a simple meal of jackfruit cooked in a pit hearth called the *aalaav*. The Jarawa created a fire at the bottom and covered it with pebbles, laid on the jackfruit, then layered more pebbles on top. They served honey stored in wooden buckets and covered with green leaves. Both men and women collected the honey by climbing tall trees. The kernels from seeds called *oomiin* were dipped in saline water and dried in the sun for months. To cook them, the natives boiled them in water and mixed them with pig fat.

Rebecca noticed that both men and women took part in fishing. While men used the bow and arrow to shoot the fish, women used hand nets. Entranced with their primitive weapons, she spent some time watching a cousin, she thought, ply his bow and arrow as if he were playing a musical instrument.

Mother and daughter returned from their trip tired but happy, having shared an experience few families would ever know. For the first time in her life, Rebecca felt at home in the world, this world.

"I don't understand," Anjale said in the tentative English she learned from Nurse Singh. "Why you want to shoot bow and arrow? Girls make baskets."

Rebecca laughed and hugged Anjale. Her mother stiffened as if she had received very little of that type of affection, but softened it with a smile. "I've never been a typical girl. I'd have more use for archery lessons than a class in basket weaving. Thanks for letting me use one of the bows you brought from the village. It makes me feel like a true native."

When not taking archery lessons, Rebecca practiced for hours, obsessed with a fevered passion she had rarely felt in her short lifetime. She did not discuss her reasons with her mother or Riya, but they stemmed from something Anjale had confessed on the return trip from the Jarawa Reserve.

With the soothing hum of the engine and the dark anonymity of Riya's automobile, Anjale told her version of the story when Thorne and Scopes visited her village nearly 30 years ago.

"I take water from the dog-face man," Anjale began, meaning Thorne. "But it didn't taste like water. I spit it out, but a fire burned inside my belly. My arms and legs floated. He gave me a red gift. We are on the beach, no one else there. He touched me. When I get angry, he pressed me down. I'm very afraid but tipsy with the drink. He gives me more fiery water. He takes the red… uh…" She spreads her arms out parallel, indicating a long object.

"Scarf," Riya said.

"Scarf… put it around my face so I am blind, not seeing anything. But I feel it. Feel him down there… searching. A long time. Then the terrible pain." Anjale's chest heaved as if she were reliving the moment.

"He raped you!" Rebecca cried from the back seat. Her mother sat in front with Riya, a dark stooped silhouette. "Thorne Mondae raped you. And that's where I came from." She wiped an angry tear from her eye. "I'm the living proof of a violent assault." Anjale's head dipped, as if in shame. Rebecca reached across the seat back and touched her shoulder. "It's okay, Mother." It was the first time she'd called Anjale *mother*. Without turning around, Anjale placed her hand, warm from wringing them together, over her daughter's.

"Something good came out of something bad," Riya said.

"And you thought I was dead all these years." Rebecca felt sick.

Anjale raised her head and turned to stare at her daughter. "No. I followed Mr. Scopes when he search for you. He tried to make me turn back, but I tricked him. I watched from the trail. I saw him take the baby from Tatehane after he want to drown her. She was kicking and crying, alive."

"You knew she was alive all this time?" Riya asked. "Why didn't you say anything?"

"You say nothing. I say nothing. Better for the baby to grow up in a civil…" She looked at Riya.

"Civilized?"

"Yes, a civilized country."

"You let me go away because you loved me?"

"Yes, I love you. You are my child."

"What did you name me?" Rebecca asked.

"Onia."

"Don't worry, Mother. Something good will come from this. I'll see that it does."

At that moment, she decided she didn't want to be called Rebecca anymore. She would take her Jarawa name, her real name—*Onia*. She worked it around in her mouth a few times, trying to get the feel of it. It sat on her tongue like a piece of hard candy but tasted good and went down smooth after it melted.

25

The morning after the night of the cowboy wedding revealed itself to a sleeping household. When dawn broke, Bodhi, who had curled up with Avery and Jay, jumped off the bed and let himself out the doggie door. Avery woke and followed him outside. In the early morning haze, she removed the newspaper clippings from the Suburban's glovebox and sneaked them into the bottom drawer of her bureau. She wasn't quite sure why she had stolen the clippings. They seemed such a personal thing belonging to someone else, and now they were in her possession. She felt as if she had a right to them, had become their official caretaker and protector. Hoped they would give her some insight into the life and character of Thorne Mondae. Maybe even a clue to his death. As quietly and gently as they could, she and Bodhi slipped back into her king-sized bed next to Jay.

Several hours later, with the late morning sunshine flooding her bedroom, Avery gazed at the treetops visible through the top layer of windows of her 20-foot walls. As a strong wind swayed the pines, they clacked together like battling soldiers. Pinecones shaken from the trees hit the metal roof with dull thuds, but the thumps were nothing compared to the divebombing vultures.

The first few weeks the sisters had lived in Rancho Exotica, they had very little furniture. They wanted to start their new life from scratch, to change everything including their surroundings. Avery slept on a mattress on the floor. One night, she woke from a deep, dreamless sleep to a fierce glare burning into her eyelids, as if someone had turned a monstrous spot-light into her face. But when she looked up, a gigantic full moon shining through her windows lit up the whole room. She took it as a sign, like a blessing on her new life. She remembered feeling so happy and content, two elusive emotions with which she had little experience.

Jay shifted onto his side. In the unforgiving daylight, his face appeared more lined than usual. Avery longed to ask him what he and his wife had discussed during the wedding reception, but she didn't want to appear as insecure as she felt. She really had no hold on the guy, not like his wife did. They had made a life together, with a house, kids, and a shared history that she and Jay didn't have. She cautioned herself to be ready for the end, but was it possible to prepare for being dumped? Would recognizing its inevitability make it any less painful?

The last time she had been in love, many years ago and long after her divorce, the end had come as a complete surprise. Very few events in her life had been as agonizing. Determined to steel herself against becoming too involved, she vowed to always keep up her guard. Not get blindsided again.

When she curved into him, Jay woke. From behind, she trailed kisses down his neck. One thing led to another, and they began to make love. Thanks to infrequent YouTube chair yoga video sessions, she managed to perform a nimble move or two despite her arthritic knees, but nothing that could be considered acrobatic. *Note to self: next time wear knee braces beneath filmy apricot nightgown.*

After freshening up, she headed to the kitchen to turn on the Keurig. She checked Claire's door to make sure it was closed. It had been ages since the sisters had boyfriends at the same time. It was fun, being able to share the joys and tribulations with each other. Jay came out of her bedroom rubbing his eyes, his dark hair tousled like a child's. He looked a bit grouchy. Bodhi followed and, being gifted with the sleep of the truly innocent, looked wide awake and chipper. Avery shoved a mug of freshly brewed coffee in Jay's hand and a bowl of kibble in front of Bodhi.

Later, when Claire and Tom joined them at the kitchen island, Tom made cinnamon toast from scratch, and they ate it with a raw fruit salad. Afterwards, Tom relaxed on Claire's sectional with Bodhi's head on his thigh.

He told them he had to return to Little Mountain. There was work to be done, and he didn't trust his employees to maintain things for very long.

"Before you go," Avery said, "would you share what Lianne told you last night?"

"You had her eating out of your hand," Claire said.

"I don't know about that," Tom said, but he looked pleased. "We just started talking, and I figured I'd take advantage of the situation. See if I could find out something that would help."

"Very clever, Tom," Avery said. "Glad you thought of it."

The sisters exchanged looks.

"They owned an internet provider business together." Tom tore a bite off his cinnamon toast and popped it into his mouth. A light sprinkling of sugar and cinnamon fell on Bodhi's head. "Thorne and Lianne, that is. When they were married."

"Do you think he might have left her the business, in the will, I mean?" Avery asked.

"I doubt it. Lianne said Thorne voted with the shareholders to kick her out of the company. One she helped build. Really upset her, I could tell. She cried a few tears in her champagne. Although he did come up with big bucks to buy her shares. Left her a millionaire."

"She told you that?"

"Not in so many words. Not the part about being a millionaire. But she wore some expensive jewelry and designer clothes. She even told me about her Bentley Continental Convertible. Didn't tell me how old it was, but it's an expensive car regardless."

"Like more than $50,000?"

"Like four times that or more."

"Really? Can't imagine spending that much money for a vehicle." Avery never had understood what rich people spent money on.

"That's nothing," Jay said. "Jay-Z spent nearly nine million."

"Dollars?" Avery's mouth dropped open. "On a car?"

"Nothing we plebians will ever be able to comprehend," Claire said.

"Now that I've had a mini-stroke," Avery said, "let's get back to the issue at hand. Lianne Rhinehart."

"She dumped Thorne not long after he voted to kick her out of the business," Tom said, "but they still worked together. She had some stake in his real estate business, played a role in its management."

"I take it that was years ago," Avery said. "Would she hold a grudge that long?"

Tom sat for a moment, his forehead wrinkled, as though deciding how to respond. He absently patted Bodhi's head, and the sugar he'd dropped earlier came off in his hand. When Claire handed him a napkin, a look passed between them. Rarely had Avery seen her sister gaze at a man with such affection. It didn't hurt that their beloved dog stared at him in much the same way. Tom wiped off the sugar. "She's still pissed. But since she's making money from the real estate business, she's not mad enough to kill the guy. That's what she said, what she wanted me to believe anyway. I tended to believe her, but that's just my opinion. Don't take it to the bank."

"Do we know if she has an alibi?"

"She claimed to be home alone," Tom said. "She volunteered that, but I have no idea if it's true or not."

"All I learned," Avery said, "is what we already suspected. That Adrianna and her personal trainer... she called her a health coach... are having an affair, probably started before Thorne's death. And they are each other's alibis. For whatever that's worth."

"And all I learned," Claire said, "is that Isaac knows Onia is his half-sister and apparently has no problem with her. And Onia claims she was not angry enough at Thorne for failing to acknowledge paternity to kill him. And her Uncle Scopes seems to be devoted to his niece."

"Sounds like he adheres to that old adage," Tom said, "that when you save someone's life, you become responsible for them forever."

After a short silence, all eyes turned to Jay. He had been sitting at the island absentmindedly sipping coffee, not contributing to the conversation about suspects. When the silence became overwhelming, he looked up and saw three pairs of eyes staring at him.

"What?" he asked.

"We're waiting to hear your contribution to the suspect information gathering at the wedding," Claire said.

Remembering the amount of time he'd spent with his wife, Avery avoided looking at him.

Jay fidgeted on the barstool, then twirled around and leaped off.

"I got nothing!" His voice rose, defensive, as if he had been accused of something. "I need to go home. I'll text later." He shot Avery a quick glance, then headed for the door.

"Aren't you going with us Monday to take the trail camera to Detective Castellan?" Avery wished she could get the desperation out of her voice.

Jay looked back. "You sisters are perfectly capable of doing that on your own. You should have done it weeks ago." To Tom, he said, "Have a safe trip home." And strode out the front door to his red golf cart.

26

With Tom on his way back to Little Mountain, and Jay bowing out for whatever reason, the sisters ended up on their own. It wasn't the first time and wouldn't be the last. They had always depended on each other and never doubted the other sister would be there whenever needed. The burden of proving Claire's innocence landed like a falling rock squarely on their shoulders. Monday morning, the frustrated and exhausted sisters drove to the Sweetgum Police Department and requested to see Detective Castellan.

They had arrived at a point in their investigation—Claire laughed when Avery classified what they had been doing as an "investigation"—where they had a photo of the possible murderer but couldn't identify the Shadowy Figure. After withholding the sim card for a month, they were petrified to turn it over to Detective Castellan. But they had been floundering around too long and, while they had gathered quite a bit of information, none of it pointed definitively to the killer. Maybe they *should* leave it to the professionals.

"Detective Castellan wants to know what your visit is about." The front desk of the police building's lobby sat behind a bulletproof glass with a small opening through which the assigned officer communicated. The cop's ruddy face rose from a burly neck and popped out of his dark uniform collar like the blazing sun rising above the azure sea. He sounded bored and tired, probably at the end of a long shift.

"We have evidence in an ongoing murder investigation." Avery gave him her friendliest smile.

The officer made a call, but the sisters couldn't hear the conversation. After he finished, he said, "It'll be a few minutes. He's in a meeting."

"We'll wait," Claire said. To Avery she said, "It's like waiting in a doctor's office. I think they do that just to put you at a disadvantage. Make you feel your time is not as important as theirs."

"Don't know if it's quite that calculated, but it's working." Avery fingered the sim card in a plastic freezer bag at the bottom of her purse. "Are we sure we're doing the right thing? I mean, the right thing for us? I understand it's the law, but we might go to jail. Who would take care of Bodhi? What would happen to our house? Could we afford to post bond?"

"Stop, Avery. Everything's going to be all right. Quit obsessing." Claire settled back in the hard chair, grabbed her cellphone, and paged through her texts. Probably expecting a message from Tom.

Avery swung her legs impatiently and scanned the room for something to entertain her. No point in checking her cellphone. She knew Jay hadn't texted. Nothing but gray, windowless walls met her gaze. She squirmed, bumping Claire's chair, and received an irritated glance.

"Claire?"

Claire refused to look up from her phone.

"Claire!"

"What?" Her sister raised her head and rolled her eyes a couple of times to signal her irritation.

"Why do you think Jay left so abruptly Sunday morning?" Avery wasn't sure she wanted to know but knew her sister would tell the truth even if it was painful.

"What do you think?" Claire set her phone aside and studied Avery.

"What do you think I think?"

Claire shook her head. "I'm not playing that game, Avery. I have a feeling you already know, or at least think you do. Spit out your theory and quit wasting time."

"He's decided I'm too old and complicated and has decided to go back to his younger wife and uncomplicated relationship." She pulled a forlorn look that was probably wasted on Claire.

"He's what? Maybe 10, 12 years younger than you?"

"Almost 10, but no one's ever asked if I was his mother. I don't think we look weird together. Do you?"

"No, but that's beside the point. I can't pretend to know what he's thinking, but I would be surprised if he goes back to the wife. He strikes me as a rather serious guy who knows his own mind. Don't think he would have left in the first place if he wasn't fairly sure."

"Really?" Avery began to feel better. She lifted her chest and gave her sister a slight smile.

"On the other hand…"

Avery's stomach sank. "What? What other hand?"

"Detective Castellan will see you now." The receiving officer signaled them to follow.

Claire dutifully tracked him with Avery tagging behind.

"What were you going to say? Don't leave me hanging like this. Claire!"

Her sister ignored her while the officer led them along a corridor with closed doors on either side. Near the back of the oblong building, they reached an open door. Inside, Detective Castellan sat behind a metal desk with very little on it. A family photo, a name plaque, a computer, and several files spread like fallen leaves across the top. A gray metal filing cabinet lurked behind with two guest chairs parked like soldiers in front. It wasn't the first time they had been there.

"What can I do for you ladies?" Detective Castellan asked after they had been seated.

"I'm Avery Halverson, and this is my sister—"

"I know who you are. The officer said you had evidence. I assume it has something to do with the death of Thorne Mondae. What is it?" No pleasantries for Castellan. Straight to the facts, Ma'am.

"I just want to say," Avery began, "that we're really sorry we broke the law, I mean I think we broke the law. But if you decide to send us to jail, could you just send one of us? Let the other one go home to take care of Bodhi, and—"

"Avery!" Claire said. "Just give him the card."

Avery struggled with her purse, and its contents spilled onto the concrete floor. She picked up the plastic bag with the sim card and passed it to

Castellan. After dropping into the guest chair, she bent over to pick up the fallen objects. With her bad knees, she didn't dare kneel on the hard floor. She'd never get up again.

"What's this?"

"In our forest, we strapped a trail camera to a tree facing our metal storage shed." Claire spoke in a steady voice. "After Mr. Mondae's death, the forensics team overlooked it. We used it to trace feral cats so we could trap, neuter, and release them. I remembered it much later. When we recovered it and looked at the photos—it's motion activated—we realized it captured the victim and possibly the killer."

Castellan's head shot up; his eyes widened.

"Can you pull up photos on a sim card on your computer?" Avery asked.

"Yes, I've done it before." Castellan pulled a surgical glove out of his desk drawer, popped it on his right hand, and pulled the sim card out of the plastic bag. He inserted it into the proper slot on his computer. "Talk me through what I'm seeing here."

What was he going to do? Check the sim card for fingerprints? Proof that they had possession of evidence and withheld it. Avery stiffened and held her breath. Maybe she was reading too much into the action. She tried to force herself to relax. Or was forced relaxation a contradiction in terms?

Claire calmly ran him through the times when Thorne Mondae had passed the field camera, then Claire, and finally the Shadowy Figure appearing from behind the shed. When she had finished, he looked dazed, as if he'd been watching a boring movie and then, all of a sudden, the monster popped up in front of the screen. He whirled in his chair to face the sisters.

"Where's the actual camera? It might need to be checked for time accuracy."

"We didn't bring it," Claire said in a slightly shaky voice. "We'll give it to Jay Vidocq so he can deliver it to you."

Avery shook her head in a subtle motion.

Castellan concentrated a heavy look at each sister as if he suspected something nefarious going on between them.

"We'll get it to you as soon as possible," Avery said quickly.

Castellan contracted his brow and slowly nodded. "Have you two heard of Texas Penal Code Statute 37.09?" He picked up what looked like one of the legal tomes the sisters used to see in their bosses' offices. The open page had been marked with a sticky note. Castellan read, "'Tampering with or Fabricating Physical Evidence: a person commits an offense if, knowing that an investigation or official proceeding is pending or in progress, he: (a) alters, destroys, or conceals any record, document, or thing with intent to impair its verity, legibility, or availability as evidence in the investigation or official proceeding.'" Castellan must have researched it while they waited in reception.

"It does specify '*he*.'"

"Avery, be quiet," Claire said.

Castellan made a face that said he might need a laxative. "I'm extremely upset with you ladies. I'm normally a patient man, and I pride myself on my fair dealing. But you two have pushed me to the edge."

"Detective," Avery said, "our names are Claire and Avery. And we're neither children nor are we senile. We know what we did was bad, but we were afraid. These photos put Claire in the forest at the same time Thorne Mondae was murdered. Surely you can understand why we withheld it."

"Let me tell you a story." Castellan leaned back in his chair, staring them down with his stern glare. "Not only are amateur detectives dangerous, but they can ruin a case beyond prosecution. Years ago, we had a woman who thought one of her co-workers looked like the composite of a fugitive homicide suspect. She actually carried his personnel photo to our witness, the one who helped create the composite, and asked her if that was the guy she saw. The witness said 'yes,' which sounds like a good thing, but the identification was tainted. The cops would have shown her five to 10 pictures in a photo lineup before allowing her to identify the perp."

"Did the guy walk?" Naturally, Claire would be concerned whether justice prevailed.

"No. By some miracle, they had enough other evidence to convict, so it turned out okay in the end."

"Maybe this will too." Avery moved around Castellan to point to the computer screen. He drew back as if no one had ever invaded his personal space before. "We surmise that the Shadowy Figure behind the shed is the murderer. See the photos before the figure appears. Nothing that could have activated the motion detector. We couldn't figure out why they had been taken since some motion is needed. I believe an arrow was shot from behind the shed, obviously by the Shadowy Figure, and the arrow activated the camera. But it moved too fast for the camera to capture a picture."

Castellan heaved a heavy sigh, looked resigned. His eyes never left the computer screen. "The victim, Mr. Mondae, was shot by someone almost directly in front of him. The shooter was opposite Mondae, whereas your sister… Claire… was coming from the same general direction as the victim. I'll have these photos enlarged and enhanced, but the unsub was wearing a ski mask in addition to a camouflage outfit. Impossible to tell if it's a male or female. Hopefully, the enhancements will give more details." He sounded as excited as the detective ever seemed to get when he wasn't reprimanding the sisters.

"Couldn't it be his son, Isaac?" Avery asked. "If I remember correctly, he didn't sign out at the barn until 12:30 p.m."

"Too soon to make any assumptions." Castellan rose quickly as though anxious to get them out of his office. "Okay, *Claire* and *Avery*." He lasered them with his homicide detective x-ray vision. "This does not necessarily clear Claire from any involvement in the murder of Thorne Mondae."

"But you said—"

"I *said* that playing amateur detective puts a target on your back. No matter how unsuccessful you may be, the perp will still feel threatened. And, it sets up the possibility of thwarting justice. Don't forget my story about the lady who played amateur detective and nearly helped a murderer escape. You don't want to be that person, do you?" He waited until both sisters vehemently shook their heads. "I'm confident there will be no more meddling from you two—Claire and Avery. Am I right?"

Avery stuck her hands behind her back and crossed her fingers.

"Absolutely!" the sisters said in unison.

"Good. Now, wait here a minute. I'll be right back."

When he left the room carrying the sim card, a flood of relief filled Avery. She had felt an anxiety attack coming on, but it passed quickly. The deed was done, and they had gotten off with nothing but a reprimand. She glanced at Claire, who still looked shellshocked.

"Looks like we skated on this one." Avery would have held her hand up for a high-five, but she thought white people looked ridiculous imitating gestures and expressions originated by African-American culture. Especially two extremely white and totally uncool old biddies like themselves who could count the Black residents in their neighborhood on one hand.

The door creaked open. Claire sat up post-straight, and her face turned as white as new bedsheets. She stared at the man who entered the room with round frisbee eyes. It was the chunky duty officer who sat behind the window in the police lobby. He gripped a pair of handcuffs in each beefy mitt.

"I need you ladies to stand up and put your hands behind your back," the officer said.

Behind him, Detective Castellan began reading from a rectangular blue card. "You have the right to remain silent. Anything you say can and will be used against you in a court of law…"

27

The worst thing was the smell. The odor of confined human flesh permeated the concrete block walls of the city jail. Avery's first instinct was to hold her nose but with her hands cuffed behind her back, that was impossible. She tried to hold her breath, but she'd stopped breathing properly the minute she heard the handcuffs snap around her wrists.

Fear, confusion, shock. Was there one word that combined all those emotions? Because each and every one of them undulated up and down her body like multiple tsunamis attacking a beach. When she glanced at Claire, the same feelings appeared in her flushed cheeks and crazy eyes. Never had Avery felt so helpless and hopeless.

Before entering what looked like a community holding cell, she read the inscription above the barred doors, "Sobering Cell #2," and wondered how many cells it took to sober up the population of a small Texas town like Sweetgum. More than one, apparently. This one did not appear to be holding inebriated people, so they must have misnamed it in their enthusiasm for rounding up town drunks. The room spread across the back wall of the police station, its concrete floors a foreboding gray, and a bench poured adjacent to the walls stretched opposite the barred double doors. They closed against Avery and Claire with a loud clang.

Aside from the sisters, the holding cell housed three other people, all women, since she assumed the rules required gender separation. One was a middle-aged white woman who looked as if she had spent the night in the local ginmill before passing out in a dirty gutter and ultimately busted by the local constabulary, an African American female who resembled a suburban housewife, and a Latina woman who looked to be middle-to-late thirties dressed in a tight tank top over shorty-shorts and a thick layer of makeup. Avery recognized none of the women, thank goodness! She had no desire to share the unique experience of being thrown unceremoniously in the town jail with an acquaintance from Rancho Exotica. The neighbors already thought the sisters were strange. Wait until they found out about this!

Claire could have played a zombie extra in an episode of *The Walking Dead*. Avery suggested they sit on the bench seating against the wall, and her sister followed with a shuffling gait.

"Claire!" Avery said. "You need to snap out of it. Remember the time we got caught in that 4-wheeler on those mining trails in the Rockies? On the one rated *intermediate* when neither of us had ever been on an off-road mountain trail before. And I'd never driven a jeep in my entire life?" She waited a beat to see if Claire responded. It took some time, but she finally received a minute nod from her sister. "We were stopped at a 45-degree angle, with ten-thousand-foot drops on both sides and barely six inches between our tires and the edge. And you turned, looked back toward the bottom of the mountain, and started screaming, 'Oh my god, oh my god, oh my god!'?"

"Holy crap, Avery!" Claire seemed to have woken from the undead. "If that's your attempt at making me feel better, it's gone woefully awry."

"Wait until I get to the point."

"Make it quick unless you want me to flop down on this bench and curl into a fetal position."

Avery huffed an impatient sigh. "Do you remember what I said to you then?"

A calmer Claire said, "We're gonna die?"

"I told you we were trapped on top of a 14,000-foot mountain—"

"I'm not feeling better."

"—and it would take both of us to get us down. I couldn't do it by myself. You had to calm down and help me navigate, or we would be stuck there until somebody found us. And who knows when that would be? We'd be a Donner Party replay."

Claire swiped a bead of sweat off her forehead. "I assume your point is that we need to work together to solve this problem."

"You got it in one, sista'!"

"Isn't that how we wound up in this mess in the first place?"

Avery was losing patience—which implied that she had any to begin with. "We were trying to absolve you of first-degree murder and a possible death sentence."

"I hadn't been indicted for murder or manslaughter or anything else. Now I'm charged with evidence tampering which, according to Castellan, is a third-degree felony carrying a penalty of two-10 years and a fine up to $10,000."

"Don't think that's comparable to lethal injection."

Claire folded her arms across her chest. "I can't talk to you unless you're taking this seriously."

"I am serious. Tell me specifically what Mary Mayberry said when Castellan let you make the call to our attorney."

Claire unclenched her teeth. "She said that the perpetrator… us… had to *know* that an investigation was going on in the first place. Which we did. And have the *intent* to impair the availability of evidence to affect the course of the investigation. Which we did. We had no lack of knowledge or intent."

"So, we're guilty as hell."

"You got it in one, sista'!" Claire's attempt at mimicking Avery fell a bit short of lightening the mood. "She's going to find someone to get us out, though. She said having criminal defense representation in Texas was imperative, the earlier the better."

"We forgot something," Avery said. "They record everything you say in jail. And we just admitted our guilt. We're screwed."

"I know they record phone calls to the outside, but inside cells?"

"Jails aren't considered private places, so we can expect to be filmed at any time. I assume that means recorded as well."

Claire looked skeptical. "Regardless, based on the fact that we brought the sim card to the investigator-in-charge, there wasn't much doubt."

"You didn't suggest Mary call Jay, did you? I'd be mortified if she asked him to post our bail."

"No, she's getting Tom to arrange things."

"What about Bodhi? He won't have his supper."

"We'll be out of here soon. I don't think he's going to starve to death in a few hours."

"He does have a bit of a spare tire."

"There's nobody to check on him since you refuse to let Jay know we're here. It's unrealistic to think he won't find out. He works with the police and lives in Rancho Exotica."

Avery stood and paced, beating a path in front of the bench seat. "I know. Guess it doesn't really matter now. I don't think I'll ever see him again. Speaking of which, what did you mean by that 'on the other hand' remark before we went to Castellan's office?" She stopped pacing long enough to wait for the answer.

"I meant that you couldn't predict what anyone would do, especially a man. But—"

"But what? Don't start that again!" Avery tried to calm herself. They were both on edge.

"Maybe Jay left because he didn't think you really cared one way or the other. Don't be offended, but you are so self-protective, always trying to keep from getting involved and possibly hurt, you tend to freeze people out. I'm not saying that's what happened with you and Jay. I'm just throwing it out as a possibility."

Avery's body went limp as if she had deflated. "Wish I had a counter-argument for that, but I don't. Except to say that it's because our mother always loved you best. You were more like her, and the two of you ganged up on me, disapproving and critical. No wonder I'm insecure."

The truth of that statement did not brook a response from Claire who sat in awkward silence while Avery resumed pacing.

"Excuse me." Avery looked up to see the three other ladies in the holding cell hovering close enough to have heard the sister's exchange. The one in the shorty-shorts had spoken. Avery backed up until her calves hit the bench where Claire sat. The group of women gathered nearby made her feel uncomfortable, challenged.

"Can I help you?" Claire asked.

"We couldn't help overhearing your conversation," the suburban housewife interjected. "We're just curious why your mother—I'm assuming you two are sisters—likes you better than the other one. You kind of left the story hanging."

The lady, who looked as if she'd spent the night in a local alleyway with her muddy dress and disheveled appearance, drew closer as though anticipating the response. Avery suppressed her urge to back farther away since she had nowhere to go. She glanced at Claire, who looked cool and unaffected by the gathering group of women. They exchanged glances, and she wondered if Claire read the unease in her eyes.

"It's a valid question," Claire said in a calm voice. "My name is Claire, by the way, and my sister is Avery."

"I'm the *younger* sister." As if that would protect her from any harm the mob might be contemplating!

"I'm Bertha," the woman in the shorty-shorts said, "and my mamma didn't like me either." She accompanied the statement with a boisterous laugh. The other inmates giggled appreciatively.

Avery searched the holding cell for an escape route and found none.

Bertha scanned the sisters up and down. "Pretty sure you two aren't working girls. Whatcha in for?"

"Obstructing justice," Avery blurted out. Give them what they wanted, and maybe they would leave the sisters alone.

"Well, technically, tampering with evidence," Claire corrected.

"I got a good lawyer," the suburban housewife said.

"We have one already, but thank you."

"So…" The woman in the dirty dress who hovered a little distance from the others moved closer. "What's the story? About your mother, I mean?"

"Oh, nothing too Freudian." Avery hoped she didn't sound too intellectually superior. "It's just that when Claire was born, everybody considered her a little princess. Curly blonde hair, big dimples, and an uncanny resemblance to the Gerber baby didn't hurt. Both our father and mother adored her. They had done such a good job, they decided to have another one, who turned out to be me. I came out a little no-neck monster who looked like a bowling ball with an apple on top. They declared a moratorium on any more kids. After our dad died, my mother learned that she had more in common with Claire than she did with me. I was a mischievous handful and Claire was an angel." Her oversharing tendencies always came out when she felt anxious.

"Our mother loved you just as much as she did me."

"Maybe, but she didn't approve of me. Neither did you. It was a long time ago. It's okay if you admit it."

"So that's it?" Bertha said. "You're in jail because your mother disapproved of you?"

"Is that a punishable offense?" the suburban lady asked.

Bertha huffed, shook her head. "No hooking to supply a nasty heroin habit, no running away from an abusive home, no neglected kids removed by CPS, no gangbanger boyfriends threatening you with a gun to your head? Nothing but a little parental disapproval?"

Avery's cheeks flushed hot. She actually felt guilty for not being bad enough. Relief replaced guilt when the three inmates moved away, grumbling amongst themselves.

"You two are the most boring jailbirds I ever met!" Bertha fired back at them.

"Based on the source," Avery said to Claire, "I'm guessing that was an insult."

28

As the day stretched into evening, noises in the Sweetgum Jail began to rise and drift into the cell—a cacophony of coughs, shouts, harsh arguments, creaking walls and clanging doors, skids across hard floors slick with humidity, and unidentifiable low murmurings that could be voices of police officers quietly discussing their cases or whispers of former inmates' ghosts who passed fitful nights in the dark recesses of the oblong building.

When the doors of the holding cell clanked open, Avery jumped a foot off the bench where she slept with her head against the cool wall. Beside her, a fierce-faced Claire maintained a wide-awake stance as if she thought at least one of them needed to stand guard and protect them from whatever evils lurked in one of the most awful places they'd ever been. Not quite as bad as a closed casket, but paranoia-inducing nevertheless.

Deputies showed a young woman in her late twenties through the open door. She strode regally inside wearing an outfit Avery described as the sexy secretary look—form-fitting black pencil skirt, white collared blouse with rolled up sleeves, and heels that ranged into the stiletto stratosphere. The matron detained her and swapped the stilettos for the orange slide-on Croc knockoffs like all the inmates were wearing. Guess shoes could be a weapon, which was certainly the case with the sky-high heels. With her sleek, shoulder-length strawberry-blonde hair, the new inmate could have been a high-priced call girl or a graduate student at the college located in the only nearby city which was large enough to have one. Turned out, she was both.

Apparently, there was something about being a senior citizen—a similarity to everyone's grandmother, perhaps—that made them seem instantly trustworthy. Or maybe it was their proximity to imminent death. Realistically, how much damage could oldsters do with the short time they had left? Within minutes of discovering who Claire and Avery were, the woman began to talk. Her working name was "Crystal Diamond," which sounded like a contradiction in terms, but she instructed them to call her by her real name, Amber. Not far removed from the sex trade, but far enough.

Amber had been working on her Master of Arts in Clinical Mental Health Counseling and decided to do her thesis on "A Psychoanalytic Study of the Working Girl." She hypothesized that knowledge of the problems of the call girl might help illuminate the relationship between personality and the kind of occupation an individual chose, plus emotional factors involved in that choice. During interviews with her subjects, she quickly determined that the high-class ladies managed by a call service made more in one night than she would make in a week, even after she earned her degree. With mounting school loans, the cost of living off campus with no means of income (her parents were supportive but poor), and a deep-seated curiosity that wouldn't be satisfied by individual subject profiles, she had her first "date" within weeks of beginning her studies.

She explored the social and professional lives of the women, including their men, illustrated by two studies of a pimp and a compulsive, frequent client of call girls. And that's when the sisters really became interested.

"You ladies live at Rancho Exotica, don't you? Sounds like an exotic sex retreat." Amber had positioned herself next to Claire on the bench and held their rapt attention while she spoke about her life.

"That's what I always thought," Avery said. "Unfortunately, it's not."

"Or fortunately," Claire said, "depending on your point of view."

"I know several people who live there." Amber's intonation hinted that she knew these particular RE residents intimately.

Claire squirmed in discomfort, but Avery decided this might present an opportunity to learn a few things about their neighbors which might help in the investigation.

"Did you know Thorne Mondae, the guy who was murdered in our forest?" Avery asked.

"Well... didn't know it was your forest... but I'd be sorta uncomfortable naming names." Amber put on a knowing but coquettish smile. "My associations might not have been exactly legal."

"Two consenting adults? Nothing illegal about that." Avery wondered if Amber knew their conversation was being recorded by CCTV cameras. Depended on how much true crime TV she watched. "Besides, wouldn't you want to help in the investigation of a murder case if you could? It would be your civic duty."

The young woman had an innocent quality that made her unsuspicious and eager. And probably just a touch of insecurity that compelled her to please others or do whatever was needed to get and keep their attention. Not uncommon traits for women in the sex trade. Avery felt a little guilty trying to take advantage of the woman's naïveté but decided it was for a good cause. Did the means justify the end? That remained to be seen.

"I suppose." Amber drew closer and lowered her voice. Avery doubted it was low enough not to be recorded, but it didn't really matter. If the police learned any useful information, they were welcome to it. "Mr. Mondae... the dead guy... he was a special friend of mine. Like a regular." She cast her eyes around the room as if looking for eavesdroppers. "He was kinda cheap though. I'd tell him up front what it cost to be with me for an hour or however long he'd booked the session. But he always tried to bargain me down no matter how many times I told him the price wasn't going to change." She emitted a little giggle, then put her hand over her mouth as if she feared calling attention to herself. "And he was a rich man. Don't know why he was such a tightwad."

"Guess that's how they stay rich," Claire said.

"He even wanted a twofer."

"What's a twofer?" Avery asked.

"Two-for-one. He wanted me to make it with him and his son. And just charge the single rate. I refused, of course."

"His son, Isaac?" Claire's big baby blues bugged out of their sockets.

"Yes! Can you believe that Scrooge? He even wanted me to be with both of them at the same time! It was disgusting."

"A three-way twofer," Avery said. "Sounds confusing." She could tell Claire was resisting the urge to close her eyes, cover her ears, and curl into the previously-threatened fetal position.

"Thorne would menace me when I refused him, try to scare me, but it never came to anything. He was pretty much all talk. The kind of guy who creates mischief and expects somebody else to get him out of it."

"Did Thorne talk much about himself? Tell you anything about his past; if he had any enemies or something like that; someone who may have had reason to want him dead?"

Amber scanned the room again. Her gaze stopped on an object that could have been a closed-circuit camera but was dome-shaped like a light bulb rather than oblong. Avery couldn't be sure.

"We found some old newspaper clippings," Avery said, "hidden in Thorne's home." She didn't admit to stealing them. "One is about criminals profiting from the sale of handguns in Chicago—"

"He admitted to being a gun dealer in his early life. Didn't say he was a criminal exactly. But he seemed proud of the fact that he made money off of the dumb lowlifes he associated with. That's where he met his friend, Scopes."

Avery's ears pricked up. "What did he say about Scopes Redfield? Was he a gun dealer too?"

"He didn't say Scopes was a criminal, but he was always bragging about his power over Scopes. How he escaped detection many times thanks to Scopes's loyalty. Did you hear about the oil rig disaster in the early 90s? I think it was near Scotland or Ireland or some country like that. Thorne claimed it was all his doing. That he caused the rig to collapse by forgetting to report something broken during the previous shift. I didn't understand all the technical stuff, but the gist was he was the only one who knew about the breakdown. He claimed he 'forgot' to tell the supervisor, and the equipment was turned on when it shouldn't have been. Scopes worked there too and knew Thorne had caused the disaster, but he never told anybody. Although they both barely escaped alive—a bunch of other men didn't—they were expecting a big payment from the oil rig owner's insurance company. Both of them kept quiet and became wealthy men."

"Now that's disgusting," Claire said.

"I'm a psychology major," Amber said, "and I've studied a lot of subversive behavior in humans. But Thorne's description of Scopes gave me the chills. He was one of those creepy characters who live in the shadow of someone who has a bigger, more persuasive personality. Thorne described him as *protective*, but it seemed to me a better word would have been *submissive*. In those old *Dracula* movies, there's a character who Scopes reminded me of; you know, the guy who ate bugs to try to be like his idol the Count? Even though I never met him, I was more afraid of Scopes than I was Thorne. Character studies are my specialty, and those two would have been a whole thesis in themselves. But whatever ailed Scopes was hidden in a dark place in his soul."

"Do you think Scopes could have killed Thorne?" Avery asked.

Amber rubbed her temple as if stimulating her brain for an answer. "I doubt it. He sounds like too big of a wuss."

The barred cell door squealed open, and a female officer announced, "Would Claire Halverson Browning and Avery Halverson please come forward and follow me?"

"Maybe they're releasing you," Amber said. She looked disappointed.

"It was nice to meet you," Claire said, "and good luck with your studies."

"Thanks for the info," Avery said. "Stay in touch." She exchanged numbers with Amber in case she thought of more questions. That is, if she could actually remember a whole telephone number. She asked Claire to repeat it to give them a better of chance of pulling it from their mutual memory libraries.

Tom had posted their bail, and they were released around midnight.

"Wish I could have worn those orange Crocs home," Avery said to Claire.

Her weary sister rolled her eyes and trudged toward the Ody which still sat in the jailhouse parking lot brooding beneath a streetlamp.

29

Back home at Rancho Exotica, Avery and Claire felt like two egg-laying hens who had been released from a commercial battery cage—ecstatic to be free to flap their wings and soak up the light and warmth of the sun. And forever grateful to their liberator, Claire's cowboy, Tom Wellman, who had ridden up on his white horse and plucked them from the arms of their evil jailors.

"So, to spring us from the joint, Tom had to pay 10 percent of $10,000, which was the bail amount. That's just $1,000. We can manage to pay him back for that." Avery began to feel more optimistic.

"That's just for one of us. It's $1,000 *each*. We're not stuck together, you know."

"Some people think we are." Avery wrinkled her brow. "I wonder... if we were conjoined twins... would the bail be $1,000 for one person or $2,000 for two?"

"I don't know, and I don't care."

"Would you ask Mary Mayberry the next time you talk to her?"

"Absolutely not."

Avery didn't know if she felt relieved after turning over the field camera photos to Detective Castellan, or if her primary emotion was anger for him putting them in jail. Whatever the feelings, the practical part of her brain told her they needed to decide whether to continue looking for Thorne's killer or not. Her incarceration had certainly put a damper on her enthusiasm for the task. She reminded herself that the threat of imprisonment still hung over Claire, but wasn't as much of a threat as it had been before they showed Castellan the sim card. But the tampering charge still hovered over them with the annoying stealth of a drone. Avery couldn't help but believe that issue might disappear if they were able to uncover the real murderer or, at the very least, help them in their defense. Ultimately, the realization they would never regain their former peace and serenity until the murder was solved convinced Avery, and she hoped her sister, they must continue their investigation. Oh, yes, *and* the vengeful idea that finding the killer before Detective Castellan would give him his comeuppance for throwing them in the slammer.

Before any of that happened, however, Avery had another hurdle to jump. Her neurologist wanted her to take an ambulatory EEG. When she left the doctor's office and climbed into the minivan with Claire, her first words were "Beam me up, Scotty."

After preparing the area with glue, the physician's assistant had attached electrodes all over Avery's scalp. She funneled the resulting wires protruding from her head like tentacles through a white gauzy material and plugged them into a portable computer that Avery carried around like a shoulder pack. The PA wrapped her head in a gauzy helmet to cover the electrodes. She looked like an alien from outer space or, more accurately, a mummy.

She had to eat, sleep, watch TV, and manage all other daily activities while wearing the getup for a mandatory 72-hour period—three whole days that dragged by like a three-toed sloth crossing the highway. Avery's biggest fear was that someone might see her in the outfit, most especially Jay Vidocq. She chastised herself for her fear, reminding herself that she hadn't seen or heard from Jay since the cowboy wedding. The odds of him suddenly appearing now, a week later, seemed miniscule. She asked Claire to take Bodhi for his daily golf cart ride and walk around the lake, while Avery hid behind drawn shades in their house of 66 revealing windows.

The evening before the doctor intended to remove the electrodes and analyze the data gleaned from the computer, Avery watched Claire drive off with Bodhi in tow. Bored, she wandered onto their back patio to sit in the cool evening breeze and watch the autumn leaves flutter to the ground. She tried not to dwell on the next day. The not-knowing was the worst part. If the doctor found irregular brain activity, Avery would have to stay on the powerful medication she took every day. Its terrible side effects impacted all areas of her life. It impaired her hearing and vision and created the brain fog that often clouded her thought process. On the other hand, if her brain were declared normal, she could withdraw from the meds and go back to living a normal life—whatever that was.

As she sat there watching the falling leaves, something niggled at the back of her brain. "Oh, good grief!" After everything that had happened, she had forgotten to study the newspaper clippings she'd stolen from Thorne Mondae's trophy room credenza. She leaped from the lawn chair, checking herself when she remembered the portable computer she had hooked over her shoulder, and pulled the shabby box from her bedroom bureau. Back on the patio, she thumbed through the clippings trying to decide which one to read first. Probably best to read them in chronological order. She selected the earliest one and read:

Chicago, Illinois:
Gangbangers with Vehicles Profit from New Handgun Ban

In 1981, receiving strong support from Mayor Byrne and her allies, and coming in the wake of the assassination attempts on President Reagan and Pope John Paul II, Chicago became the first major city to enact a handgun freeze in United States history. Only residents who purchased and registered their handguns prior to January 1982 were allowed to keep the weapons.

As expected, it reduced the flow of illegal weapons to the city's underground market, and gang members experienced difficulty getting guns, stymied by the fact that Chicago had no gun shops.

The ban, however, created an unexpected effect. Urban criminals, up until the ban, had no need for vehicles and were subsequently unable to drive to the nearest suburb and buy arms from gun shops. The few who owned cars became neighborhood entrepreneurs, making a business of bringing in guns from the 'burbs. But they insisted on being

compensated for the service, which raised the price. Some didn't want to
pay the extra and disputes among gangs became more frequent. Further
perpetuating the increase in gang-related crimes, thefts of handguns
from individuals who acquired them before the ban increased, and the
spoils were sold to gang members for their nefarious purposes. The stolen
guns were registered to the original legal owner and couldn't be traced to
the thieves. And, unless the users left fingerprints, couldn't be traced to
the gangbangers either.

It was a win-win for the middleman.

Avery thought about the article for a minute, but nothing about it pointed her to the murderer of Thorne Mondae. Amber had mentioned that Thorne and Scopes had made money selling guns to gangsters. It sounded like they could have been the "middlemen" who stole the legal guns and resold them to gangbangers in the article. Even if they were, that was forty years ago, and the statute of limitations had surely run out unless they had killed somebody during a burglary. It was beyond her why Thorne saved the clipping, unless it was a reminder of happier times. If being a thief could be classified as happy. Amber said he was a narcissist who was unashamed of his criminal past. It appeared as if he might actually be proud of it.

A slight breeze stirred the fallen leaves scattered across the small lawn. She looked up from the article and noticed that her herb garden needed watering. Holding the plants, the standing wooden container had been sectioned into eight compartments that held potting soil. Each compartment sprouted a different herb. Avery—being Avery—had planted them in alphabetical order—basil, cilantro, dill, oregano, parsley, rosemary, sage, and thyme. She observed that people who gardened appeared to be healthier than her and believed working the soil might help her avoid another seizure. Leaving the box of clippings in her chair, she turned on the hose and let fresh water sprinkle over the plants from the spray head.

A shadow appeared from the other side of the garage, and Avery paused when a little tingle of fear ran up her spine. Through the fence, she watched a figure creep toward the patio gate. She gasped, jumped back, spun, and darted for the patio door, leaving the hose flip-flopping across the concrete. With the computer attached to her electrodes tugging at her, she didn't make it fast enough.

"Avery!" Jay called. "Wait!"

OMG, OMG! The last person in the universe she wanted to see.

Jay pushed open the fence gate and rushed toward her, barely avoiding the dancing water hose. She jerked open the sliding glass door and jumped inside, ducking behind a supporting wall. Jay caught the door before she slammed it shut.

"No! Please!" Avery cried. "I don't want you to see me like this." She had never felt so hopeless and ashamed.

"It's okay. I want to talk to you. That's all."

"Don't look at me."

"I won't."

"What do you want?" she asked.

"Come back outside. Let's sit on the patio."

"No!"

"I've already seen you. It's okay. What's happened?"

Avery heaved a heavy sigh. Too late to hide now. She stepped onto the patio. Jay turned off the hose and pretended not to stare, but she caught him taking surreptitious glances. She gathered up the box of clippings that had been soaked by the wayward hose, stuck them inside on the kitchen island, then collapsed into a lawn chair. Jay sunk into its twin.

Avery dropped her head into her hands, careful not to disturb the electrodes jutting from her forehead, and cried with broken sobs. Jay said nothing, letting her get it all out.

"This is the last way I wanted you to see me," Avery said after she was able to stop sobbing.

"Do you have any tissues?" Jay asked.

"Inside, the side table by my chair."

When Jay returned, he dropped the box of tissues into her lap, never mentioning the wet box of clippings on the island. Avery wondered if he recognized it from Thorne's trophy room. She blew her snotty nose with a big honking sound. He probably didn't need to hear that either.

"What's going on?" Jay asked. "What's wrong with you?"

Avery sucked in a deep breath. "Remember when I told you I retired after that attorney told me to quit talking?" Jay nodded. "That's not why I retired."

"It's not?"

"If I had quit every time an attorney acted like an arse, I'd have been quitting every week. Not that the majority of them weren't nice, but there were the few. The truth is, one day when Claire and I drove home after work, I had a seizure during rush hour traffic. Big mess in the HOV lane. Cars piled up for miles. Which I found out about later since I was totally out of it."

"A seizure. Is that like a stroke?"

"No, it's different, but I spent weeks in the hospital. They were treating me for things I didn't even have, like a stroke, as well as overdosing me on powerful anticonvulsants. I didn't begin to snap out of it until Claire took control and demanded the doctors take me off everything except the medications directly related to the seizure. I went to a rehab facility for 10 days, then Claire brought me home. That's when we decided to retire and moved here."

"What's happening now?"

"My neurologist is having me take this 72-hour ambulatory EEG—that's an *electroencephalogram* that records electrical activity in the brain—to see if mine is functioning properly. If it is, she'll take me off my medication."

"You only had the one seizure?"

"Yes. Seizures can be caused by lots of things. If you continue to have them, they label it epilepsy, but no one knows what causes them. Since I only had the one, chances are I'll never have another. No guarantees, of course. But the prognosis is good. I'm still recovering and sometimes don't think straight. Forget things."

He laughed. "Don't we all?"

"That's what Claire keeps telling me." She sighed. "Anyway, I didn't tell you because I didn't want you to think of me as a sick old lady." Avery felt her face flush, because that was exactly what she looked like in the alien mummy outfit.

"I don't think of you that way." He lowered his voice and gazed straight into her eyes.

Uncomfortable, she turned away. He was just being nice. She had a feeling that any minute he'd walk away, and she'd never see him again. Not on purpose anyway.

"Why are you here?" Avery wondered if it had anything to do with her being in jail. She had an idea he'd had more to do with their release than Tom admitted. Especially after finding Bodhi's food dish half-full when they arrived home from the jail at 1:00 a.m. She guessed Jay had snuck through the patio door, which they sometimes neglected to lock, and fed the dog his dinner.

Claire and Bodhi pulled into the driveway and distracted them. Jay told Avery to let him know how the EEG turned out. He said hello to Claire, scratched Bodhi's head, and disappeared down the driveway.

"How did that little meeting come about?" Claire asked Avery. "I thought you particularly wanted to avoid him while your EEG was going on."

Avery spread the wet newspaper clippings across the kitchen island to dry. She realized she'd have to confess to her sister that she stole them from Thorne's house. Her new well-constructed world seemed destined to crumble around her.

And for the second time that day, Avery burst out crying.

30

Avery backed the golf cart out of the garage. When she jumped off to load up Bodhi, a misty haze that clung to the pine branches dripped onto her head. She dried with an old towel, then used it to wipe the dog's thick coat. Afterward, he shook himself and looked as contented as a damp dog could.

With Thanksgiving two weeks away, the deciduous trees still hung tenaciously to their green leaves. After the holidays, they would turn fiery red, orange, and yellow and begin their annual descent to the ground.

Two agonizing days after she removed the electrodes, the neurologist had called Avery. And for the third time in a forty-eight-hour period, unexpected tears gushed from Avery's eyes, a personal-best record. She hadn't cried as much when she was a baby. The doctor declared Avery's brain to be completely normal. Although some might dispute that finding, Avery's neurologist would attest to it. An ecstatic Avery gladly went off all medication. It didn't take long before her hearing unclogged, her blurred vision cleared, a chronic urinary tract infection disappeared, and most of her memory returned. Now, she could operate the washing machine, oven, and TV remote all by herself.

Avery's euphoria from having her brain declared normal lapsed into gloominess shortly thereafter. She had envisioned a comforting Thanksgiving Day with relatives in their small hometown and a speedy return to the arms of her inamorata. But she hadn't heard from Jay since the evening on the patio and was too proud to text him. Better to let things end before they became too involved, too complicated. That's what her head told her, but her emotions said something else. Impossible to define her exact sentiments, except that Jay had made her feel safe and valued.

When her dog saw Bitty Binaila waiting at the barn door, Bodhi swished his tail back and forth across Avery's face with a dozen wags. It comforted her to see that somebody in her world stayed happy all the time. The Wildlife Chairperson had agreed to meet her at the community's storage barn, a sizeable metal building that housed feed for the exotic animals. When the weather permitted, large group meetings could be held inside the barn, but an enclosed air-conditioned space at the far end of the building hosted the board meetings.

"Hey, Bitty," Avery said. "Thanks for meeting me. I know you're busy, so I appreciate it."

"No worries." Bitty had drawn her long dark hair into a braid. She pulled a rope hanging from one of three overhead doors, and the door slid open. A long table-like shelf had been attached to the barn's sides, and papers were strewn across it. "Here's the sign-in sheet for the day of the murder." She opened a ledger book and turned to the day in question. She handed the open book to Avery.

Avery scanned the rows for a few minutes. "Other than Thorne and his son, Isaac, it looks like only four other people were hunting that day." Using a yard-long CVS receipt she found in her purse, she wrote down the hunters' names while making a mental note to cut off the usable coupons.

"That's correct."

"Can you take me through the process? Beginning from when the hunters signed in."

"Everyone meets at the barn in the morning, and each hunter is given a map showing available hunting properties. The lots where the property owners don't allow hunting are clearly marked. After each hunter signs in, he... or she... is assigned an area. When they leave, they sign out after recording what they killed that day."

"*Who* they killed." Avery hated it when people spoke as if a sentient being were an inanimate object.

"Yeah, that's what I said."

"Is the barn locked afterwards?"

"The door's not locked during the day."

"What about the log book?"

"It's left here, on the sign-in table."

"So, anyone who lives here or is visiting could come in and find out where a hunter was located."

"It's not a secret."

Avery saw that Thorne Mondae had been assigned to the property adjoining hers, so he probably staggered onto their property after being shot.

"Did you see anyone hanging around, anyone not on the list, who looked suspicious?"

"Suspicious? In what way?"

Avery knew it was pointless to describe the Shadowy Figure on the trail camera. He or she had been wearing a ski mask and being dressed in camouflage was irrelevant. So had every other hunter who signed up that day. "Didn't look like they belonged. A stranger, maybe. Someone who wasn't a resident."

Bitty shook her head. "They all look suspicious to me. Like little kids dressing up for Halloween in those ridiculous outfits. But, no, nobody that looked out of the ordinary."

"I agree with you. Not sure why they call hunting a sport. In sports, aren't both sides supposed to understand and agree to the rules of the game? Pretty sure the deer are clueless as to what the humans are up to. Nothing sporting about that."

Bitty nodded. "Wish I could have been more helpful."

"Did anyone sign up to hunt that had never signed up before? Someone new or surprising?"

Bitty wrinkled her forehead in thought. "No, but Thorne said his friend, Scopes Redfield, would be hunting with him that day. But he failed to show up."

"Anybody else fail to show?"

Bitty shook her head like a sparrow shaking off raindrops. "Not that I remember. Sorry."

That's okay, Bitty. You helped. Really."

"Do you think they'll catch him? The killer, I mean? It's put the whole neighborhood on edge."

"I'm sure they will. Don't worry." She squeezed Bitty's arm in reassurance. "One other thing. I know you were born in the United States, but have you ever heard of the Andaman Islands? Located in the Bay of Bengal near India? Maybe heard your parents talk about it or something?"

"I've heard of the Andaman and Nicobar Islands, of course. The Indian government protects the indigenous people who live there. That's about all I know. Why?"

"Nothing, really. Just wondering if you might have any information on weapons—bows and arrows, to be specific—that the indigenous people use. Would you recognize them if you saw them?" Avery was thinking about the display they discovered in Thorne's trophy room during the cowboy wedding.

"Sorry." Bitty shook her head. "Wouldn't have a clue. I'm not being much help, am I?"

"It's fine. Just a long shot. Give me a call if you think of anything. Thanks!"

She called Bodhi who had been sniffing zebra poop in the weeds, and he leaped onto the cart.

"Hey, Avery," Bitty said. "This probably won't help you…"

"Tell me. You never know what might turn out to be useful." Avery had heard that on every detective show she'd ever watched.

"Well…" Bitty chirped in her birdlike voice, "some of those property owners treat Rancho Exotica like their own personal hunting ranch. You know Angela Hickson? Her husband, Bob, is some big shot at the oil company where he works. He brought one of the other executives with him, and I'm pretty sure that guy killed a buck and didn't record it in the harvest record. You know they're required to kill two does first, before they're allowed a buck."

"If they didn't record it, how did you know about it?"

"How else? Rancho Exotica gossip. Another resident saw the dead buck in the back of Bob's trailer and reported it to me. Wasn't much I could do about it. The animal was already dead."

"Could Thorne have been murdered to cover up the fact that they had killed a buck? Seems a bit drastic."

"The problem is, it wasn't a whitetail. They actually killed one of the Axis bucks and lied about it. That could be a criminal offense because the Axis are considered property of the RE residents. Killing one could be interpreted as destruction of private property, or theft, or something like that."

"So, if Thorne saw them do it, maybe he threatened to report them or held it over their head as a form of blackmail."

Avery and Bitty exchanged thoughtful looks. Bitty looked doubtful, but she probably didn't watch as much true crime TV as Avery did.

"I've heard of people killing each other for a lot less," Avery said. "Thanks for the info. I'll give it some thought."

She waved at Bitty as she and Bodhi drove onto the main thoroughfare.

31

Several hours later, Avery and Bodhi climbed back onto the cart for what she hoped would be the last time that day. They had visited the homes of the men on the hunting list the day Thorne was killed. All had been willing to talk but none had anything worth telling. Of course, Bob Hickson denied everything regarding the Axis buck, as Avery knew he would. According to him, he and his partner drove to their assigned area and never left until they signed out that evening. No one saw anything suspicious. Which meant the killer either had to be someone from Rancho Exotica or had sneaked in another way. Not easy in a gated community surrounded by a high game fence with a required sign-in and sign-out for contractors, vendors, and guests.

Avery huffed out a big sigh, then heard her cellphone ding indicating a text message. She didn't stop to read it until she saw the name Jay Vidocq.

Are you busy right now? Can you come by the RV?

Avery caught her breath and parked the cart onto the grass. Bodhi looked as if he didn't know what to do. Seeking comfort, she encircled him with her arm and laid her head against his. The day had worn her out. It had been a fruitless search, a whole day wasted. She hoped this wasn't one of those meet-ups, the ones where the guy dumps the girl claiming: *It's not you. It's me.* Oh, well. It wasn't like she hadn't been there before.

She texted Jay telling him she would be there in 30 minutes, then dropped by her own house and freshened up. She reassured Claire she'd be back in a couple of hours. Bodhi whined and watched her with liquid brown eyes as she walked away.

Sitting beside the RV, Jay lounged before a firepit which hadn't been there before. Must be one of those things his wife threatened to throw out if he didn't come get it. He dragged another lounge chair next to his, facing the flames. The evening had turned crisp, and Avery felt grateful for the warmth.

"Wine?" he asked after she settled in.

"Do you have anything stronger?" She had a feeling she was going to need it.

"Margarita?"

"No thanks. Had too many of those at the cowboy wedding."

"I have some grapefruit juice. How about a salty dog?"

"It's been ages. Sure, if it's not too much trouble." She could at least delude herself it was healthy.

"No problem." He climbed into the RV, and Avery pretended not to notice the curve of his tight jeans or the way his short-sleeved T-shirt clung to his biceps. When he returned, he passed her the drink, then spread a fuzzy throw across her legs. The simple, thoughtful gesture made her want to cry.

"Thanks. It's getting cool out here." She sipped the drink. It refreshed her after her long day. "It's delicious."

"How did the EEG go?" he asked.

"According to the neurologist, my brain is completely normal." She eyed him with a warning grin. "No wisecracks please."

"Glad to hear you're… *normal*."

"Why did you come that night? Did you know about the EEG?" When he didn't answer, she said, "Did you want to check in with me after learning I'd been arrested? I have a feeling you knew more about that than you let on."

"Did Tom tell you—"

"No, no. Tom never said a word. I thought he might have asked for your help since you lived here and could post the bond fee more easily than him. Made sense. Besides, you left a tell-tale clue by putting food in Bodhi's bowl. Thanks for doing that. I was worried about him. I appreciate… Claire and I… appreciate what you did… getting us out of that hellhole. You're a very kind person." Avery willed herself into silence. Fought the need to fill the void. Fearing he would say something that would make her sadder than she already felt.

"Glad I was able to help." Jay took a drink from his beer, then let it hang in his hand beside the chair arm. "Are you okay now? Recovered from your time in jail?"

"Well, you know, prison kinda changes you." She shot him a quick grin to show she was kidding, her way of coping with a tense situation.

He stared into the firepit as though in a trance. They sat for a few moments listening to the logs crackle. "Avery, listen…"

She bit her lip, said nothing.

"Sorry I haven't texted or called in a few days, but I needed to make some decisions. And I needed to be alone. Can't think straight when I'm around you."

"Jay, you don't have to apologize." She steadied her voice, hoping it wouldn't break. "You don't owe me anything. I have no expectations. I—"

He put his free hand on her forearm. "Please, don't interrupt. Just let me get this out."

She nodded.

Another drink from the beer bottle. "I got married fairly late for most men—middle-thirties. I was finally ready to settle down, have a family, live a life not strictly for myself. Macy, my wife, came along at just the right time. She was from a good family, not quite 30, and she was ready too. We married, raised two great kids, both of whom are married. My son has a little girl, my first grandkid. I've had a good life."

"You're lucky. I can understand why you want to go back. It sounds perfect." Avery flicked away a single tear before he noticed. She sipped her drink and held her breath.

Jay shook his head. "That's just it," he said. "I don't want to go back.

"You don't?"

"Since I've gotten older… it's hard to explain… I felt stifled. Like I had lived somebody else's life. Or at least the one expected of me. I'd done what everyone else wanted. I followed the rules, and it never occurred to me that whole time to ask myself what I wanted. I lived for my parents, my wife, my kids. The only thing I ever did for myself was become a homicide detective. I threw myself into the job, so I never had to think about the other aspects of my life. And that sustained me for a long time." He sighed deeply. "Until it didn't."

"It's aging." Avery turned her arm over and slipped her hand into his. "It takes you by surprise. One day you're walking down a garden path lined with trees and flush with flowers. The path before you is bright. You're a child eager to roll down a grassy slope. Endless possibilities." She gripped his hand tighter. "Then it happens. This dark hole opens up, and you realize it's your grave. You're going to die. You'd given lip service to the idea, been to plenty of funerals, but never really believed it was going to happen to you."

"And you're out of chances. No more opportunities to change. It's over, and you didn't see it coming. I don't want to spend the rest of my life doing what I was doing."

They sat in silence for a minute, about as long as Avery could stand.

"When I retired," she said, "I told all my friends—from this moment on, I don't intend to do anything I don't want to do."

"Except die."

"Not that either." Jay laughed like he thought she was kidding. She paused for a beat, enjoying the sound of his laugh. "So," she said, "you're not dumping me and going back to your wife?"

"Are you kidding? For the first time in years, I'm having fun! So, no, not dumping you. Not going back to Macy."

"Want to retreat to your RV and go at it like rabbits?" Avery asked. "I'll fill you in on what Claire and I learned in the slammer later."

Jay hauled her out of the lounge chair. "How can I say no when you asked so nice?"

32

Avery scuttled down the driveway wrangling the leaf blower as it propelled everything in its path, including branches, leaves, pinecones, and an ant or two, in every direction except the one she intended. Half of it ended up on her clothes and in her hair. Just as she reached the mailbox at the end of the pavement, Jay pulled up in his golf cart.

"Hey cutie!"

"Jay." Avery flipped off the leaf blower, painfully aware of her lack of makeup, her ponytail, and the baggy jeans and T-shirt she sported. She reminded herself that Jay had seen her in her alien mummy outfit, so she probably looked like a movie star compared to that. She still needed to have that showing-up-without-calling-first talk with him.

A strong wind whipped through the tops of the trees, and it sounded like a truck speeding down the hill. Jay had to raise his voice to be heard above the wail.

"Are you guys busy?" he asked. "I need Claire to give Tom a call. Have some new information regarding the arrow used to kill Thorne Mondae, and I understand he did some bow hunting in the past. I'm thinking he might give us some details, answer some questions."

Avery glanced down at her dusty clothes.

"I caught you at a bad time." He studied her for a moment. "You're trying to blow the leaves against the wind. Better to go with the wind direction."

"Yeah, I'll keep that in mind."

"Sorry, I'll come back later." He looked like she'd hurt his feelings.

"No, it's okay." Avery climbed into the cart's passenger seat. "Let's go to the house. Claire's working on her forest trails, but I'll call her."

"I don't want to interrupt—"

"She could probably use a break." The surrounding pines moaned as the wind whistled through them, and their trunks clacked together like barking seals. "It's too windy for her to burn anything today."

They followed the winding driveway as it turned through several 100-foot trees and curved into the back of their house. Avery phoned Claire, who drove their old golf cart across the bridge and met them on the parking pad behind the garage. Green sulfur powder she had spread in the forest to discourage ticks covered her clothes. Although a severe problem in the summer, the ticks would disperse in the fall. Except the weather was unseasonably warm, and they wouldn't give up until it turned cold.

Inside, Avery settled Jay with a glass of iced tea and Bodhi at his feet while Claire retreated to her bathroom to wash up. Avery excused herself to hit her underarms with a dab of deodorant, and her face with a dusting of powder, a touch of blush, and a swipe of mascara. That was all she had time for, but it would have to do. When she returned to the common area, Jay was apologizing to Claire for not calling first, while she politely assured him it was alright. She had planned on coming back to the house in a minute or two anyway.

While Claire tried to hook up Tom using Zoom, Jay sat at the kitchen island with Avery.

"I talked to Bud Tengle," Jay told her. "The guy you met at the funeral. One of Thorne and Lianne's commercial tenants who claimed he was on the other side of the country when Thorne was murdered?"

"At Thorne's funeral, he also said he was glad Thorne was dead and wished they had killed Lianne as well." Avery offered Jay a vegan brownie she'd bought at Walmart, which he declined. "Did you speak to him in a legal capacity?"

"Well, kinda." Jay's eyes crinkled up with a short laugh. "When I interviewed him, he might have thought I was a detective."

"Why would he think that?"

"Because he assumed, but never asked, and I never told him otherwise. Just said I was from the Sweetgum Homicide Department. Not that Sweetgum actually has a homicide *department*."

"What did he tell you?"

"Basically, the same thing he told you. That he did have a lawsuit against the company, but that Thorne's death wouldn't do him any good. He wants to pursue it and needs either Thorne or Lianne alive to keep things simple. I guess the suit could be against whoever inherits the real estate business, since technically it's against the company, but either of their deaths would complicate matters. On the other hand, the heirs might be more willing to settle out of court. No way to know since Lianne is still alive."

"He said he was on the other side of the country when the murder occurred." Avery ate the brownie Jay had turned down. Not bad for a pastry alleged to be healthy.

"On vacation in San Diego with his family. I confirmed it with the airlines and his hotel. Which makes everything else a moot point. Guess that takes him off your suspect list."

"One little Indian down," Avery said, "only nine little Indians to go." Jay looked as if he didn't get the literary reference.

Claire placed the laptop computer in front of Jay and sat next to him. All three of them could see the screen when Tom's face appeared. A fluffy Persian-type black cat stretched across his lap.

"Who's your friend?" Jay asked.

"I'm cat-sitting for my daughter." The feline meowed, reached out sharp claws and kneaded Tom's leg. He grimaced. "His claws are like f-ing talons." He pulled the huge paws away from his thigh and gently dropped the cat to the floor.

"What's his name?" Claire asked.

"Mopsey."

"That sounds like a bunny rabbit's name," Avery said.

"I call him Pita," Tom said. "Short for 'Pain-In-The-Ass.'"

Claire and Avery laughed.

"He's a big, handsome devil," Jay said. "Tom, I need your expertise. I saw Thorne Mondae's autopsy report. The arrow they pulled from his body had some type of irregularity."

"Irregularity?" Tom said.

"Not like anything normally used by modern hunters. Very crude, primitive almost. I don't have any particulars, although I'm sure it was booked into evidence. I understand you bow hunted in the past. Wondered if there was something you could tell us about the arrows."

"Didn't bow hunt for long. Not for me. But I do know that bows don't leave a ballistic signature on arrows like guns and bullets do. But, things like the whisker biscuit—"

"What's that?" Claire asked.

"Sounds disgusting," Avery said.

"A whisker biscuit is where you rest an arrow. Its bristles form a ring around the arrow and hold it in place. When you release the arrow, they leave tiny scratch marks on the shaft. The more you shoot the arrow, the more pronounced the marks become."

"Did you Google that when we weren't looking?" Avery asked.

Tom ignored her. "When a manufacturer produces an arrow, they print a serial number on the shaft that is barely visible to the naked eye. If you hold the shaft away from direct light and slowly turn it, the serial number appears. It can be traced."

"The arrow recovered from Thorne Mondae must not have had a serial number, or Wendy the coroner would have seen it. I'll ask her if she checked for a serial number."

"Will she let you look at the arrow?" Tom asked.

"Even better," Claire suggested, "take a photo of it on your cell phone, if you can do it inconspicuously."

"The only thing is," Jay said, "they called the arrow 'primitive,' so it's possible it was homemade, which would make tracing it back to someone through the manufacturer impossible."

"Why does there always have to be a 'yes, but' every time we discover something new?" Avery asked in whiny frustration, but didn't receive any sympathy. "If it's a primitive or homemade arrow, then it probably wasn't the visiting hunter who killed Thorne, the one who poached the Axis."

"Probably not," Tom said. "But, more importantly, does it look anything like the arrows on display in Thorne Mondae's trophy room?"

Mopsey leaped onto the desk and traipsed across the computer keys. Tom's computer went blank.

33

Jay had hung around the Sweetgum Police Department way past his shift time. He intended to sneak into the evidence room when the place cleared. Unfortunately, Detective Castellan interfered with Jay's plans by sticking around to do some paperwork.

While he waited for Castellan to leave, Jay skimmed his emails and thought about the puzzling Thorne Mondae case. Based on the interviews with family and friends, the victim had not been a popular guy. Murder subjects usually received the "He'd give you the shirt off his back," and "Her smile would light up a room" accolades from interviewees. Seldom did a murder victim get reviled with such malevolent enthusiasm and universal lack of caution as Mondae. It created a suspect pool as big as the Olympic-size swimming pool at the Sweetgum Community Center.

Jay fidgeted and glanced at his watch, wondering if the detective would ever leave. He didn't want to spend the night here. When Castellan left his desk for the breakroom, probably to secure a cup of the swamp mud the Department called coffee, Jay decided to tiptoe down the hall toward the locked evidence room. Just to check it out. As a trusted police volunteer, he had received a master key he hoped fit the room's lock. Time to find out how much they trusted him.

Success! The key worked perfectly. Jay checked both ways down the hall and made a snap decision. He stepped inside the room and closed the door. Rather than switch on the light, he engaged his cellphone flashlight. He tugged on a pair of powder and latex free Nitrile gloves, the material thin enough to allow extra protection if the wearer needed an additional pair. Not necessary at this particular crime scene. He quickly located the Mondae file and withdrew the bag containing the arrow shot into Mondae's chest and removed by the ME. Because the head had not been imbedded into bone, it had been extracted without detaching the shaft. A couple of quick pics, and his task was completed.

Well… not quite. Jay heard the squeak of rubber soles as they traveled along the hall's linoleum floor. Hairs tingled along the back of his neck. The door, which he had locked when he entered, rattled as if someone tried the handle. The hall light glowed steadily in the space where the door's bottom edge failed to reach the floor. A shadow flickered across the threshold—or did he just blink? Immediately, he flicked off his mobile's flashlight. He heard the jangling of keys, the knob slowly turned, and the door squeaked open. A ripple of fear punched into his belly. His throat tightened. The door spread wide. Light spilled from the hall into the evidence room. A man wearing dark clothes popped through the opening.

"Vidocq!" Castellan spilled hot coffee down the front of his starched white shirt. "Damnation, man!"

Jay jumped so high his head almost hit the eight-foot ceilings. "Butler! You scared the hell out of me."

"You scared the hell out of me, too."

"Sorry." His eyes widened as he watched Butler Castellan holster his gun.

"Instinct," the detective explained. "What are you doing here?" He pulled a handkerchief from his pocket and dabbed at the brown stain on his shirt.

"I was here earlier researching a case for the Chief. At home, I realized I'd left my cellphone in the evidence room." Jay held up the phone in his hand. "Found it!"

A disapproving look passed across Castellan's face. Jay hoped he hadn't noticed the Nitrile glove. "Ever since you started volunteering here," the detective said, "I've had the feeling you missed being a detective." When Jay didn't say anything, he continued. "Are you working overtime on a case and trying to keep it from the Chief?"

Jay stood, half-turned toward the squad room, ready to flee as soon as he had the opportunity. "No, sir."

"Did those sisters ask you to find out information about the Mondae case? That would explain why you're acting so anxious."

"Listen, Butler, I've got to run." Jay felt as if he stood poised at the blocks waiting for the starting gun to go off.

"I warned the Misses Claire and Avery to get out of the detecting business. You need to tell them if I catch them butting in again, they're going back to jail. I thought that would've at least taught them a lesson."

"Okay, right. I'll tell them. Now be sure to rub some Neosporin on those burns when you get home." Jay tucked the phone into his back pocket and shot down the hall.

"Wait!" Castellan called after Jay's retreating figure, but he didn't turn around.

* * *

Avery watched through the glass strips running across their double front doors as Jay rang the sisters' buzzer. She made a note to curb his tendency to show up unannounced. In the hand not smashing the doorbell, he waved his cellphone in the air. When no one came immediately, he knocked. Bodhi barked like an alarmed seal.

Claire, who had been working at the office computer, opened the door, and Jay dashed inside.

"I've got it!" he said, waiving the cellphone.

Avery, who had been making lunch, wiped her hands on a cup towel. "Got what?"

"A photo of the arrow used to kill Thorne Mondae. It's on my cellphone." He flopped into the barstool at the kitchen island and began swiping through photos on his phone. Bodhi sat at his feet whining to be noticed. Jay lowered his free hand and stroked the dog's head.

"How did you get it?" Avery was catching Jay's excitement.

"Last night, I sneaked into the evidence room by telling the guard I left my cellphone there. That I was researching something for the Chief. I found the file and snapped a photo." His eyes sparkled. "I thought I was the only one there, but Detective Castellan caught me."

"Do he know what you were doing?"

"No. Totally clueless." Jay found the photo he had been looking for and laid the phone on the island for the sisters.

"Claire's been researching bows and arrows used by the Jarawa in the Andaman Islands," Avery said, her animated voice an octave higher than usual.

"They use a type of flatbow and at least three varieties of arrows," Claire said. "Apparently, there's one for fishing, one for hunting, and untipped ones for shooting warning shots."

"Warning shots?" Jay asked. "At who?"

"At intruders," Avery said. "Anyone who's not native Jarawa isn't welcome in their reserve."

Claire studied the photo on Jay's cellphone. "This looks like their hunting arrowhead to me. The fishing arrows have forward-pointing prongs, but the hunting arrows have ovoid heads."

"Ovoid?" Avery had never heard that term before. "Does that mean it's shaped like a regular arrow? Or something different?"

"Sharp at one end and rounded at the base," Claire said. "Just like the common arrowheads used here. They're made with iron and attached to arrows over three feet long, almost as tall as a Jarawa tribesman, but they're pretty short." From the office, Claire carried two color photos printed on typing paper. She showed them to Avery and Jay. "Your picture looks very much like these."

The first printout showed a primitive man walking along a sandy beach with a long bow and several arrows thrown across one shoulder. The other featured the closeup of a native honing the edge of an arrow tip made of metal. Several children watched the man working, and in the background a plain-vanilla dog roamed free. Avery hoped the dog was a well-fed pet.

"Where do they get the metal?" Jay asked. "So-called 'primitive' arrows are usually hewn from stone."

"'Hewn'?" Avery said. "I love it when you use sexy words." They exchanged meaningful looks.

"Gross," Claire said. "I'm gonna forget I saw that. Back to business. The Jarawa are not exactly sophisticated metal workers, but they have some cold-smithing and iron sharpening skills. Apparently, they find metal objects that have washed up on shore. I read about a container ship that ran aground on the coral reefs. For years, the Jarawa were able to scavenge metal from the ship."

"This doesn't look like an arrow the bowhunters we know would use," Avery said. "And you're beginning to sound like Tom. He must be rubbing off on you." A complicit smile from Jay.

"I texted it to him," Claire said, ignoring her sister's innuendo. "He said this one is made of…" She glanced at her cellphone. "…and I quote 'crudely honed metal notched into the arrow as compared to the modern steel process used for today's bowhunting arrows.' End quote."

"Our Tom," Avery said, "Mr. Wikipedia. Does he still have Mopsey?"

"His daughter picked the cat up a couple of days ago."

While the sisters discussed the cat, an intense Jay studied the photo on his phone and Claire's printouts. "Correct me if I'm wrong," he said with delight, "but I believe this narrows down the suspect list considerably."

"Well," Avery said, "it does and it doesn't."

"What do you mean?"

"Apparently, the murder weapon was made in the Andaman Islands by its primitive people, most likely the Jarawa. Which means the killer is probably someone who has visited there at one time or another."

"But?"

"But," Claire picked up where Avery left off, "anyone who had access to that person's possessions could have taken the bow and arrow and used it without the owner's consent."

"And," Avery said, "it's not just the people who are still alive, visited the islands, and have access to the weapons, but remember that collection of bows and arrows in Thorne's trophy room?"

"What about it?" Jay asked.

"I'd bet they came from the Andamans, and I'm pretty certain they look just like these pictures."

Claire thumbed through her cellphone photos. "And you'd be right." She showed the other two the photo she'd taken from Thorne's trophy room. "Thorne Mondae could have been the source of his own demise. He could have owned and unknowingly supplied his killer with the murder weapon. And that could be anybody who came into his home, including family, friends, vendors and workers, or guests."

"Wasn't one of the newspaper clippings we found at Thorne's about the Jarawa?" Avery knew her theft was a touchy subject, but all the evidence, if indeed it was evidence, needed to be shared and explored.

"I'd check the photo on my phone," Claire said, looking at her sister as if she were a naughty child, "but I happen to know somebody here has the original."

"It's a bit waterlogged." Avery went to her room to retrieve the clippings leaving Claire with Jay to tell him the story of her thievery. When she returned, her boyfriend had joined her sister in a shared Avery-is-a-naughty-child look. She decided to ignore them. Watermarks covered the box, and the clippings were a bit crinkly, but still intact. Out loud, Avery read the one about the Jarawa to her decriers.

Port Blair, Andaman Islands:
Baby Killing Tests India's Protection of Aboriginal Culture

When members of the isolated Jarawa tribe on South Andaman Island venture into the surrounding villages to snatch rice, cookies, bananas or, for some unknown reason, red garments, the police send them back into their forest Reserve, where for millenniums they have survived by hunting and gathering. The Inspector whose precinct includes the Reserve is under orders to interfere as little as possible with the tribe— the last remnants of a Paleolithic-era civilization.

The inspector was not prepared for the criminal complaint registered in the fall of '93. A five-month-old baby was reported missing and presumed dead. Witnesses who came forward left the police no choice but to arrest a Jarawa tribesman on suspicion of murder.

The 400 remaining Jarawas are believed to have migrated from Africa 50,000 years ago. Dark-skinned and small in stature, until recently they lived in complete cultural isolation, shooting outsiders who came near with steel-tipped arrows. After the tribe made peace with its neighbors, India took steps to minimize contact with them, hoping to avoid the catastrophe that befell the aboriginals of Australia and the US. Nevertheless, contact is occurring. Outreach workers visit the tribe's camps, and Jarawas receive medical treatment in isolation wards at hospitals. Poachers strike up illicit relationships, trading food for help in harvesting crabs or fish.

When a baby girl with blue eyes was born to an unmarried Jarawa woman, a welfare officer feared the tribe had carried out a ritual killing. Infants born to widows or fathered by outsiders are breast-fed by each of the tribe's lactating females before being strangled by one of the tribal elders. Although the dead child haunted him, the officer declined to interfere with tribal customs.

Taking a different view, a hospital nurse claiming to have witnessed the baby's birth posted a social worker near the camp to watch her. Months passed before the nurse received an alarmed call from the worker. She discovered the baby missing and her mother crying, claiming a tribesman had stolen and murdered her child. The baby's body was never recovered.

The three friends uttered a communal sigh of frustration.

"That's an interesting story, but it doesn't really help us," Claire said.

"Who knew India had an indigenous tribe on an Island right off their coast!" Jay said.

"Wait a minute," Avery said. "Wasn't that article around the time Onia Redfield was born? The clipping was found in Thorne Mondae's house, who she's claiming to be her father."

"That sounds like a pretty big coincidence," Claire said, cocking her head to the side like she was doing some hard thinking. "But the article said the baby was dead."

"No. It said the body was never found. The baby was *presumed* dead."

"But who saved her, and how did she end up here?" Jay's face had the glow of a man on a mission.

"Remember my talk with her during Thorne's funeral," Claire said, "after Adrianna kicked her out? She said Scopes Redfield saved her from being drowned by the tribal elder and brought her to the U.S. She was adopted by his brother and his wife."

"Interesting," Jay said. "Could this somehow be related to Thorne's death?"

"There're too many possibilities. My head is spinning!" Claire slipped off her reading glasses and rubbed her eyes.

"How often could that happen?" Avery asked. "A mixed-race baby being born to an indigenous woman?"

"Probably more often now than it did back then." Claire studied her sister. "What are you thinking?"

"That the odds of that article being about Onia Redfield are pretty darn good. It specifically states she had blue eyes. And the time frame fits." Avery gave her cohorts a mischievous grin. "Time to bring out the wanted posters!"

Bodhi jumped up wagging his tail while Avery pulled the suspect corkboard from the office to the island where Jay and Claire sat. They rolled their eyes heavenward, but she ignored them.

"Can't we at least have lunch first?" Claire asked.

"Yeah," Jay said, "what are we having?"

"Southwest pasta salad with chili-lime dressing," Avery said. "Won't take long. I guess we could eat first."

"My stomach's growling," Claire said.

"Mine too," Jay said.

Avery resigned herself to feeding them, but as soon as their bowls were empty, she snatched them away. Claire and Jay sat dazed at the island while an oblivious Bodhi snored on the sofa.

"No dessert?" Claire asked.

"No, like you said, back to business." Avery stood next to the cork board and pointed. "Here are our suspects. First, let's take Bud Tengle, the Mondae's commercial tenant, off the board and throw him away. He's been cleared by

Detective Jay Vidocq, who confirmed him to be in California at the time of the murder."

"Check," Jay said, looking pleased that she called him *detective*. "Thorne's death doesn't really benefit him much."

"Agreed," Claire said. "Anyone want something to drink? Coke, tea, orange juice?"

"Margarita?" Jay asked with his most charming grin.

Avery tore Bud Tengle's photo off the corkboard and threw it in the trash. "I'm good."

"I'll make you a margarita," Claire said to Jay. "Keep talking," she said to Avery. "I can make a drink and listen at the same time." She moved toward the beverage bar, but stopped in front of the corkboard. "You still have that unflattering photo of me up here. I think we can remove my photo and tear it up now. Don't you?" She gave Avery a pointed look.

"Oh, alright." Avery ripped Claire's photo off the board, tore it into tiny pieces, and tossed it into the trash. "Happy?"

"Thrilled. I think I'll have a margarita to celebrate."

"Did you put Thorne Mondae, the murder victim's, photo on the board because he might have committed suicide?" Jay asked.

"You guys decided it was possible, even using a bow and arrow, so that makes him a suspect, doesn't it?" It irritated Avery to have to defend her actions.

"I vote we remove him, since it's unlikely he killed himself," Claire said. "He'd have to have been an archery expert, which I doubt he was."

"You should know." Avery ignored a pissy look from her sister.

When Jay agreed, Avery jerked Thorne's photo from the board, ripped it to pieces, and threw it into the trash next to Claire's. "That narrows the list from 10 to seven. Anyone else?"

"Before we take anyone else off the list…" Claire took a sip of her margarita. "…we need to discuss what, if anything, the police discovered regarding the victim's phone records. And, if Thorne's financial records turned up anything. Jay, can you help with that?"

"I'm not privy to everything that goes on at the police department, but I do know that no one spoke with the victim before his death. They found his cellphone on the body, but it had been turned off. No suspicious activity in his records, as far as I know."

"What about financial records? Surely, they've had a will-reading by now, if people outside of television and movies actually have those."

"He wasn't popular with his residential and commercial tenants," Jay said, "and had a number of lawsuits filed against him. None of those had escalated to murderous proportions, except Bud Tengle. And we've already excluded him. In his will, assets were doled out with his ex-wife, Lianne Rhinehart, getting most of the real estate holdings. His present wife, Adrianna Mondae, received the house here in RE and their Dallas condo and his share of their seafood restaurant. The son, Isaac Mondae, inherited the online security firm, as well as a 25% interest in the real estate business. No one has much reason to complain, as they are all left well-off by Thorne. Of course, that also gives them a good reason to kill him."

"The ex-wife, Lianne, probably wouldn't have access to the primitive weapons we saw at Thorne's house," Claire said, "much less know how to use them."

"Unless there were others she had taken before the divorce," Avery said.

"Unlikely," Jay said. "Besides, she didn't look like the athletic type. Can we take her off the list?"

After they all agreed, and Avery had removed her picture from the corkboard, Claire said: "What about the son and daughter-in-law? Both of them would know where the bow and arrows were displayed, and Isaac would certainly know how to use them."

"True," Jay said, "but couldn't we clear the daughter-in-law, what's her face? Named after some country and western singer. We could clear her on the same basis as we did the ex-wife. She probably wouldn't have a clue how to shoot a bow and arrow."

Avery pointed to the photo of Isaac's new wife in her cowboy wedding outfit. She'd replaced the old one she'd found in the online Sweetgum High School Yearbook with the more up-to-date wedding photo: "Shania. She's married to Isaac, so rich by association. She might have been an accessory, but I'm willing to take her off as a primary suspect. Everyone?"

Both Claire and Jay nodded their heads, and off Shania came from the corkboard.

"Wait a minute," Avery said. "What about his friend and business partner, Scopes Redfield? He managed their financial investments, which I'm sure Thorne held at least half interest. And wouldn't Scopes have held half interest in the other businesses as well?"

"If I understand it correctly, Scopes sold his half-interest in the other businesses to Thorne years ago, and just kept the investment business. Even though Thorne still held a half-interest in the investments, he willed that back to Scopes. So, he inherited, but he didn't need the money. He was already rich."

"Five photos left on the board," Claire said. "I don't think we can remove any of the people who inherited money from Thorne, which includes Adrianna, his wife, Isaac, his son, and Scopes, his business partner. Since we are not able to eliminate Adrianna, we have to keep her alibi as well, her personal trainer, Delia Adair."

"I disagree," Avery said. "The same can be said of Isaac and his wife, but we eliminated Shania."

"I interviewed Adrianna personally," Jay said. "I asked her to repeat what she had told Detective Castellan regarding her alibi. She kept to her story about attending the charity breakfast after spending the night at her Dallas condo. She admitted that Delia Adair is also her lover, and that they were together both the night before and the morning of the murder. The problem is, in Delia Adair's statement, she claimed that their morning training session happened at Adrianna's home here in Rancho Exotica, not at the Dallas Condo."

"Their alibis contradict each other," Claire said. "More reason to keep them both on the suspect list."

"Adrianna said that Delia had trained her at both locations, and she just forgot where she was that day—at the condo rather than the house. I believed her."

"Of course, you did," Avery said. "A beautiful woman tells you a story, it's only natural you believe her." Avery wondered if what she was feeling

might be jealousy. She dismissed the idea, telling herself she was merely acting the way a dispassionate and analytical citizen detective should act.

"Fine, leave them up there." Jay looked a little miffed. "I need to be
getting home. I just remembered that Detective Castellan has a message he
wanted me to give you two."

"What was it?" Claire asked.

"He said to tell you to butt out of the detecting business. He's threatening to put you back in jail."

Both Avery and Claire laughed.

"Bit of an idle threat, isn't it?" Claire said.

"Aren't we forgetting one thing?" Avery announced in an authoritative voice.

Claire and Jay gave her their full attention. *What, oh world's greatest
citizen detective, are we forgetting?*

"Onia Redfield. She's the only family member who didn't inherit a
thing. Thorne refused to even acknowledge her as his daughter. The news-
paper article shows to my satisfaction she had every reason to want him dead.
Assuming she's the Jarawa baby who disappeared and was presumed dead.
The three main reasons humans commit murder are money, sex, and revenge.
In one way or another, didn't she have an issue with all three?"

34

Still in the Andaman Islands and not yet legally "Onia," Rebecca Redfield had realized the name fitted her better than she could have predicted. While taking down the target she used to practice the archery skills she'd acquired during her weeks-long visit to Port Blair, she felt as if she'd found the meaning of life. Her life, anyway. She rubbed her foot across the shooting line she had spray painted on the grass. Having crossed it so often, only a barely visible smudge remained.

Since she had made the decision to change her name, she asked both her mother and Nurse Singh to call her by her new name, Onia. She'd make it legal when she returned to the United States, which was in—she glanced at her sports watch—six hours. Riya had offered to drive her to the airport, but she preferred to take a taxi. After an early morning breakfast in the hotel's Juniper Berry restaurant, they said their goodbyes. Promising to visit again soon, Onia shared with Riya her plans to bring Anjale, her mother, to the United States.

"Are you sure she'd be happy there?" Riya asked.

"I think so." Onia had a moment of doubt. "Besides you, I can't see that she has that many connections to people here. There, she would have me. And I could take care of her. Protect her. And when I have children, she would meet them, be a grandmother to them."

"If she agrees, then I wish you both great happiness."

"You can come visit."

"Of course."

As she watched her friend's car pull away, Onia felt fairly certain she'd never see Nurse Singh again.

Anjale distracted her when she emerged from the apartment building carrying a cloth bag filled with food she'd prepared: Amritsari Kulcha stuffed with mashed boiled potatoes and spices, samosas with tamarind chutney and mango achaar, Jhal Muri, a popular street food made of puffed rice and an assortment of spices, vegetables, chanachur—a mixed snack food—and mustard oil, and coconut water.

She placed it on a picnic table near a mangrove tree just beyond Onia's target area and spread out its contents along with plastic utensils and paper napkins. They snacked in companionable silence for several minutes until Onia spoke.

"Is it hard for you to call me by my new name?" she asked her mother.

With a crisp napkin, Anjale wiped the corner of her mouth. "I always call you Onia. That is who you are."

"My father…" Onia hesitated when Anjale made a distasteful face. "His name is Thorne Mondae. He's not a nice man, as you well know. As far as I can tell, he's never paid for any of the bad things he's done over the years. Everyone hates him, even his own wife and child."

"Some men are born bad."

"Do you want me to make him pay for what he did to you?"

Anjale looked out over the blue sea where seabirds dived for fish. Dapples of light fell on her cheeks like bright tears. "Pay how?"

"With money. I want to bring you to America. To live with me, meet my future husband, be there when I give you grandchildren. We need cash for that. I know Uncle Scopes gives you a monthly stipend, but I doubt if it's enough to live on the rest of your life. Thorne owes you back child support from the time I was born until I left my adopted home. He's rich and can afford to compensate for his neglect. If he refuses, I'll take him to court." Onia dipped a samosa in chutney and held it poised to take a bite. But when she put it to her mouth, she couldn't eat. She had lost her appetite remembering what Thorne Mondae had done to her mother and gotten away with all these years.

"Court?"

"Sue his ass off, file a lawsuit for everything he's worth. After the world hears what he did to you, his name will be rubbish in business circles. Not that he gives a hoot what people think about him."

"No," Anjale said. "The world does not need to know about me."

Onia thought for a moment. Thorne wasn't afraid of lawsuits. And shaming him wouldn't be an easy task. She might have to find a different approach, like shaming someone in his family. Well, she'd worry about the particulars later. Form a specific plan when she got back to the States.

"I do not need rupees," Anjale said.

"What do you need?"

"I believe the English word is 'justice.'"

"I guarantee you'll have it, one way or another."

35

Claire loaded Bodhi onto the golf cart, and Avery pulled it out of the driveway. Because Bodhi took up so much room, he rode shotgun beside Avery while Claire sat in the second row of seats. A dignitary being chauffeured by her trusty bodyguard. Around dusk, when they took the dog on his walk by the lake and ride around the neighborhood, it wasn't unusual to meet their neighbors. RE residents used their carts to seek out the exotic wildlife, and a friendly neighbor often rewarded Bodhi with a jerky treat.

The zebras had become the most popular with not only the residents but also any visitors to the ranch. The first time he saw them, Bodhi had barked but, being the good dog he was, ignored them after that. The herd grazed across from the brood pond, and Avery stopped the cart to watch the two youngest herd members frolic together. When young, the zebra's stripes were brown rather than black but darkened with age. Claire videoed their romping to post later on Facebook. It amazed their friends and relatives that zebras often foraged in the sisters' front yard.

"Uh oh," Avery said. "Here comes PAM."

Penelope Viktor drove her plain white golf cart with beige upholstered seats. Just as plain vanilla as its driver and passengers. Angela and Mabel rode shotgun and backseat passenger, respectively. They pulled up next to the sisters and gave Bodhi a bone-shaped dog biscuit. He looked at it for a moment, about to turn his nose up, thought better of it, and began gnawing on the treat.

"Say 'thank you,' Bodhi," Claire said, and they all waited a beat as if expecting him to do just that.

Avery had announced to Claire that PAM served as undercover agents to gather information from sources unavailable to the sisters. The sisters had no idea from whom PAM's wealth of data came and, even if they did, lacked the interrogation skills to extract it from them. Apparently, PAM had that talent down in spades, and Avery intended to make use of it.

"Penelope," she said, "is that a new hairdo? It looks nice." She knew Penelope sported the same short neckline 'do she'd always worn. The plan was to establish a rapport with the interviewee, soften her up, and catch her off guard before zeroing in on the essence of the cross-examination. A technique Avery learned from watching true-crime television.

"I just had it done." A skeptical frown proclaimed Penelope's wariness of her neighbor's attentions.

"All you ladies look nice this evening."

Six eyes stared from beneath unmascared lashes, scrutinizing Avery as if she'd just walked naked among the zebra herd.

Okay, maybe compliments weren't the way to go.

"Have you ladies ever met Onia Redfield?" Claire asked. "The young lady adopted by Thorne's business partner's brother?"

Claire to the rescue. Nothing like the direct approach, although Avery gave herself credit for loosening them up and getting them ready for the direct hit to the middle. When alerted to a nice bit of gossip, PAM snapped to attention. They moved to the edge of their seats.

"We saw her at the funeral, but we had already seen her a long time ago," Penelope said.

"Really?" Avery asked. "When?"

"We were at dinner with our husbands at the Clubhouse," Angela took up the narrative.

"About a year ago," Mabel filled in.

Angela frowned at her sister, then continued. "Thorne Mondae was having dinner with a young African American girl—"

"She's Jarawa from the Andaman Islands," Avery said.

"I don't even know where that is," Angela said with a touch of indignation.

"It's not important," Claire said. "Go on."

"I remember we were having chicken fried steak—"

"I don't think so," Mabel corrected her sister. "John was trying to stay away from fried foods back then. That was just after his heart attack. We were having the baked chicken with mashed potatoes and gravy and—"

"No, you weren't," Penelope said. "I'm sure we all had the catfish. It was on special because it was Catfish Friday. We had hush puppies and French fries. I remember because it was Calvin's turn to pay." She looked at Avery and Claire. "We take turns paying when we eat out together."

Avery resisted the urge to jump off the cart and ring their collective turkey necks.

"Please," Claire said. "Can we settle the food question later? Did you hear any of the conversation between Thorne and Onia?"

"It seemed friendly, at first," Angela said. "But in the middle of dinner—he was having steak and a baked potato, and she was having a Caesar salad because I saw the croutons—"

"Could we just stick to the conversation between Thorne and Onia?" Avery failed to keep the impatience out of her voice.

"Of course. I'm getting to that," Angela said.

"When?" Mabel asked. "The next millennium?"

"You had your turn." Angela turned an angry glare on her sister.

"Ladies, please." Claire used her most soothing voice. "Can we just hear about the conversation? Thank you. Now, Angela, you were saying…?"

Avery was impressed that her sister could tell the PAMs apart.

Angela harrumphed. "I was saying that they got into a loud argument in the middle of dinner. I heard her say 'I'm your daughter. You owe me!' or something to that effect."

"He was laughing at her," Mabel said. "You could see she was furious."

"And humiliated," Angela said. "I remember, he said 'You can't blackmail a man who doesn't give a—he used a naughty word that starts with an 's'—who doesn't *care* what other people think.'"

"Then she jumps up and throws a whole glass of tea on him. I know it was tea because she hadn't ordered a mixed drink. And the liquid was too dark to be water." Mabel puffed up like a rooster about to crow, pleased with her powers of deduction. "She ran out of the Clubhouse crying."

"And he sat there wiping the water off with a table napkin."

"Wiping the *tea* off."

"He had this creepy look on his face, kind of a smile, but not quite."

"A half-smile," Claire volunteered.

"You mean smug, self-satisfied, like an Angel Clare look?" Avery said.

PAM stared at her with blank expressions, not an unusual look for them, but she was getting the same vacant gape from Claire.

"Who's Angel Clare," Penelope asked.

"Nobody you know," Claire said.

"Are you talking about your sister, Avery?"

Avery sighed and shook her head. *Claire an angel? Hardly.*

"We must be off," Claire said. "Bodhi needs his walk."

Later, Avery defended herself when Claire accused her of trying to make PAM look stupid. "It was a literary reference!"

"I'm an English major, and I don't know who that is." Claire slipped into her big sister lecture mode.

"He's a character from *Tess of the D'Urbervilles*. He was this morally superior guy who condemned Tess for doing the same thing he did, i.e., have unprotected illegitimate sex with someone other than their spouse."

"Was there such a thing in those days as 'protected' sex? They didn't have condoms, did they?"

"I guess not, but you know what I mean. It's okay for the man but not the woman."

"*Anyway*," Claire said, "back to the problem at hand. "Was Onia angry enough at Thorne to kill him? And, if so, how could she have entered our gated development without being invited by a resident?"

"Obviously," Avery said, "Thorne invited her and cleared her at the gate when they had dinner, but he wouldn't do that again once he knew what she wanted."

"He might even have had her name put on the blacklist of people who are not allowed entry."

"I don't think so. Remember Adrianna, Thorne's wife, asked Jay to put Onia's name on the blacklist at Thorne's funeral. So, it must not have been on there before. Nevertheless, she still wouldn't be admitted unless a resident had invited her."

They drove down the tree-shaded sidewalk that ran by one of the development's lakes, then stopped to let Bodhi jump down. The trio headed toward the dock. From the pier, the dam that separated two lakes rose into view. Its paved surface served as a passageway connecting one section of the development to another and only golf carts or ATVs were allowed to use it. Thick forests of trees lined both lake banks, broken occasionally by a private dock jutting into the water like a long arm.

"The high fence surrounding the Ranch would be a hindrance but not impossible to get over or through if someone were determined enough. A wire cutter could make a hole big enough for a human to pass through." Claire continued their conversation.

"Except no hole was found in the fence. If it had been, Jay would have known about it. Maybe she climbed over. It wouldn't be difficult for a young, athletic woman like Onia."

"But she would have been carrying a bow and arrows. Remember the photo of the Jarawa hunter? He slung the weapon over his shoulder with nothing to carry it in, like a quiver. I guess she could have thrown the bow and arrows over the fence, but it would be difficult. Maybe she put it all in a duffle bag or something."

"There are a lot of 'yes, buts,' and 'maybes' to this scenario," Avery said. "She would have had to know where there were security cameras, besides the ones at the front and back gates. Some people have motion-detector lights over their doors and garages." Avery blushed, remembering the motion-detector light that caught her snooping at Adrianna's the night she and Jay hooked up.

"If she didn't drive into the development, where would she park?" Claire called Bodhi, and he followed them down the pathway leading from the dock. A venue of vultures perched in the leafless branches of an old oak tree. A few flew away when the sisters and their dog came near, but several others held their posts.

"Remember that drug-crazed relative of one of our property owners? When he couldn't get in through the front gate because his aunt had put him on the blacklist, he had his friend drop him off down the highway, and he climbed the fence. It's conceivable that the killer could have done the same."

"But then the friend who dropped them off would know about them being here and consequently about the murder. As we know from watching true crime TV, if you don't want to get caught, do not include anyone else in your nefarious plans, and don't open your own big mouth." Claire called a wayward Bodhi from sniffing in the pine forest and back to the paved path.

"But if they brought their own car, they would either have to park on the highway or on one of the two country roads that run perpendicular to the highway. If anyone abandoned their car for any period of time either place, someone would report it to the police. You can't do anything in a small town without somebody knowing about it." Avery sighed.

"The big question now is: Did anyone notice an abandoned vehicle at that time of day?"

* * *

"Yeah," Bart Downs told the sisters. "I saw an abandoned car parked on the highway shoulder that runs in front of the development." He gave Bodhi another dry bone-shaped treat, at which Bodhi sniffed and turned up his nose. He'd already had one of those today, and he certainly wasn't lowering himself to eat another one.

"Did you tell Detective Castellan about it?" Claire asked.

"Who's Detective Castleton?"

"*Cas-tell-an.*" Avery couldn't believe what she was hearing. "Did he not interview you? Talk to you about the death of Thorne Mondae?"

"Why would he? I had nothing to do with it."

Avery heaved an exhausted sigh. She and Claire had driven all over the development in the last several hours, catching anyone they could at home to ask them the same question. "Did you notice an abandoned vehicle between 9:30 a.m. and 12:30 p.m. on either the highway or the adjacent county roads the Thursday Thorne Mondae was murdered?" They had been making their weary way home with dozens of "nos" filling their heads, when Bart Downs's cart came meandering down the hill as they turned into their own driveway. Even though bone tired, and Avery determined to make a quick getaway, Claire insisted they ask him.

"Did he have to ask you personally?" Claire asked Bart. "Didn't that seem like something the police might like to know?"

"No, it didn't occur to me."

"Can you tell us exactly where it was parked, what kind of vehicle?" Avery asked.

"A white late model SUV. Maybe a Ford Edge. Too far to be sure. Parked on the highway right next to the treeless lot over on Gazelle Street. Want me to show you?"

"We know where it is." Avery was tired and losing patience, not that she had started out with any. She reminded herself that a good citizen detective remained patient and objective. "Why did you notice it? Did it stand out in any way?"

"I had company, and we were looking for the zebras. We drove down Gazelle Street. I could see the highway because that lot has no trees to block the view. Don't often see an empty car parked there, but I figured somebody had car trouble and called for help. Wasn't my problem. Didn't occur to me it happened the day Thorne Mondae was murdered. If my memory serves me right, that is."

"Thank you, Bart," Claire said. Avery felt disinclined to be polite and said nothing.

After he had driven away, Avery suggested they go look at the treeless lot. Although Claire stared longingly at the house, she agreed. When Bodhi realized they were not going home, and he wasn't getting his supper anytime soon, he decided to rethink the dry bone treat. He must have ruled in its favor, because he gobbled it down as they traveled toward Gazelle Street.

"Wouldn't the cops put an abandoned car notice on the vehicle?" Avery asked Claire.

"Probably not enough time passed. It's not often you see an empty vehicle along that highway. But they're not as scarce as cop cars. I don't ever remember seeing the police on the highway."

"It would probably be the Highway Patrol, but I don't remember ever seeing them either. Of course, we don't get out much."

Claire laughed. "True. Especially since neither one of us can see worth a damn at night."

The sun began its descent and a dusky twilight settled around them. A spectacular sunset lit the lakes ablaze and set the sisters' faces aglow. They arrived at the treeless lot, which had been denuded from the uncontained and contaminated runoff from the Highway Department's two-to-four lane highway expansion. The State had offered to pay for replanting the trees. The owner of the property, a widow who lived in another state, did not care whether trees grew on the property or not. Had, in fact, not even known she owned it and never contacted the State. Surrounding it, hundreds of trees reached for the skies, but the lot lay naked and bald and unashamed. Beyond the high game fence, cars, pickups with trailers, and trucks sped by on the highway elevated on a rise above the fence line.

"The car must have been tagged with an abandoned car notice, or someone would have called it in." Avery pushed her sunglasses on top of her head to get a better view. The gesture triggered a memory that remained just out of reach. She knew better than to force herself to remember. Best to let it go, and the answer would materialize later. "Even if a cop or highway patrolman never saw it, some irritated driver would have. Nothing is beneath people's notice, and nothing is beyond complaining about."

"Maybe the perpetrator already had a notice, put it out when they left the car, then took it down when they returned." Claire looked pleased with this suggestion.

Avery frowned and pursed her lips. "Yeah, but where would they get one? Park their car on a highway, leave it long enough to get a ticket, then reuse that ticket? Wouldn't there be a record?

"You're dating a cop. Ask him."

"Is that what we're doing? *Dating*?"

"What would you call it?"

"Distracting ourselves in order to forget the inevitability of our imminent demise?"

"Avery." Claire spoke with her impatient big sister voice. "Quit being morbid and admit you're having a good time with a great guy."

"Okay, I will." She dialed Jay and put him on speaker phone.

"Hey, sweetie," he said.

"Jay, just wanted to let you know I'm having a great time and not thinking about dying at all," Avery said.

"Huh?"

"You're on speaker and Claire's here," Avery warned. "Don't say anything... uh... incriminating."

"Hi, Claire. Like what could I possibly say that your sister doesn't already know in intimate detail?"

"Not a thing," Claire said. "You know Avery can't keep a secret."

"One of my most endearing qualities. Anyway, here's the latest scoop." Avery explained about the parked white SUV Bart had seen and their theory that the driver could have used a secondhand abandoned vehicle notice.

"You're in luck, ladies," Jay said. "One of my duties as a volunteer at the police department is to tag abandoned vehicles. Don't think I tagged that one, though. I'd probably remember because it was the day of the murder. I can check to see if someone else did."

"Walk us through the process," Claire said.

Jay cleared his throat. "When they find an empty vehicle, an officer will first check to see whether it was reported stolen. We place a warning tag on it giving the owner 48 hours to move it. If the vehicle isn't removed, the city impounds or disposes of it. Members of the public can fill out an online form about an abandoned vehicle in their neighborhood and submit it electronically. They're posted on the police website. If you ever decide to do that, by the way, be sure to provide as much detail as possible for a quicker response."

"We'll keep that in mind," Avery said. "What I'm hearing is that if a person gets a notice but removes the vehicle within the 48-hour time period, the physical tag is never retrieved by the police. Isn't it possible that they could have saved it for a future use?"

"Like using it to preserve their vehicle while they murdered Thorne Mondae?" Claire said.

A silent moment from the cellphone, then, "It's possible, assuming no one looks close enough to see the original issue date."

"Here's the scenario," Avery said. "Let me know if I leave out anything. The Unsub parks their car on the side of the highway—"

"Unsub?" Claire laughed. "Sorry, but it's funny when you play citizen detective."

Avery ignored her sister. "—the *Unsub* checks both ways for oncoming cars, exits the vehicle, and places the abandoned vehicle notice under the windshield wiper. They descend the incline toward the game fence. They're either carrying the bow and arrow over their shoulder, as the Jarawa tribesman did in Claire's photo, or they put it in a duffle or gym bag, which would be less noticeable. Once out of sight of the highway, they throw the weapons over the game fence, or maybe put it over their shoulder, and climb the fence into the treeless lot."

"What about security cameras or motion detector lights?" Jay asked.

"We're at the lot right now," Claire said. "There aren't any. No homes on either side or opposite the property."

"The terrain is easy to walk across because there aren't any fallen limbs, no foliage, and the land is flat all the way to Gazelle Street," Avery said. "If you remember, that's the street where Thorne's UTV was parked while he was hunting. The Unsub could have walked right to it."

"Except," Claire said, 'how would they know where Thorne would be hunting that morning?"

"Because," her sister said, "the barn where the hunters sign in would be right in the path where the approaching murderer crossed. All the Unsub had to do was check the sign-in log. No one would be around the barn because the hunters had checked in much earlier. The Unsub could travel straight to Thorne's hunting spot."

"Probably someone who had been invited here before and had a map to the place." Jay said.

"Not sure they would even need that. I think you can find a Rancho Exotica map on the Internet. Onia would have one from when she met Thorne at the Clubhouse to extort him," Claire said.

"Thorne's wife and son would obviously have one, as would his friend, Scopes, who had hunted with him before," Avery added.

"So, now all we have to do," Jay said, "is find somebody who has a late model white SUV and a used abandoned vehicle warning notice."

"Yep," Avery said, "that's all."

"I just thought of somebody who drives a white SUV. It might even be a Ford Edge.

"Who?" Jay and Avery asked like a pair of hoot owls.

"Onia Redfield."

36

When Onia Redfield walked into the Rancho Exotica Clubhouse, she experienced a disturbing sense of *déjà vu*. She had not seen Isaac Mondae since his father's funeral, but had scheduled this meeting with him in the same place she had been rejected by Thorne. Good thing she didn't have a superstitious bone in her body, or any other body part, for that matter. She wasn't the sort of person who went around saying: "Everything happens for a reason." Bad things just happened; there wasn't any universal justifying excuse for it.

Onia looked around the room but didn't see Isaac. A few people sat at the tables, but since it was early afternoon, there were no dinner guests. She slid onto a bar stool and ordered a glass of dry white wine, his choice, from the bartender. Wearing a vest with long-sleeved blue shirt turned up at the cuffs and a bar towel thrown over his shoulder, the young man reminded her of the Sam character in the long-running comedy *Cheers*. She often caught the series in the early morning hours when sleep evaded her. The Clubhouse did not embrace her with the same warm comradery as the sitcom.

Now that Thorne was dead and had willed his illegitimate daughter— her, Onia Redfield—absolutely nothing, she doubted she'd ever be able to bring her mother to the United States. She decided to talk with Isaac. See if she could appeal to his better side, if he had one, that is.

Onia despaired over what seemed to be happening to her. Her frustration and anger, emotions she had rarely experienced in her short life, overwhelmed her. Never knowing the circumstances of her birth, she had promenaded through life in a smooth flow, taking advantage of the opportunities offered her, of which there had been many. Slowing down to think about where they came from and why never occurred to her. She did not recall having doubts or insecurities about being adopted or being a minority. Self-confidence had always been present, she assumed, in her DNA. Now she wasn't so sure. Not about anything.

Since finding her birth mother and learning the facts of her conception, she consulted the always accessible Internet to educate herself about the multitude of issues which might arise when a child realizes she's adopted. Her grief over the loss of her birth parents, particularly the rejection from her father, had given rise to a deep sorrow and sense of loss she had never known. Although given every advantage an American-born child could have, she still longed for the cultural and family connections that would have existed with her native Jarawa mother. Most of her friends would laugh if they learned she craved the true tribal experience with all its striving and deficiency to the luxurious and struggle-free American way.

When she had finally confessed that very thing to her fiancé, Rafael Valencia, he looked appalled.

"If you'd stayed in the Jarawa Reserve, we never would have met!" An upset Rafe's voice rose to a shout. "You're wishing away the first 30 years of your life. Good years, rewarding, happy years. What about your adoptive parents? They love you. What about me? I love you. You're acting as if that means nothing."

Warm tears had rushed to her eyes, and she tried to put her arms around him. He pushed her away. "I do love you," she said. "Of course, I do. But this is something new I don't understand. Please, just give me the opportunity to follow it to its conclusion. To see how it ends."

He hesitated longer than she expected.

"I'll wait," Rafe said, "but not forever."

The quarrel with her fiancé occurred before she had challenged Thorne Mondae, and he rejected her. But it was not over. The all-consuming anger that ate at her guts stifled her, and she had to find a way to conquer it. She just didn't know how. Episodes remained to be played out. Stay tuned.

"Give me whatever you've got on tap," Isaac Mondae said from behind her. "Hey, there, Rebecca. What's happening?"

"It's Onia, now," she said. "I changed it. It's a Jarawa name."

"Uh, oh yeah. Sorry. Heard about that. Didn't really think it would stick."

"Well, it did."

Isaac seated himself on the barstool next to Onia, and the bartender served his beer. He slugged down a big gulp as if preparing himself for whatever bad news or major surprises she had in store. Onia noticed he wore an Audemars Piguet Royal Oak men's watch in rose gold.

"Hope that came with papers," she said, indicating the exorbitantly expensive timepiece.

He glanced at his wrist, cocked an eyebrow, and smiled. "Course it did. Got it from eBay."

"Sorry about your father. It's tough. A violent death like that."

Isaac shrugged.

"I would have asked to meet at your house, here in Rancho Exotica, but I didn't want to make Adrianna uncomfortable. We had a few words at the funeral, as I'm sure you know."

"No worries. She doesn't live there anymore." He eyed her with a combination of suspicion and nonchalance. Onia suspected the nonchalance was an act. "She gave me and Shania the house as a wedding present, deeded it over to us. Then she moved into the Dallas condo with Delia Adair. I assume that's no surprise to you or anybody else."

Onia wondered which part he meant—that she deeded a valuable property to her stepson or that she moved into her condominium with her lover.

"I have no feelings about either one of those things."

"You here to talk about my father?"

"He's my father too."

Isaac rolled his eyes. "If you say so."

"Thorne Mondae rejected me, even though he knew what he had done to my mother. He took advantage of her naivete, got her drunk, and raped her. If it had been the United States, he would have got what he deserved. He'd have gone to jail."

"Rape?" He cocked his head, and the false bravado left his voice. "That's news to me."

"My mother, Anjale, I met her in Port Blair. She told me."

"And you believed her?"

"Of course! Why would she lie? She had nothing to gain."

"If that's true… and I'm not saying it is… sounds to me like he did get what he deserved. He's dead." He narrowed his eyes to thin slits, stared as if he were trying to read her mind. "Look. Let's cut to the chase. I didn't like the guy any better than you did. So, just tell me what you want, okay?"

Onia breathed from her diaphragm and let it slowly out her nose. "My mother, Anjale, the one in Port Blair, was let go from her job at the hospital. They could only afford to retain essential personnel, and her job as a nurses' assistant was dispensable. Bottomline, I need money to bring her to the United States. She is in grave danger from Covid and wouldn't be able to afford an illness should she get one."

"You want money."

"When I was in Port Blair, my mother asked me for nothing but justice." Her voice hardened. She studied his indifferent features. Appealing to this young man's soft heart wouldn't sway him. Nor would asking him to do the right thing. She had to play hardball, the only approach that worked on a privileged white boy who had never earned a penny on his own.

"What, exactly, is your interpretation of justice?" Isaac's reedy voice had hardened to match hers, as if he were determined not to let her get the best of him.

"Just this: A house for my mother in a middle-class neighborhood, furnished nicely, and supplied with all the necessities. In addition, she needs a lifetime income. I'm thinking fulltime employment with one of your companies, without her ever having to show up, of course, making a minimum of $50,000 yearly, adjusted for inflation, including health insurance, bonuses and 10% annual 401(k) contributions for the next 20 years. A car, preferably hybrid, every five to 10 years, depending on wear and tear on the vehicle, insurance, and roadside assistance. By making her an employee, she'll be an asset."

"Thanks for thinking of me." Isaac's mirthless laugh sounded more like a disgusted grunt. "You are kidding, aren't you? There's no way in hell I'd make a deal like that. Why don't you get your precious Uncle Scopes to help? He's got plenty of dough. Especially since he inherited my dad's half of the investment business."

Onia inhaled a deep breath. "It's the fair thing to do, make up for what your father did. But if you don't care about fairness, then I'll claim a right to part of your inheritance and contest the will. I'll file every lawsuit possible against you personally, your wife, your mother, your stepmother, and all of your companies. I'll keep you and your company and your relatives and your future children tied up in court until the next millennium. It will be generations before you or anyone else sees any of Thorne's money. You will never have a moments' peace and neither will the people you love. You will go to your grave fighting me, and you will never win because I will never give up."

Isaac's face had turned beet red. "You are my father's daughter, aren't you?"

Onia bit her lip, realizing she had turned into someone she didn't recognize. But Isaac saw through her, and it made her sick to think about it.

"I don't even know if you *are* my sister!" Isaac's knuckles turned white as he clutched the beer mug. He signaled for another beer, pursing his lips into a thin line until it arrived, then took a big swig. "I'll tell you what, *Anita*, or whatever your name is now. If you can prove to my satisfaction that you are truly my half-sister, the daughter of my late father, I'll discuss it with my mother and Adrianna. Maybe we can work something out."

"Really?" Onia couldn't believe it. Could it be that easy? She didn't trust him for a minute, but it appeared as if her threats might work on Isaac, whereas they had not on his father. "I'm happy to get a DNA test. I'll give you the written report as soon as I get it."

"Is that justice for you, then?" Isaac rose, an exhausted look on his face, and threw enough money on the table to cover both their tabs. "My dead father and a big chunk of his money?"

"Shot through the heart with a bow and arrow fashioned by some primitive arrow smith? That's my mother's Jarawa justice." Onia got in his face. "The money? That's just good ol' red-blooded American revenge."

37

Avery dropped Claire off at the community center for a water aerobics class. She would have gone with her sister but had a late breakfast meeting with Jay at the Thunderbird Café. Weary of the tension she felt to solve the mystery of who killed Thorne Mondae, Avery wanted to tell Jay it was over. Not between them but the search for a killer who seemed as elusive as ever.

Maybe Jay would be relieved too. In addition to her exhaustion, Avery had begun to feel as if she were using Jay and wondered if he felt that way. It hadn't been intentional. Who knew he would prove so useful? In fact, who knew that she would ever be involved in the search for a murderer? She wondered if their relationship might be based solely on the adrenalin rush of the hot pursuit of a killer. Not that their investigation could in any way be considered a hot pursuit.

She also wondered if her constant tiredness resulted from growing older or if the seizure she'd had months ago still affected her. Occasionally, she sought words to complete sentences that escaped her, and her sister had to supply them. Claire insisted everybody within their age group had the same problem, but Avery still worried that she might be going senile. Or more realistically, close to another seizure. But since the ambulatory EEG, that fear had been more or less alleviated. As a year since her seizure approached, she hadn't had any other symptoms. The odds of her having another decreased proportionally to the amount of time she'd gone seizure-free. The prognosis looked good.

As for Jay, the big question loomed: did she really like him or was she just using him?

He waited for her in a booth. Not much at the café for her to eat, but the biscuits and gravy usually worked. She waved, then slid into the opposite seat. Looking as fresh as the chilly breeze outside, he gave her a big smile. She wished she felt and looked that chipper. What a difference 10 years made. Jay leaned across the table and kissed her on the lips.

"Did you find out if any of our suspects got an abandoned car notice recently," Avery asked.

A shadow passed across his face. "What? No 'hello,' or 'how are you,' or 'yes, Jay, you're the hottest guy I know'?"

"Yes, Jay, you are the hottest guy I know." She gave him an embarrassed grin, wondering if he could read her mind. If he knew she had been feeling guilty about using him. She leaned across the table and kissed him. The sweetness of the kiss went a long way toward convincing her of her sincere affection for this lovely man.

"That's better!" he said. "Still looking through the records. Since I don't have a precise date for when the notice was issued, if there even was one, it's a lengthy process. All I can do is start from the day of the murder and work backwards."

He held his coffee cup in one hand. Avery covered the other one with hers. "I can't tell you how much I appreciate all your hard work."

He looked at her curiously, as though not expecting such a heartfelt expression of appreciation. "You're welcome. I'm enjoying myself. Aren't you?"

"I'm just tired. Don't worry. I'll snap out of it." She squeezed his hand, pulled away. After taking a couple of bites of biscuit, she pushed the plate to the side. Too much grease made her stomach queasy. To be honest, even more than the biscuits and gravy, Jay's nearness still affected her that way—excited, not queasy.

"Aren't you going to eat that?"

"No, do you want them?" She shoved her plate toward him, and he scraped the leftovers onto his plate. Sure, he worked out at the gym every day. He could afford a couple of greasy biscuits and gravy. She envied him.

"I told Detective Castellan about the arrow, how Claire identified it as probably coming from the Andaman Islands. He acted like it wasn't news to him. Guess he had already figured that out."

"We can only hope he's progressing better than we are. The existence of the mysterious primitive arrow pretty much narrows the suspect field to the victim himself, Thorne Mondae, who may have killed himself out of guilt and despair for the people he hurt during his lifetime."

"Not freaking likely, based on what we know about him. Besides, we already covered that. Took his name off the suspect board. No need to cover that ground again."

"Okay, then there's Onia Redfield, his daughter by a Jarawa woman whom he refused to acknowledge. We know she's been to the Andaman Islands based on her passport records and her own admission. Of course, other people had access to the weapon in Thorne's house, but none of them have a compelling motive to kill him."

"What about that guy who claims to be Thorne's best friend, Scopes Redfield?"

"He doesn't seem to have had much of a motive." Avery looked out the restaurant's front windows facing Sweetgum's main street. The old court-house—every county seat in Texas had one—loomed above them like an antiquated castle with gargoyles and other ancient beasts perched on its pinnacles. Creepy.

"He was in the Andaman Islands the same time Thorne was. He would have access to the weapon, and his passport shows a couple more visits there. Nothing recent, though."

Avery stared at the gargoyles who looked as if they were about to fly off the building and attack the passersby below. They made her think about the vultures in her forest, hovering above Thorne's body, waiting for an opportunity to feast. The forest reminded her of something she had forgotten.

"Jay," she said, "I've thought of something." She had his undivided attention. "Remember when Scopes Redfield spoke at Thorne's funeral?"

"Read a poem, if I remember correctly. I hate poetry."

"We have that in common," Avery said.

"And a couple of other things." Jay gave her a mischievous grin.

Avery rolled her eyes. "An obsession with sex and murder. The elements of a deep and long-lasting relationship." They both laughed.

"So, what about Scopes and what he said at the funeral?"

"He said Thorne died in a forest that reminded him of the Jarawa Reserve in the Andaman Islands. But, as far as I know, he's never been to our forest."

"You sure about that? Maybe he saw it one of the times he went hunting with Thorne."

"And maybe he saw it the day he killed Thorne?"

"It's a stretch," Jay said. "But I'll keep it in mind. Gotta' get to work." He pulled the pair of Maui Jim sunshades he'd pushed above his cap brim and shoved them across his eyes.

Something about the gesture resurrected a memory in Avery's brain, but it floated away as quickly as it had arisen. She also realized she'd forgotten all about telling Jay she wanted to stop their murder investigation.

38

After her water aerobics class, Claire showered, blow-dried her hair, and threw on a minimum of makeup. She wanted to give Avery and Jay a little more time to be alone. After finishing her toilette, she called her sister's cellphone. It rang and rang until it went to voicemail. Not unusual for Avery, who always left her phone in her purse and never heard it ring. Claire knew the odds of her checking her voicemail were small to none.

The cafe where Avery and Jay ate breakfast was several city blocks from the Sweetgum Community Center. A little farther than Claire had planned on walking, but she decided to strike out anyway, hoping Avery called her sooner rather than later. She headed toward downtown carrying her gym bag, but hadn't gone far when she realized it had been a mistake. The wind blasted her with cold air, and her bag felt like she'd stuffed an anvil inside. A small city park loomed in the near distance. As soon as she'd staggered there, she collapsed onto a bench bordering the main street. A cold wind nipping at her spine kept her from fuming at her sister.

She dialed Avery again; still no answer. Claire steamed at her sister's irresponsibility. Or was it just forgetfulness—a byproduct of her seizure? Possibly, but Claire didn't feel inclined to give Avery the benefit of the doubt. While dialing again, a white SUV pulled up just beyond the curb and honked. Something about the vehicle rang a bell inside her hippocampus. When she saw Onia Redfield sitting behind the wheel, she remembered being with its owner inside that very automobile during Thorne's funeral. Plus, it looked like the vehicle Marcus Downs saw parked on the highway the day Thorne died.

Onia rolled down her window and called to Claire: "Need a ride?"

Avery's cellphone went to voicemail again. Claire made a quick decision. She circled behind the white SUV surreptitiously observing the word "Edge" written across it's rearend, and climbed into the passenger seat next to Onia. The young woman's face glowed with excitement.

"You look like you're about to burst," Claire said. "Good news?"

When she'd stopped, a line of cars had stacked up behind Onia. One or two of them impatiently honked.

"I'm going home for lunch. Would you like to join me? I'll tell you all about what I've been doing."

Onia looked as eager as a puppy begging for a walk. As if she couldn't wait to pass on her good news to a friend. Claire didn't consider them friends exactly, but she had made a connection with this young woman at her father's funeral. And besides, what better opportunity would she have to interview a potential suspect than an open invitation from that suspect herself? Claire couldn't pass up the chance, although she might not be able to eat what Onia provided. Before she could express her doubts, Onia resolved the issue.

"Don't worry," she said. "I know you're vegan. It's just a salad from a bag and bottled dressing. Some fruit on the side. Maybe a frozen dinner roll, if you'd like. That's alright, isn't it?" Car horns behind her honked an angry refrain.

"That's fine, but we'd better get out of here before there's a road rage incident, and we come out the losers."

Onia laughed, put the car into drive, and took off.

While Onia drove them to her house in Sweetgum, Claire texted Avery to let her know where she'd be and with whom. She wasn't stupid enough to be alone with a potential murder suspect without telling anyone. No response from Avery, but she'd surely look at her phone soon.

Onia lived in a middle-income part of Sweetgum in a basic one-story ranch that had been recently renovated. Gray-painted brick with bright white trim on the outside, open concept inside with a small island separating the kitchen and dining, both connected to the living room. Decorated in a transitional style contrasted with contemporary and a few rustic details added. Claire noticed a collection of woven baskets, seashells, and pottery displayed on a buffet table. A half-dozen arty looking photographs hung above, matted in white with black frames featuring either Africans or, more likely, Jarawa natives from the Andaman Islands.

Onia caught her staring at the display. "I visited Port Blair, the capital of the Andaman and Nicobar Islands, where my birth mother lives. She helped me find these mementos. This is a photo of her and a few of my relatives." She indicated a middle-aged dark-skinned woman with beautiful cheekbones and an athletic build wearing an Indian sari. Surrounding her, several mostly naked native men and women looked straight into the camera without smiling.

"Your mother's wearing traditional Indian clothes?"

"She's lived in Port Blair, the capital, since she lost me and, until recently, worked at the hospital where I was born. Her father brought her there to go to school. Guess he thought it best, given the tense situation at the Jarawa Reserve. Tatehane, one of the tribal elders, tried to kill her baby—me." Her blue eyes flashed with a white light that looked like pure hatred.

"I remember you telling me the story at Thorne Mondae's funeral. I can't believe someone could get away with killing a baby regardless of where it happened."

"No one is allowed to interfere with the tribe on their reserves. I'm mixed race, and they want to keep the tribe pure. The authorities just look the other way. At least, they did back then. It's a little different now, but not much. There's lots of controversy about how much the natives should be left to their own devices, and how much the modern age should be allowed to interfere with them."

"How do you feel about that?" Claire asked.

Onia looked as if she mulled it over. "I admire the Jarawa, the simplicity and naturalness of their life." She removed her mother's photo from the wall and stared at it for several seconds. "But is it really possible to stop the encroachment of so-called civilization? Is it even right to do so? The young Jarawa want cellphones, to drive cars, be educated, and learn about other worlds. Who are we to deny them?"

"It's a dilemma." Claire had never thought about it and had no idea how to respond. Best to be noncommittal. "Your mother is beautiful. I can see the resemblance." She realized that Onia just confirmed Avery's speculation about the newspaper article she had stolen from Thorne's trophy room.

"Yes, she is, thank you." Onia hung the photo back on its hook. "I hope to bring her to the United States soon."

They ate mixed greens salad with Italian dressing, a fresh pineapple that Onia peeled and sliced, and dinner rolls. She removed a bottle of wine from the refrigerator, and they drank the sweet-tart beverage from wine glasses that felt light and fragile.

"A housewarming gift from my Uncle Scopes," Onia volunteered. "He likes nice things, even though he came from a rough background." She knocked back a large drink of wine. "He saved my life, you know. He never abandoned me, even if my own father did."

"I'm sorry about that." Claire sipped the wine, not knowing what to say. Feeling both sad and suspicious of the young woman. She seemed to have strong negative feelings about Thorne, but were they strong enough to kill him? "Weren't Scopes and Thorne good friends? Didn't they have a long history together?"

"Being my uncle was more important to Scopes than staying friends with Thorne." Onia's lip wrinkled when she mentioned her father's name. "Besides, he was becoming disillusioned with Thorne before he brought me to the States. I'm sure you've heard that Thorne Mondae was not a nice man. Some, including Uncle Scopes, said he had committed a number of evil acts over the course of their life together. And my uncle had spent most of that time protecting Thorne, rescuing him when he got into trouble, covering up for him. I think Uncle Scopes had grown quite weary of the whole thing."

"He didn't seem all that upset at Thorne's burial," Claire said. "Although, neither did anybody else. I've never been to a more tearless funeral."

Onia laughed, which seemed a bit inappropriate. "Just shows you how disillusioned he was with Thorne." Onia spent several seconds in what looked like deep thought. When she spoke, her voice had become raspy with emotion. "Ever hear of that North Sea oil rig disaster in '92?"

"I've heard of it." She remembered Amber, the college girl/call girl they met in jail, had mentioned it, but didn't feel it necessary to share that with Onia.

"One of the worst disasters ever. A rig exploded, killed dozens of men. A faulty valve was involved, but the main culprit was negligence by the production company."

"What does that have to do with Thorne and Scopes and their relationship?"

"Uncle Scopes claims Thorne was directly responsible for the whole disaster."

"Wow, really?" Claire played dumb to get as much information out of Onia a possible. To jog her memory, Claire pulled up the newspaper story on her cellphone and presented it to Onia. "Is this what you're talking about."

Onia studied the clipping. "Where did you get this?"

"Uh… just part of some research my sister and I've been doing into Thorne's life."

Onia raised an eyebrow, but said nothing. She began reading.

North Sea, Aberdeen, Scotland:
Oil Rig Disaster Blamed on Company

An explosion and resulting oil and gas fires destroyed an oil production platform in the North Sea off the coast of Aberdeen, Scotland, killing hundreds of workers and a rescue vessel crew. It was the site of one of the world's most lethal offshore disasters. Although a subsequent Inquiry Board found the company guilty of inadequate maintenance and safety procedures, no criminal charges were brought against them.

Despite making a major upgrade, the company decided to continue operating the platform rather than temporarily shutting it down. On the day of the disaster, a condensate pump's pressure safety valve was removed for routine maintenance. Although the condensate pipe had been temporarily sealed, the work could not be completed by 6:00 p.m. when the day shift ended. Forced to allow the hand-tightened cover to remain, the on-duty engineer filled out the required permit stating that the pump must not be switched on under any circumstances.

On the evening of the explosions, the rig's fire-fighting system had been under manual control. When a blockage of an alternate pump caused it to stop, documents were searched to ensure the pump stopped by the engineer earlier could be turned on. The valve and pump were located in different places, and the permits placed in separate boxes. Based on the documents he read, the manager assumed starting the pump would be safe. No one noticed the missing valve.

A man who claims the engineer told him about the pump and he neglected to tell the manager, spoke on the basis of anonymity.

"I'll never forget the noise," he said. "Deafening, like a blowtorch magnified a hundred thousand times. The whole world was on fire, and it was my fault. I don't know if anyone was still alive at that point… but that sound was them going right down to the bottom of the sea. It's a thing I'll carry to my grave."

Survivors were eventually compensated by the carrier that insured the rig.

"That's Thorne, alright." Resentment tainted her voice like raw sewage. "The one who didn't tell the manager about the pump. He never suffered any consequences. In fact, both he and Uncle Scopes received big compensation from the insurance company. That's one of the things that helped finance their investment company."

"That's quite a story. I guess Scopes didn't hold it against Thorne, though. He did give him a lovely tribute at the funeral." Claire realized Onia was confirming all the information they had received in the jail from Amber.

"Uncle Scopes isn't heartless. Just sick and tired. I think they went to the Andaman Islands after the rig disaster, but that was the last adventure they took together. After what Thorne did to my mother, Uncle Scopes had had enough." She suddenly brightened. "But I do have good news. Even though his evil father rejected me, Isaac Mondae agreed to help me bring my mother to the States!"

"He has?" Claire had not received good vibes from Isaac, who seemed like a dissatisfied and angry young man. Maybe inheriting his father's money had put him in a better place. He didn't seem the type to want to share any-thing with his unrecognized illegitimate sister. There had to be a catch.

"Once I prove to him that I'm Thorne's biological daughter."

Ah, there's the rub.

"When I picked you up, I'd just come from my doctor's office. Had a DNA test which will prove Thorne's paternity. As soon as I get the results, Isaac and I are going to enter into a written agreement about my mother moving here and him putting her on his company payroll… among other things." It sounded like Onia was holding back details of their contract.

"That's wonderful!" Claire felt happy for her, since it appeared as if she wanted it so much. But it didn't take the focus off her as a suspect for Thorne's murder. Apparently, she had drawn from the victim's son what she had been unable to elicit from the victim. "Onia, did Isaac agree to this before or after Thorne's death?"

"After, of course. He wouldn't have had the finances to do it before." A cloud passed across Onia's face; a veil meant to hide what she truly felt from an observer.

But Claire caught the surprised look before it changed into a blank. Onia realized she had said the wrong thing. Admitted Thorne Mondae's death directly benefited her. She failed with the father, gotten rid of him, and been successful with the son. Is that how it had gone down? Claire didn't know. She needed to talk it over with her sister. The unfocused look on Onia's face gave Claire a creepy feeling. A shiver went up her spine, as if a bug crawled up her back. She wanted to go home.

The doorbell rang, and Onia excused herself to answer it.

Claire quickly dialed Avery, who picked up immediately and apolo-gized for not calling sooner. Claire gave her the address and told her to hurry.

A befuddled Onia returned followed by Detective Castellan and a Sweetgum PD uniformed officer.

"Onia Redfield a/k/a Rebecca Redfield," Detective Castellan said, "we are hereby serving you with a search warrant for the premises. Here's a copy of the warrant, a sworn affidavit signed by a magistrate. It specifies what we are looking for and where we are going to search. If evidence is found, the warrant gives us the power to seize it." He handed her several pieces of paper folded together, which she involuntarily took. "You need to sit here while the search is conducted."

"Avery?" Claire whispered into her cellphone. "You still there? Bring Jay with you. We have a situation here."

39

"The warrant looks good." After calling to say he'd be late for work, Jay sat with Avery and Claire on the sofa in Onia's living room while a cadre of police personnel swarmed over her house.

"What do they say I did?" Onia asked, although Avery suspected she already knew.

"Warrant says homicide."

"What are they looking for?"

"Electronic devices, cellphones, computers, etc." Jay checked the warrant. "Primitive artifacts, weapons, or other apparatuses which may have been used in the commission of the crime. It's pretty detailed. You can read it for yourself."

Onia shook her head. When Jay returned the papers, she laid them on her coffee table and burst into tears. Not knowing what to do, no one moved.

"Thorne's raping me, just like he raped my mother," Onia said.

Jay looked at Avery and Claire, a puzzled expression on his face.

"I need to get something from the car," Avery said. "Jay, care to join me?"

Claire looked as if she wanted to go too, but someone needed to stay with Onia and, since Claire knew her best, she was elected.

Outside, Jay and Avery climbed into her nondescript gray Honda Accord. She started the engine and turned on the heat. The weather had turned cold.

"I'm afraid this is my fault," Jay said.

"The search of Onia's residence?" Avery shuddered; the car hadn't had a chance to warm up. "Why is it your fault?"

"I told Butler… Detective Castellan… about the similarity between the photo of the Jarawa arrow to the one taken from Thorne's body. I showed him the photo Claire printed out. He didn't ask how I knew what the murder weapon looked like, and I didn't tell him. He discovered that Onia… her name was Rebecca then… had taken a trip to the Andaman Islands less than a year ago. Based on the fact that she threatened the victim and could have obtained a bow and arrow while there, he had probable cause to issue a search warrant. A judge agreed, and here we are."

"Wouldn't he have figured it out by himself eventually?" Avery had doubts about the efficacy of the Sweetgum Police Department. Like maybe they might be overwhelmed by their first murder investigation since before the flood.

"We can only hope," Jay said. "Now that we know Thorne raped her mother, that would strengthen her motive for revenge."

"I think we already assumed that since Onia told Claire he had gotten her drunk and taken advantage of her. In our world, that amounts to rape."

"True," Jay said. "But hearing the word straight out of Onia's mouth—and by association her mother's—makes the accusation more forceful. I'm anxious to find out what they discover during this police search."

* * *

The search of Onia's home took several hours. The trio of friends stayed with her, alternately consoling and cajoling her, hoping she would give something away. She never implicated herself in any way. But she looked miserable and anxious the whole time, squirming on the sofa, alternating between tearful sorrow and angry outbursts.

When Detective Castellan and his team prepared to leave, Jay followed them outside. The women waited in the living room surveying the damage. It wasn't like seeing a house demolished on TV by a brutal crime scene team. The searchers had left the home in very little disarray, almost as pristine as when they arrived.

"At least they didn't toss the place," a surprised Avery said.

"That's just for drama on TV," Claire said. "I doubt if they ever do that."

Jay returned, a perplexed look on his face.

"What did they find?" Onia looked like French royalty waiting for her turn on the guillotine.

Jay gave her a quick glance that looked as though he was trying to decide how much to reveal. "I get the impression Detective Castellan was a bit disappointed. Specifically, he was searching for a primitive bow and arrow that might have originated in the Andaman Islands, but all he found was some baskets and pottery, a few other artifacts that appear to be tourist stuff."

Avery watched Onia closely. Wide-eyed surprise came first. Then her shoulders slumped with relief, followed by a face collapsing into a puzzled frown. Her eyes darted to the credenza where the Andaman Island artifacts had been displayed. A couple of the drawers had been left ajar. Like an automaton, she moved to the chest and pulled out the drawers one-by-one, then closed each of them with neat efficiency.

"Thank you all for being here during this ordeal." Onia sounded like a hostess hinting that her guests might have overstayed their welcome. "I'm very tired now. Would anyone like a bottled water before you leave? I have some leftover fruit, if you're hungry."

Clearly, she intended to kick them out albeit in a very polite way.

Outside, Jay climbed into the backseat while Avery drove and Claire rode next to her.

"Jay," Avery said, "we were surprised the searchers didn't make a mess. Do we watch too much television?"

"Yes," Jay said without adding the grin Avery expected. "Cops do what is necessary to serve a search warrant. No more, no less. The searches I participated in—we never tossed a house, scattered belongings, or damaged anything just for the fun of it. If we opened a drawer, we'd look through it without dumping everything out, then close the drawer again. If we unscrewed a light switch to look behind it, we screwed it back. If we removed a book from the shelf and thumbed through it, we reshelved it. We avoided having to explain to our chief, the city attorney, or the media why we trashed someone's home, especially if we didn't find what we were looking for."

"Do you think Onia was withholding information?" Claire asked. "She looked disoriented when we left."

"She's definitely covering up something," Jay said, leaning over the console. "Something she expected the police to find, but they didn't. We need to keep an eye on her."

40

Onia opened the side of the credenza made for hanging clothes where she had stored the bow her mother had given her, then the adjoining drawers where she remembered tucking the arrows. Along with the other Andaman Island souvenirs she collected, she had carefully packed the weapon and checked it at the airport. Although she hadn't looked for it since before Thorne's death, Onia couldn't believe the police search team hadn't found it. Unable to locate them in the space they'd been originally stored, she proceeded to empty her closets in quest of the missing bow and arrows. Nothing.

After turning her house upside down, Onia called her mother on the cellphone she had bought for her. After speaking to Anjale, she knew who had taken the weapon.

* * *

"I think I've found what we've been looking for!" Jay's excited voice exploded from Avery's cellphone.

"A pot of gold at the end of a rainbow?" Avery pulled off her sunshades so she could see the phone screen and placed Jay on speaker. "A winning Texas lottery ticket?" What was it about sunglasses the kept piquing her memory? The autumn sun shone hot and bright through denuded tree limbs. She flicked her shades back on.

"I searched the records for abandoned vehicle notices issued prior to Thorne Mondae's murder," he said, "and located one dated two weeks before.

Didn't quite know what to make of it cause it was a rental car." Jay stopped and took a deep breath.

"Barring a long-lost relative who left me millions, that'll have to do."

"The statute states that if a vehicle has been left unattended on the right-of-way of a designated county, state, or federal highway for more than 48 hours, it can be labeled abandoned. It was never followed up on because the vehicle was removed within the allotted 48-hour time period."

"Don't keep me in suspense. Who was it issued to?" She had taken a short walk up the street, arriving home just in time to receive Jay's call. The forest still gave her a sense of foreboding she couldn't explain, so she had stopped taking her daily walks there. She settled on the steps that lead from the driveway to her front porch.

"The notices aren't issued by name, but it was a new white Range Rover Evoque."

"But Bart said he saw a white Ford Edge which, by the way, is what Onia Redfield drives."

"If you held a picture of a white Evoque and a white Edge next to each other, it would be hard to tell the difference."

"All those SUVs look alike to me anyway." Avery frowned. "What does Scopes drive?"

"According to the records, a BMW. But…"

Jay stretched it out until Avery cursed him in protest. "But what!"

"After calling the local agencies, I discovered the Evoque is a rental. Rented under the name Scopes Redfield 15 days before Thorne's murder."

"No kidding! So, he held on to it, then used it to keep the car from being reported abandoned on the highway while he was killing Thorne. If the car had been tagged, passersby on the highway would have thought it had already been reported."

"Let's not be hasty," Jay said. "Scopes could have loaned the tag to Onia, or she could have taken it. The vehicles are similar enough to pass as the same without a close inspection."

Avery shook her head. "What other reason would he have to rent a car? And, remember how Onia reacted when the search of her home didn't turn up the murder weapon? She acted surprised, then confused. I'll bet

Scopes took the bow and arrows she brought from the Andaman Islands and used them to murder Thorne. He stored the weapon in some sort of carryall, parked the Evoque, and threw the bag over the fence. Then climbed over after it."

"What motive does Scopes have to kill his best friend? Do you think he killed Thorne for monetary gain?" Jay asked.

"Onia said he was tired of Thorne's evil ways. And Amber said he gave her the chills even though she never met him. It's the obsessed inferior personality who murders his idol because the hero hasn't lived up to his inflated expectations. But there's more to this. I don't know what. You don't have to prove motive to prove guilt. I'm putting my money on Scopes as the killer." Avery's cellphone chimed. "Hold on. I'm getting a call from Claire."

"Where is she?"

"I sent her to keep watch on Onia. I'll call you back." When Avery removed her sunglasses a second time, their significance hit her.

"Holy shitowski! Jay! Don't hang up."

"I'm still here. What the hell?"

"Hold on." Avery put Jay on hold, then answered Claire's call. "Hold on, Claire. I've got Jay on the other line."

"Wait, Avery—" She cut Claire off and switched back to Jay.

"I thought of something else. The first time I met Scopes Redfield, he put his sunglasses above the brim of his golf cap."

"And—"

"Remember the trail camera photos? That's exactly where the Shadowy Figure behind the shed put his shades—stretched across the brim of his camouflage cap! The Shadowy Figure is Scopes Redfield!"

"He's not the only person in the world who does that." Jay still sounded excited.

"Maybe not, but all my true crime shows have taught me that there are no coincidences. I assume the police can track the rental car's GPS. If, on the day of the murder, it was parked on the highway in front of RE's only treeless lot, it puts a final nail in Scopes's coffin, as far as I'm concerned."

An exhilarated Avery hung up with Jay and switched to Claire's call, anxious to tell her sister that the citizen detective had solved the crime. She felt like crowing.

41

Onia was worried about Uncle Scopes. He had not shown up at the office today. Unusual behavior for him, at least in the near past. More recently, particularly since the death of Thorne Mondae, Scopes had taken to coming in late and leaving early. Totally unlike the workaholic Uncle Scopes she knew.

Built near the Sweetgum Country Club, his house looked well-manicured. All the fallen leaves had been meticulously removed from the lawn, which sparkled dewy green in the summer, but had faded to a crisp beige this December. The two-story Texas Hill Country style home had been sided with limestone and capped with a metal roof. An arched entryway introduced a large front porch supplied with dark gray Adirondack chairs.

Scopes hired professionals to execute his holiday décor with all the decadence and excess the season demanded. Hundreds of twinkling white Christmas lights lined the roof's eaves. Dozens of tall trees in the front yard had string lights wrapped around their trunks. An automated and illuminated display of a polar bear mother, father and two cubs raised and lowered their heads nodding approval at the winter wonderland surrounding them. Net lighting covered every bush surrounding the abode that flashed on and off all night every night. Leave it to Uncle Scopes to go all out to make his neighbors jealous.

Scopes had given Onia his house key, just as she had given him hers. All her life, he had been the person closest to her, even more than her parents. Which said a lot considering how tight she was with them. But she could be more honest with him than Mom and Dad, and Scopes seemed more forgiving, more understanding. He'd made mistakes in his life and was less inclined to criticize Onia for hers.

A giant pine wreath ornamented with sparkly gold and silver balls hung on his double front doors. When she slipped in the key, the door swung open. She could immediately tell the house was empty. A house without people had a certain ring to it, an echo not heard when occupied. It smelled as if the housekeeper had just left, the house redolent with lemon-scented floor wax, pine furniture polish, and lavender air freshener. The dark hardwood floors sparkled as Onia made her way into the great room where an open concept kitchen, living and dining area exposed 25-foot ceilings crisscrossed with heavy wooden beams. Floor-to-ceiling windows looked out onto the pool area and a lawn that flowed down into a babbling brook. She searched the first floor for any signs that Scopes had been there recently. A book he'd been reading rested on the coffee table, and the TV remote control lay next to it. Other than that, nothing.

Upstairs, she saw that his giant four-poster bed had been neatly made, and his grooming supplies put away in the marble-covered master bathroom. Large windows opposite the bed looked out onto the lawn and the stream, and a chaise lounge settled in a nook to take advantage of the view. Next to it, Scopes's writing desk had nothing on top except a vase of fresh flowers. His place reflected his bachelor status, although a very neat and orderly bachelor.

Onia pulled out his desk drawers and riffled through them. She found a spiral notebook with a red cover containing marketing lists and other personal items, none of any interest to her. She did notice that a couple of pages had been torn out of the notebook, leaving the tattered edges hanging onto the spirals. She wondered what had been on the pages and where Scopes and taken them. Probably just something he didn't need and threw away.

Downstairs, she prepared to leave, thinking about what she'd learned from her mother. Wondering if it meant what she thought it meant. She passed by the professional stainless steel refrigerator freezer taking up an entire corner of the kitchen. A Statue of Liberty magnet attached the two pages that had been torn from the notebook. At the top of the first sheet in large block capital letters, Scopes had written: *MY BELOVED NIECE, ONIA*. She pulled the pages from beneath the magnet and read. Her heart sank with every word, and she began to sob.

* * *

"I followed Onia to her uncle's house," Claire said into her cellphone. Hidden by a large bush planted too close to the street, she had parked on the opposite side of the road.

"Claire, Scopes Redfield killed Thorne Mondae!" A breathless Avery shouted into Claire's ear. "Jay discovered it was his rented vehicle parked on the highway, and I'm betting he used Onia's bow and arrows as the murder weapon. I realized he's the Shadowy Figure on the trail camera. Scopes pushes his sunglasses above his hat brim the same way the figure did. Do not go anywhere near him. Do you hear me?"

"Really? Don't worry. He's obviously not here." Claire watched Onia Redfield dash out of Scopes's house, tears squirting from her eyes. "Onia's coming out. She's crying. I'll call you back."

"Claire, Claire! Please be careful!" Avery shouted before her sister cut her off.

Claire caught Onia before she climbed into her car.

"Onia, what's the matter?" Claire asked.

"Claire!" Onia could barely talk through hitching sobs. "What are you doing here?"

"I was just in the neighborhood—"

She threw her arms around Claire's neck and sobbed into her shoulder. Claire patted her back, not knowing how to console her. When her sobs slowed to wet hiccoughs, Claire said: "Can you tell me what's wrong?"

Onia, a miserable expression marring her face, handed Claire two hand-written pieces of notebook paper.

Claire read the note out loud.

MY BELOVED NIECE, ONIA:

Your mother told me you planned to extort money from Thorne Mondae on the basis of him being your biological father. When he failed to acknowledge his paternity, you became so upset that revenge rather than monetary gain became your primary motive. I know you promised Anjale justice and believed in your heart killing Thorne was the only way to accomplish that. I'm not judging you and, in fact, agree.

I spent half my lifetime witnessing Thorne get away with evil deeds. Truthfully, I was instrumental in enabling him to walk away blameless from his disgusting crimes. The world is a better place without Thorne Mondae. Since my enabling created him, it became my duty, my destiny, to destroy him. Like Frankenstein and his monster.

When I learned you intended to use your Jarawa bow and arrows, I stole them from your house and followed through with your wishes. I understood the poetic justice of him dying at the hands of a native Jarawa, but I could not let you do it. When the police searched your house, I feared they would blame his murder on you. I hid the bow and arrows in my storage unit downtown along with a handwritten and signed confession for the authorities to find. It's up to you whether to show the police this letter.

Lastly, I have no intention of spending the rest of my life in prison, so I intend to kill myself. I beg you not to be unhappy. I have lived a full and rewarding life. You are the one person in the world whom I have truly loved, and I'm leaving all my worldly goods to you. I know you will become a successful business owner, a wonderful wife to Rafe, and one day a loving mother. I'm sorry I couldn't be there for those events, but it's better this way.

With all my love,

Your Uncle Scopes Redfield

Onia wailed as if her heart had burst into pieces. "After the police searched my house," she blubbered, "I called my mother, Anjale. She admitted telling Uncle Scopes that I was planning to get revenge on Thorne for raping her."

"You were?"

"He stole my Jarawa bow and arrows and did it himself. Just to save me!" She grabbed the papers, crumbled them, and threw them on the brown grass. "But I'd already changed my mind about getting revenge. I decided not to kill Thorne, not to let anger ruin my life. If I'd known Uncle Scopes had knowledge of my intentions, I would have told him I'd decided against it. He was just trying to help me. We have to stop him from killing himself!"

Claire's mind was racing. "Onia, calm down." She held her by the shoulders until she stopped shaking. "Do you have any idea where he might have gone? Does he have a favorite place? Somewhere he might feel comfortable enough to…"

"I don't know!" She chafed her forehead.

"Does he have a gun? Did he take it?"

Onia took a deep breath. "After I skimmed the letter, I ran back upstairs to check his gun safe. I know the combination to it, just like I have a key to his house. He trusted me with everything."

"Was the gun still there?"

"He has an entire safe full of them. Couldn't tell if any were missing. If he took one, it wasn't obvious."

"Is there somewhere else he might keep a gun?"

"Let me think. It's not usual, but there may be one downstairs. There's a table in the entry hall with a locked drawer. He might have one in there, just to avoid the inconvenience of going upstairs. A home invasion would come through the front door."

"Makes sense."

Onia unlocked the front door, and they checked the entry hall credenza drawer. "I don't have a key," she said, when the drawer wouldn't open.

No time to take the delicate approach. Claire marched to the fireplace, grabbed the poker, and slammed it into the drawer until it cracked open.

"Yikes!" Onia jumped back.

Inside, they found a single hard case with two snap latches, but no gun. Just the Styrofoam egg-carton-like material with the shape of a gun imprinted into it.

"Bingo!" Claire said. Then realized they had wasted precious time looking for a gun when they needed to be looking for Scopes instead. She said as much to Onia.

"I've thought of somewhere he might be," Onia said. "He's tough but sentimental. I think he might intend to kill himself where his best friend died… where he killed Thorne."

"In my forest?" Claire felt sick. "At the funeral, he said our woods reminded him of the Jarawa Reserve. A place where he and Thorne admired the natural beauty and the unaffected natives."

Onia stared at Claire, who's body had gone rigid.

"Avery!" Claire said. "We have to warn Avery."

"I don't believe he'd hurt her," Onia said.

"He'd better not." Claire stabbed her sister's number into her cellphone.

42

Avery stared out her back windows at a leafless oak tree where a half dozen turkey vultures roosted. One bird balanced on the blunt end of a bare branch, her arched wings poising her body like a ballerina's upstretched arms in a pirouette. The vultures brooded with their tucked necks and dark visages, disapproving and superior. Avery couldn't help but shudder, seeing them as foreshadowers of death. Then felt guilty remembering the big birds did the world a service by removing carcasses from the landscape and highways. They were good friends to human beings even if you didn't necessarily want to invite them to Sunday dinner.

Suddenly, the vultures flew off their perches and flapped into the sky until the air currents lifted them away. Curious to see what had scared them, Avery called Bodhi, and they strolled toward the bridge. Several white, dark brown, and spotted fallow deer, feeding on watermelon rinds she had strewn about earlier, looked not toward her and the dog, but deeper into the woods. They stood like statues, then darted across the creek, leaving the half-eaten melons behind. Unusual, because they loved watermelon and left tooth marks where they had scraped the rinds clean. Rushing ahead, Bodhi disappeared into the thick conglomeration of leafless trees.

Avery hung back, remembering that the beckoning forest had once been a crime scene. The place where a man had been murdered. From a short distance, she heard Bodhi barking. She searched inside her jacket pocket, felt better when her trembling hand gripped her cellphone. At the end of the bridge where the crime scene tape had been wrapped, she noticed something red floating with the breeze. A silky scarf of deep crimson had been tied to the bridge railing. How odd. She untied the scarf and carried it with her, following the sound of Bodhi's barks.

Standing on the embankment where Thorne Mondae had collapsed and died stood his best friend, Scopes Redfield. Bodhi confronted him, barking like a banshee, while Scopes aimed what appeared to be an automatic pistol at her dog.

Avery's phone chirped out a jaunty tune. Scopes lifted his head and stared at her. He held her gaze while Claire came on the line.

"Avery, you were right," she said. "Scopes Redfield wrote a letter to Onia confessing to the murder of Thorne Mondae, and he's going to kill himself. Onia thinks he might be in our forest."

"Get this dog away from me," Scopes yelled at Avery. "Or I'll kill him before I kill myself!"

"I know." Avery said to Claire, trying to keep her voice from shaking. "He's here now, with a gun, threatening Bodhi. Call the cops."

"Get off the frigging phone and get this dog." Scopes screamed.

"We're on our way," was the last thing she heard Claire say before she hung up.

43

Claire and Onia threw themselves into Claire's vehicle and headed for Rancho Exotica. Light traffic and a heavy foot propelled them along.

"Call the cops." Claire squelched her fear, remaining calm for her sister's sake. Remembering what Avery had said in the jail about her panic attack atop the mountain.

Onia phoned emergency services, described the situation, and demanded they notify Detective Castellan.

"Onia," Claire said, "call Jay. He might be closer than we are. And closer than the police."

"What's his number?"

"Can't remember." She tossed her cellphone to Onia. "Use my phone."

"It went straight to voicemail." She left Jay a frantic message.

Claire felt like crying. She told herself to take a deep breath. "You don't think Avery is in any danger from Scopes?" The heavy silence set Claire on edge.

"I don't want to lie," Onia finally said. "I never thought Uncle Scopes would be violent, but he isn't thinking rationally. And, let's face it, he has nothing to lose at this point."

"I wish you had lied."

After the longest 10 minutes of Claire's life, they pulled through the development's back gate. Another three minutes to her house, even driving faster than the posted 25 mph. Praying she didn't run over a deer or a possum or any other animal. Claire leaped out of the car as soon as her Honda hit the driveway. She dived onto the golf cart, yelling at Onia to wait here for the police. Rushing across the bridge, she could only hope she had arrived in time to save her sister from harm.

44

Situated on the creek bank where he had killed his best friend, Scopes Redfield held Bodhi at bay with an automatic pistol.

"Bodhi," Avery said, "come here!" The dog stopped barking and trotted up to her. She told him to sit, and he did. "Mr. Redfield, what are you doing?" Her voice sounded steadier than she felt.

Scopes guffawed. "Isn't it obvious? I killed my best friend. Now I'm going to kill myself. I'm a coward who doesn't want to spend his life in prison."

Avery glanced past the bridge to see if any cop cars had arrived. Nope, she was alone. She tried to think of what hostage negotiators said when they talked people down. "You don't have to do this." Dammit! That's what everybody said, and it sounded stupid.

"No, I'm doing it because I choose to. I'm not afraid to die. I welcome it. My life has no purpose."

"How can you say that? You're a business owner, a contributing member of the community. You have people who love and admire you. People you love."

Scopes rolled his eyes, shook his head. He didn't look upset, just impatient. "I spent half my life keeping Thorne out of trouble. My job was to remove obstacles from his path. Thorne, that little piece of crap, was always getting away with stuff. It had to stop, so I killed him." He smiled. "I'm like a working dog with no job—no blind to lead, no post-traumatic stress to sooth, no drugs to sniff. Useless."

"What about Onia, your niece? She still loves and needs you."

He smirked, indicated the red scarf Avery had untied from the bridge. "Want to know the truth about that scarf?" Avery held it up and the dropping sun shimmered through it. "Might as well tell you the truth. Let you decide what to do with it."

"What truth?" Avery took a small inching step toward Scopes.

"It wasn't Thorne who raped Anjale, Onia's mother, all those years ago."

"What do you mean?" Keep him talking until the cops arrive. Move closer.

"I did it. I'm Onia's father, not Thorne."

Avery froze, unable to comprehend what she'd just heard.

"She was tied up. Thorne blindfolded her with that scarf you're holding. Totally helpless. But he couldn't perform. I think he was still traumatized by the oil rig incident. One of the few things he'd ever done for which he'd taken emotional responsibility. When he left her alone, I replaced him. In that moment, I discovered what it felt like to be Thorne Mondae. Not worrying about consequences. Not caring what other people thought, how they felt. Only thinking about myself. The only person in the world who mattered."

"A narcissist."

"Yes, that describes him exactly. But I'm not. So afterwards, after I had hurt that innocent young girl, the terrible shame came flooding in. I convinced myself something had possessed me. The evil spirit that was Thorne Mondae had overtaken me. I had no control over what I'd done. Except when I came to myself, I knew I had to fix it. I removed the scarf from Onia's mother's eyes and kept it all these years. Rushed her to a medical center where nine months later she gave birth to a little girl with startling blue eyes. When Jarawa tribal elder Tatehane stole the baby… *my baby*… and tried to drown her, I rescued her. I've been living with the lie ever since.

"For the next 30 years, one idea never left my thoughts. Thorne Mondae deserved to die. He was cruel and dangerous. I thought I would never be able to do it myself. Until I realized my daughter, Onia, intended to do what I was too cowardly to do. To get justice for her mother. I couldn't let my precious child sacrifice herself. I had spent my entire life cleaning up after the natural disaster that was Thorne Mondae. A wrecking ball of death and destruction everywhere he went. He had to be stopped." Scopes wiped sweat from his face, or maybe it was tears. "When I murdered Thorne, it was like killing myself. Worse. I already felt like I was dead."

"But Onia needs you," Avery said. "She'll be devastated." The heavy weight of fear and the desperate need to say the right thing overwhelmed her. She remembered what Tom had said about saving someone's life, how it made you responsible for them forever. "Live for her instead of dying for yourself."

"I've given my whole life to her, loved her more than anyone. This is the last time I can save her. I'm sacrificing my life in exchange for hers. My obligations to her are over." Scopes lifted the pistol and held it to his temple.

"Scopes, please—"

Claire came hauling ass across the bridge, the golf cart churning up sand as she hit the trail and hurtled toward Scopes and Avery.

"Keep away," Scopes shouted, firing a bullet into the air. "Don't come any closer."

Claire did not even slow down. When she pulled up next to Avery, Bodhi jumped onto the cart's passenger seat.

The sound of sirens shrieked from the main road, and beyond the pines half a dozen police cars tore into the driveway. A squad of uniformed officers rushed the bridge. Scopes shouted multiple warnings at the top of his lungs.

As cops swarmed the forest, Scopes fired half-a-dozen rounds at them.

A young cop with a ruddy face pulled Claire off the cart and sped toward Scopes. Bodhi clung to the passenger seat by his toenails.

"Bodhi!" Claire screamed.

"Go back across the bridge," the cop shouted at Claire and Avery.

"Let the dog off the cart!" Avery begged.

The cop barreled toward Scopes, who shrieked for him to stop. When he didn't, Scopes fired.

Avery, close to a panic attack, swallowed her death fear and chased after the cart. Claire came flying after her, both of them yelling for Bodhi to jump. He looked petrified. He'd never ridden the cart when it went that fast.

More officers shouted from the bridge. Screaming for them to stop. Trying to gain control.

In her frantic pursuit of Bodhi, Avery ignored the sharp cracks of gun-fire exploding around her. Her knees burned as she struggled to maintain balance over the rough terrain.

Suddenly, a loud pop, and a sharp blow slammed into Avery's left shoulder. Had she smacked into a tree? She stopped cold, stumbled, collapsed to the ground, tried to rise, fell again. Prone on the damp earth, she stared straight up into the 100-foot pines swaying above. Was she dead or dying? Frozen, unable to move, she watched the treetops, wondering if she should cry, pray, or scream.

Another loud bang, and Avery managed to turn her head slightly to the side. Scopes Redfield went down, landing in the creek in much the same place as Thorne had died. Bodhi leaped off the golf cart, ran to Avery, and started licking her in the face. She was alive!

"Avery, Avery," Claire cried, "are you alright?" She rushed to her sister and knelt beside her.

"Neither of us is going to be able to get off this ground by ourselves," Avery said.

"You're bleeding," her sister said. A police officer arrived, helped pull them both out of the dirt. "Can you walk?" When her sister nodded, Claire supported Avery from one side and the female cop from the other.

"Bodhi!" Avery turned, the burning pain in her shoulder making her stop short. The dog followed close at their heels. "Good boy," she said, and unexpected tears burst from her eyes. She used the red scarf to wipe her wet face.

"Avery!" Jay rushed up, his face in a panic. "I'm… so… sorry…." He huffed and puffed trying to catch his breath. "Please forgive me for not being here!"

He scooped her into his arms and carried her across the bridge. Claire stuck with her sister, keeping close, as they had always been. Jay handed Avery onto the gurney and the EMS paramedics rolled her into a waiting ambulance.

Avery couldn't talk from crying so hard.

"It's okay," Claire said. "I'm here. We're together, and that makes us invincible."

Claire rode with her as Jay followed the ambulance carrying the sisters to the hospital.

45

With her hand on the passenger side door handle of her fiancé, Rafe Valencia's, Toyota hybrid, Onia Redfield paused, thinking how much alike they were. They bought the best vehicle they could afford but with a view toward not contributing to the environmental pollution. She admired his practicality coupled with compassion. He wasn't bad to look at either.

After settling their differences regarding her new-found heritage, they had agreed to be married within the next year. She decided she knew as much as she was going to about who and where she came from, and it was time to carry on with her life as originally planned. The death of Uncle Scopes made her realize the brevity and fragility of existence. You never knew how much time you had left. Better to take hers off hold and get on with it.

Rafe had driven Onia to the hospital to visit Avery Halverson. In some ways, she felt responsible for what happened to Avery and wanted to convey her regret as well as her best wishes. Pausing long enough to lift the hood of her rain jacket, she pulled the door handle and stepped into a mild drizzle. Rafe removed a pot plant from the back seat and handed it to her.

"Are you gonna be okay?" he asked. "I could come in if you wanted."

"I'm fine," Onia said. "I need to talk to her by myself. A third person might make it awkward."

"Especially since you're giving her the test results." Rafe outlined the curve of her jaw with his fingers. "I'll pick you up when you're done. Don't forget that I love you." He lifted her chin and gave her a light peck on the lips.

"Me too."

She watched as he drove away, feeling somewhat apprehensive about her visit with Avery but looking forward to the beautiful future she envisioned.

* * *

Avery sat in her hospital bed, an IV tube running from her arm to a bag of saline solution hanging on a hook behind her, which seemed to be standard equipment for every patient. Her shoulder throbbed slightly, but the pain injections the nurses plugged into her IV helped in more ways than one. She expected Claire to arrive any minute, mainly to bring her something edible. The hospital had her on what she called the "white diet." When she told them she was vegetarian, they didn't seem to understand the principle of vegetables, much less know what to do with them.

Her meals consisted of white bread, white cream of wheat, white potatoes, white rice, and white powdered coffee creamer. One day, she received a salad, or their version of one. Very white iceberg lettuce, but the kitchen had gone to the trouble to halve cherry tomatoes and place them in a decorative ring around the edge of the plate. Very thoughtful. Her dressing consisted of a single packet of bright white Newman's Own Ranch Dressing. She felt grateful for a dish that had at least visited the green neighborhood.

After looking at photos Claire had sent of herself, Bodhi, and Tom, who had rushed to Rancho Exotica when he heard what happened, Avery laid her cellphone on the purple coverlet and rested her head on the pillow. Claire had also taken photos of the area in their forest where Scopes Redfield had been killed by the police, once again a crime scene with yellow tape surrounding its perimeter. Avery sighed. She felt both sad and angry about Scopes. He had sacrificed himself for his daughter, but was it really necessary? Was murder ever justifiable? Scopes had decided to kill himself, but his demise ended up being "suicide by cop." Guess that was as good as doing it yourself.

She must have dropped off, because the next thing she realized was that someone had entered her room and stood over her bed. Rising quickly, a startled Avery winced from the pain in her shoulder. Her visitor, Onia Redfield, held a small potted plant in her hand.

"Sorry, did I wake you?" she asked.

"It's okay. The drugs make me nod off." She indicated the yellow bromeliad in a pot surrounded by silver foil. "Is that for me?"

"Oh, yes." Onia placed it on the dresser next to the two dozen red carnations Jay had sent. She sat on the edge of the reclining chair looking as though she wanted to say something but didn't know where to start.

Defying her usual need to fill in blank spaces, Avery waited. To distract herself, she eyed the red carnations which reminded her a little too much of funeral flowers and the near-miss she'd had with a bullet. Next to it sat a mixed bouquet of lilies, daisies, and roses sent by Rancho Exotica friends. Several plants, Claire told her, had also arrived at the house.

"I came to apologize," Onia finally said.

"Apologize?" She had Avery's complete attention. "What for?"

"I feel it's my fault that you and Claire were put in danger. If I could change things, I would. I should have dealt with my anger another way. I can't explain what got into me. There's a side of me I didn't know existed. It scared me. Sorry you were hurt and hope you get well soon."

"Thank you, Onia." Avery realized she had actually put herself in danger. "Claire and I volunteered to play detective. It was as much our fault as yours. Just a shoulder wound, went straight through without hitting a bone or major organ. A little physical therapy, and I'll be fine. But thank you."

"There's something else." Onia sat back, heaved a heavy sigh. "I did a half-sibling DNA test to prove I truly was Thorne's daughter and Isaac's half-sister." She drew a paper from her handbag and handed it to Avery. "Isaac volunteered to let me use his DNA since we didn't have Thorne's."

Avery winced when she leaned forward to accept the paper. It showed two columns of lab tests and codes which Avery didn't understand. The third column read "Sibling 1" and listed Isaac Mondae. The fourth read "Sibling 2" and listed Onia Redfield. Both columns were divided and filled with numbers. Most telling, red typing at the bottom right corner read, "Probability of Relatedness: 0%."

"Turns out, I am not related to Thorne Mondae in any way." Onia wiped a fallen tear from her cheek.

"I'm sorry," Avery said, unable to look her in the eye.

"It was all for nothing," Onia said. "All the pain, the anger, the agony of being rejected. No point to any of it. Especially Uncle Scopes's death."

"You have to remember the good things. He was a wonderful uncle and a role model, despite what he did." At that moment, Avery made a momentous decision. She put herself in the place of a mother trying to decide what was best for her daughter. Difficult, considering she'd chosen not to have children. Within that frame, as best she could imagine it, the better course seemed not to tell Onia that Scopes was her real father. Maybe one day, when some of the pain and hurt had been resolved, but not now. If the decision proved to be a bad one, Avery hoped she would be in a position to rectify it or, at the very least, be forgiven for guessing wrong.

"I suppose it's for the best. I found my biological mother. And Uncle Scopes left me everything, so now I can afford to bring her to the States."

"Onia, look in my jacket pocket; it's in the closet."

Onia looked askance, but did as she directed. "Nothing in here except this." She pulled out the red scarf Avery had found tied to the forest bridge. She held it up waiting for an explanation.

"It was tied to the bridge when I found Scopes in the forest. It obviously meant something to him. Said it had been a gift to your mother. Thought you might want it." She remembered what Scopes had told her about the scarf. That Thorne had used it to blindfold Anjale. But it had apparently been important to him, maybe symbolizing his redemption, and she thought Onia should have it.

Onia held it against her cheek. "It's lovely. I'll cherish it. Thank you."

"Keep in touch. Maybe you and me and Claire could have lunch sometime when I get out of the hospital."

"Of course, I'd like that." Onia still clutched the silky red scarf when she left.

Avery must have nodded off again, because when she woke, twilight glowed outside her window. Claire showed up with Tom and Jay following her. They had stopped at the barbecue place in town to get her some side dishes for dinner—fried okra, hush puppies, squash, cabbage, coleslaw, and potato salad. Not the healthiest, but it beat the heck out of the white diet. Jay kissed her on the cheek, Tom patted her shoulder, the good one, and

Claire opened the to-go bags and plated her food. A warm glow enveloped Avery, and she felt comforted having her beloved family and friends around her.

"How's the shoulder?" Tom asked. "Are you getting out of here any time soon?"

"It feels okay," Avery said. "Might need a little physical therapy, but that's all."

"She needs to stay until she's completely well," Claire said in her most big sisterly tone.

"And Claire doesn't have to play nursemaid," Avery said. "Don't worry. Even though Claire and I are now officially citizen detectives, I promise not to act like the stereotypical detective in novels and on television."

"How's that?" Jay asked.

"After being wounded, they check themselves out of the hospital before they are completely healed or released by a doctor. Big, brave, obsessed detective defying the pain to get on with his or her compulsion to solve the mystery. Not me. I like being catered to, having pain-relieving drugs, and no responsibilities. I might stay here indefinitely." Her friends laughed as if she had been kidding. That happened to Avery a lot. Making a serious statement others found unbelievable and humorous. She never bothered to correct them.

"Detective Castellan sends his regards," Jay said. "He dropped the tampering charges on both you and Claire."

"That's nice. I thought he might. Guess he's pretty miffed that we solved the murder before he did."

"Not really. Don't you think I gave him the abandoned vehicle tag info before I told you?"

"I guess," a slightly disgruntled Avery said. "When you checked the GPS, it showed the rental car stopped where I said it would be, right?"

Jay hesitated longer than she thought he should have. "Yes, Avery, you were right about everything." A slight sardonic tone in his voice. "*But*, Detective Castellan had it solved. He just didn't know where to find Scopes Redfield. You had the advantage… or disadvantage, depending on how you look at it… of finding Scopes in your forest."

Avery harrumphed. "Believe whatever you want. Here's some good news for Detective Castellan. As soon as I recover from the bullet I took for the posse, I'm going to do what Jay does."

"What does Jay do?" Claire asked, a guarded look on her face.

"I'm going to the Sweetgum Police Department and fill out a volunteer application. I'm going to work there!"

"No way!" Jay and Tom said in unison.

"Castellan will never consent to that," Jay said.

"He won't have a choice. His people—the Sweetgum Police—shot me. When the doctor removed the bullet, it was from an officer's gun. If they don't let me work there, I'll sue the whole city."

"I can't allow you to do that." Jay unsuccessfully tried to look stern.

"You'll get hurt again," Tom protested.

Claire looked at Avery, her sister looked back, and the unspoken words that passed between them said:

As if they could tell either of us what to do.

46

The weather had turned cool, finally deciding the time had come to declare winter. Not like February, when an arctic blast would cut a body to the bone with sharp fingers. But a southern December still struggling to let autumn go.

Avery, Claire, and Bodhi paraded across the wooden bridge and into their forest. The second round of crime scene tape had been removed, and the woods were eerily quiet. Only the murmur of a slow-flowing brook and a slight breeze teasing the treetops interrupted the silence. A small band of whitetails ran across their path, one doe stopping long enough to give the interlopers a thousand-yard stare then darting away. Bodhi looked interested but had learned not to chase the deer. He had been outrun too many times and was sane enough to stop doing the same thing over and over expecting different results.

"The forest keeps us safe," Avery said.

"Not too safe for Thorne Mondae and Scopes Redfield," Claire said.

"That proves nothing. Their deaths were unnatural, caused by human nature. Death may be inevitable but is not necessarily imminent."

"Someone's waxing philosophical today. Still taking that Oxycodone?"

Avery ignored her sister's jab. "Thorne and Scopes weren't listening. The animals warn us of danger. Remember the rustle of the leaves when the whitetail flees, the scream of the fox, and the fussing of the crows when a hawk is nearby? I feel safe here, in the forest."

"Nowhere is perfect, but this feels like our home now."

Suddenly, with sheets of muddy water pouring off his back, Bodhi leaped out of the flowing creek and rushed toward them as if he wanted to jump into their arms.

"Bodhi! Stop!" They cried in unison while scrambling away from the mucky dog. He sat, staring at them with big eyes, totally ignorant of what he had done wrong.

"Somebody's getting a bath when we get back to the house," Avery said, as they turned toward the bridge.

Bodhi whined.

"Guess we'll never get to solve another murder." Avery sighed wistfully. "Both of us could die before a Sweetgum local kills somebody else."

"Cheer up." Claire patted her sister's shoulder. "We may get lucky and Rancho Exotica will produce its very own serial killer."

She laughed when Avery's countenance illuminated with joy.

Available Fall 2024

Check the author's website at www.patsystagner.com for details.

A DAZZLE OF ZEBRAS
THE RANCHO EXOTICA MYSTERIES—BOOK 2

The Rancho Exotica zebra herd is accused of stomping a woman to death. Claire and Avery must uncover the true killer before the animals are sold to a Chinese zoo or worse, slaughtered.

Dear Reader:

I hope you enjoyed this book and are looking forward to Book 2 featuring the beloved Rancho Exotica zebra herd. Your help in leaving a review would make a huge difference to this up-and-coming author. Just return to the Amazon link where you originally purchased it and leave your thoughts and feelings on A VENUE OF VULTURES. Very much appreciated.

If you would like to receive news regarding new books, stories, signings, giveaways, or other events, or read my blog which focuses on mystery, animals, and senior citizens, go to my website at www.patsystagner.com and sign up for my newsletter. No spam, guaranteed. You can unsubscribe at any time.

Joy and best wishes,

Patsy Stagner